# ◈ONCE UPON A REALM

## REMIXED FAIRY TALES BY DIVERSE VOICES

CURATED BY
**KESHIA MCENTIRE**

K. R. S. MCENTIRE, MONTREZ, ALICIA ELLIS,
R. L. MEDINA, E.M. LACEY,
KRYSTINA COLES

Copyright © 2024 by K. R. S. McEntire

Copyright © 2024 by Montrez

Copyright © 2024 by Alicia Ellis

Copyright © 2024 by R. L. Medina

Copyright © 2024 by E.M. Lacey

Copyright © 2024 by Krystina Coles

Once Upon A Realm: Remixed Fairy Tales by Diverse Voices

Published by: Diverse Books With Magic

Edited by: Jennifer Roachford at Curly Tales Publishing

Formatted by: Keshia McEntire

Character art by: Ian Sebastian

Cover Design: Miblart

Paperback ISBN: 9781939452580

Ebook ISBN: 9781939452597

*To those who searched for their reflection in the enchanted mirrors of classic tales in vain, yet refused to accept the limitations placed upon their stories.*

*For the brave souls who dare to rewrite their endings, turning their fates into fairy tales.*

*For the seekers of magic in a world that forgot how to believe.*

*These stories are for you. Welcome home.*

# TABLE OF CONTENTS

# INTRODUCTION

Dear Readers,

I've always been captivated by fairy tales. What's not to love? They have adventure, romance, magic, and almost always a guarantee of happily ever after ... At least they do in our modern versions.

The truth is, these "tales as old as time" have been reimagined time and time again, growing from dark and dangerous cautionary tales to the safe love stories we consume as children. Despite these revisions, it seemed as though the majority of these stories were confined to portraying only one type of heroine, often the story of a rich princess with skin as white as snow.

That's why I'm thrilled to introduce "Once Upon a Realm: Remixed Fairytales by Diverse Voices," an anthology that breathes new life into classic tales by offering fresh perspectives from six writers of diverse backgrounds. With each story, we shatter stereotypes and challenge the traditional narrative, inviting readers of all ages to embark on a journey where every voice is heard and every person is valued.

In these pages, you'll find tales that resonate with universal themes of love, courage, and resilience, reminding us that regardless of our backgrounds or circumstances, joy can always be found. These stories were written with teen readers in mind, but these themes are universal. We believe that seeing oneself reflected in the stories we tell is empowering—it builds confidence, reaffirming that our voices matter and that our stories can have happy endings.

Each story is crafted to be bite-sized—novella length—allowing readers to immerse themselves in a complete and satisfying tale in one sitting. And the best part? If you find yourself falling in love with the worlds we've created, know that all of these stories are connected to full-length books or series by each author.

We are excited to welcome you to embark on six fairytale-inspired fantasy and sci-fi adventures. We hope you find new favorite authors within these pages and that our stories inspire you to dream, to believe, and to embrace the magic within.

Welcome to "Once Upon a Realm."

- Keshia McEntire

# K. R. S. MCENTIRE

## RED IN THE WOODS

In a dystopian world where the boundaries between predator and prey blur, Fable wasn't just Liam's lover—she was his sanctuary. Their cozy cabin in the secluded woods was the only refuge where Liam could exist without the threat of death for being who he was. But on the fateful night of the full moon, a wolf enters their sanctuary, a relentless pursuit shatters their haven, and Fable vanishes without a trace.

Now, Liam embarks on a perilous mission:
Sneak into the city
Infiltrate the Wardens' lair
And reclaim the woman he loves

The city may be full of ruthless killers, but Liam harbors a deadly dark secret within himself. Can he outwit the predators and bring Fable home?

A dystopian adventure loosely inspired by the tale of Little Red

Riding Hood. This story takes place in the world of The Eden Saga book series by K. R. S. McEntire.

# LIAM

*L*iam burrowed beneath threadbare blankets, his tiny fingers clutching his favorite book of fairytales. He squinted as his flashlight flickered like lightning, illuminating the pages in bursts. Between spells of total darkness, he devoured stories the way other kids devoured sweet treats. Liam loved stories where darkness was defeated by light and heroes found their happily-ever-afters in the bleakest of circumstances. He savored the light he found in the heroes, heroines, and magical worlds. Someday, he promised himself, he'd go on an adventure and find the same type of light in the real world.

As Liam read, he wondered what it would be like to be a hero or to rescue a damsel from her distress. But mostly, he wondered what grass would feel like under his toes or how the sun would feel if it touched his honey-brown skin.

There wasn't much grass left outside. At least, that's what he'd been told. He'd never had the opportunity to investigate that claim himself—the underground tunnels beneath the Chicago settlement were the only home he'd ever known.

His makeshift bed—the inside of a weathered wooden shipping crate—did little to shield him from the sound of his parents whispering outside. On most nights, he tuned them out and focused on the stories in his book. He'd just finished one about a tin soldier and was starting a new one about a mermaid. But his parents typically whispered about low rations and dangerous raids from Wardens, not him. At the mention of his name, his ears perked up and his attention was pulled to their words.

"Liam's not like us," his father, Gregory, whispered. "He can live a good life out there with regular people."

His mother, Hanna, sighed. "The best kind of life is one where you are surrounded by people who love you. He is just a kid, and a kid needs family."

Liam put the book down, unraveled himself from his blanket fort, and peered out of the crate. His parents were sitting on a sleeping cot, huddled close to the light of a dull lantern, with their backs to Liam.

"The Resistance offered to help him enroll in the settlement school," Father said. "They will give him a free place to stay. He will find new people to love him in the Resistance and at school. He doesn't have any mutations, so he doesn't need to live down here. He will not be killed if he enters the settlement. No one would choose the type of life we have for themselves if they had a better option."

Unease gnawed at Liam's insides, causing his brow to furrow. He put his nose back in his book and decided not to trouble himself with his parents' confusing words. His flickering flashlight abruptly sputtered out, leaving him feeling disheartened. It might be months until the Resistance could spare him a new battery. The darkness permitted him to drift off to sleep.

HANNA ROLLED A STICKY BLUE TARP OVER THE DAMP AND DIRTY ground. Her snake-like blue skin caught the light of Gregory's small fire pit and glistened in a way Liam thought was beautiful. His father held a boiling pot atop the fire, letting its contents bubble over and spill onto his fingers and hands. Liam winced. Even though he knew the fire and hot water would not hurt his dad, it still looked painful.

Rose and Risa, two tall and broad-shouldered twins who lived with their family, broke open a large crate of rations with their oversized bare hands and pulled two servings out. Liam grabbed spoons and mugs from a large metal tin where they kept cups and silverware away from bugs and rodents, and everyone gathered on the tarp to eat. Liam stepped onto the tarp, using his foot to feel for a spot that wasn't too dirty or sticky. It had been a while since they'd washed the tarp—they had other uses for what little water they had.

He plopped down next to Rose, who gave him a smile after wishing him a good morning. As rations for two were split between five and broth was poured into mugs, Liam couldn't help but notice how unusually quiet all of the adults in his unit were.

"I've been reading a new story in my book," Liam said, breaking the silence. "It's about a mermaid who goes to live with humans."

Hanna's eyes softened. "I've read that one. Did you like the story?"

Liam nodded. It was his mother who'd gifted him the book of fairytales with beautiful illustrations of what the world looked liked once upon a time. Most people who lived in The City Below didn't have any books. Sometimes Liam would read to the other mutant kids, and sometimes their parents would listen in, equally excited to hear the stories.

"Six years old and already reading." Hanna's yellow eyes grew misty. "I have such a smart boy."

His mother and father exchanged a look, then Hanna sighed and moved to sit next to him.

"Liam, I want to ask you a question. It's a hard question, so you can think about it for as long as you would like before answering." She fidgeted with her hands and forced a tight-lipped smile. "If you could move above ground, go to school, and read lots and lots of books, would you want to go even if that meant you can't see Mommy and Daddy anymore?"

Liam frowned. "Why wouldn't I be able to see you?"

"Well, people who live up there don't really speak with people who live down here, and traveling back and forth can be dangerous. The people without mutations who live above ground are afraid of us."

Liam scoffed. "Why would they be afraid of us?" His eyes couldn't help but drift to Rose and Risa, with their large hands and incredible strength. "They are the ones who come down here to hurt us."

Mother nodded. "I know, baby. Most mutants aren't dangerous to humans, yet they act like we carry a deadly plague. But that is why Freedom brings us these rations each month so that we can survive in peace. But you are not like Mommy and Daddy, honey. You were born from two mutants, but you don't seem to have any mutations yourself. There is no reason you couldn't go to school and live above ground. You don't have to hide here with us unless that's what you want."

Rose whistled and shook her head. "That's a big decision for a little guy."

Liam crossed his arms over his chest. Even though he was young, he knew the world was very different than it was in his books. His mother had done her best to explain how wars, biological weapons, and genetic experiments had almost wiped out all of humanity. What was left of the world was divided between people without mutations who lived in settlements, and mutants who lived in the woods and, in their case, underground. It was almost unheard of for two mutants to have a kid without any mutations, but here Liam was.

Liam had always wanted to see the sun in person and to see if the world was as bad as his mother made it sound. If Freedom could come to The City Below to bring food, he was certain that he could find a way to come back and visit his parents.

"I would like to go to school," Liam said, though his chest tightened as soon as the words left his mouth.

A tear slipped down Hanna's cheek as she pulled Liam into an embrace. "You are so brave. You are going to make us all so proud."

LIAM SAT IN HIS MOTHER'S LAP AND WATCHED FREEDOM APPROACH, a large box of food rations balanced atop her head in one hand and a bright flashlight in the other. The bright light of her flashlight bounced around the walls and the floors of the dark tunnels they called home. Butterflies did somersaults in his belly at the sight of her.

This was it. He was leaving home.

Freedom was a tall, blonde woman with sage-green eyes and a stoic face, her iron-clad exterior a shield against the world. For as long as Liam had known her, she'd never been overly friendly, but she had always been eager to help anyone in need. She walked through the dark tunnel with fearlessness, stepping over oversized rats and a three-eyed toad without flinching as she brought their food.

"Your unit's rations may be a little bit low this month," Freedom warned Gregory. "Hasey and Daniel just had twins, so I gave them a bit of extra food as she recovers from the birth and tries to keep those babies fed."

"Understandable," said Gregory. "I've met the twins. Adorable little ones."

Freedom plopped the box down in front of them. "You guys can keep the box, too, if you need it for anything. You are my last stop today."

Liam peered into the box. There looked to be only half of what they usually received. Liam hoped that after he was gone his unit would have more food to eat.

"How are you feeling, baby?" Mom whispered in his ear, wrapping her arms around him tightly. "You know you don't have to go if you don't want to."

"I want to go," Liam assured his mother.

Mother leaned in closer to Liam. For the past couple of weeks, she'd been going on and on about how Liam would grow up to make the world a better place if he did well in school.

"There are good things in the world that you have the chance to experience out there. I know leaving home is scary, but I don't want my fear to keep you from all the light and love this world has to offer. You can use what you learn to find a way to help heal this world. You'll come back to The City Below someday when you are all grown up and tell us about all of the brave things you have done, right?"

Liam nodded.

Freedom knelt beside the box so she was closer to Liam's height. She offered him something he'd rarely seen her offer anyone—a smile.

"Hi, Liam," Freedom said. "I hear you are coming with me today."

Liam nodded. "Mommy says I can go to school."

"You'll be living with me at the Resistance headquarters. You are going to get so much love as the baby of the family. We have a few mutants living with us, but none as young as you."

"Mommy says I'm not a mutant."

"Right. Well, that's fine. At the Resistance, you'll be living in a rare community of both humans, like me, and mutants, like the people you know here. Everyone who lives at the Resistance is working to help mutants. Maybe when you are older you can be a part of that mission."

Liam smiled. Someday, he'd help his mom and dad. He'd help Rose and Risa, too. "Will I get to see the sun?"

"Yes, of course!" Freedom laughed.

Liam turned back to his parents. "I'll come back to visit you."

"Not until you're a little bit older. Right now, I just want you to stay safe."

Liam nodded in agreement.

"Let's go, kid." Freedom took off the way she'd come. Liam scurried behind her. A quick glance over his shoulder revealed his mother blowing him a kiss. He blew one back, then ran to catch up with Freedom. She was tall and quick, and every step for her was about three for him.

Liam followed freedom through the darkness of The City Below, past units scarfing their rations, crying babies, and loud mutant animals growling and snarling. Sadness swept over him as he wondered if he'd ever have a chance to read stories to the mutant kids again.

"How are you feeling, kid?" Freedom asked.

Liam forced himself to stand a little taller and he kept his tone casual. "Happy, I guess."

Freedom led Liam to a rusty metal ladder and climbed to the top, where she opened a tiny trap door. Liam knew this trap door was one of the exits of The City Below, but he'd never dared to approach it. As

Freedom opened the door, a dull light seeped in. He watched as Freedom climbed the ladder quickly and peered down at him. He took a deep breath and griped the cool metal bars of the ladder and made his way up to Freedom.

Before climbing out, he peered into the room and saw an office full of computers, desks, chairs, and a couple of unfamiliar faces. Liam had never seen a computer or a desk chair, unless he counted old broken computers and furniture parts in a junk pile in The City Below. His eyes scanned the strange room with curiosity as he climbed from the ladder into a new world. The room was brighter than any room he'd ever seen. The air even felt different.

As Liam followed Freedom into the room, he noticed two women who looked younger than Freedom. The shorter of the two girls wore a knee-length blue dress, her curly dark hair falling halfway down her back. The taller girl had her hair in dozens of braids and pulled back away from her face.

"Hi, Liam." The girl in blue grinned from ear to ear. "We've been looking forward to meeting you. I'm Angela, and this is my friend Lilah."

Liam thought Angela's smile was pretty.

Lilah moved closer to Angela and smiled. "Aww, he's so cute!"

Angela stepped closer to Liam and extended her hand to him. "We've got your bedroom all set up. Would you like to see it?"

Liam nodded, and Angela took his hand and led him into the hallway. It felt nice to walk with Angela. Freedom had raced ahead during their journey, and he liked the comfort that holding Angela's hand brought him. He didn't need to rush to keep up—she matched her pace to his and made sure he was comfortable.

"A new home and a new school all in one day! Those are a lot of big changes."

"I'm feeling brave." Liam thought of his favorite fairy tale characters as Angela led him to a small room with a bed and a dresser inside. He knew that if he was to be anything like the heroes in his favorite books, bravery was a trait he'd need to always have.

Liam had never had a real bed, but he read about them in books. Tears flooded Liam's eyes, and Angela held his hand tighter.

"Are you okay, love?"

"I wish Mommy and Daddy could live here, too, and come to school with me."

"I'll be happy to walk you to school," Angela said, giving Liam's hand a reassuring squeeze and leading him back to the computer room. "Everything is going to be okay, I promise. I'll take you to school. I'll pick you up."

"But aren't the Warden's outside?" Liam's voice was shaky as he thought of Wardens raiding The City Below, capturing, killing, and kidnapping mutants. His mom never told him what happened to the mutants who disappeared without their bodies ever being found, but he had a very active imagination.

"Yes, they are, but they won't hurt you. You'll be carded. It's kind of like a fake ID. Before you can go to school, Freedom needs to make you a CitCard. It's a card that proves you don't have any mutations, and that you are a citizen of this settlement. Our fake CitCards look close enough to the ones the Wardens create for us to get by."

As Angela spoke, Liam studied her face. Angela's soft brown skin, pretty dark curly hair, and bright smile showed no signs of mutations.

"Are you a mutant like my mom and dad?"

Angela nodded. "I am. I grew up in isolation in the forest in a big garden. My dad told me that he and I were the last two people alive on all the earth. Turns out, that wasn't true. That's a story for another day. The point is, mutants who live above ground are often isolated. I know The City Below can feel bleak and depressing at times, too, but it's a blessing that you have grown up around so much love and community. Not everyone has that."

Freedom stepped into the bedroom and handed Liam a change of clothes. "Hop in the shower and then change into this. You'll need to clean up if we are going to pull this off."

"Shower?" Liam asked.

"I'll run him a bath," Lilah said, rushing off to the bathroom. "I'll set some soap and washcloths out for him."

After Liam cleaned himself up and got dressed, Angela took a picture of his face. A large printer purred as it created Liam's CitCard. Liam's mouth fell open in shock as he looked at his card.

"How did you get my face on it?" Liam asked.

"It's a camera. After school today, I can introduce you to some of the technology we have here. Cameras, computers, cars." Angela chuckled to herself. "I still remember the first time I saw a car. I was so scared and confused."

"Angela's going to take it from here and walk you to school." Freedom handed Angela the small card. "You are in good hands with that one, kid."

"Do you know what an elevator is?" Angela asked.

Liam shook his head.

"Well, we are in a basement right now, and the elevator is how we get up to ground level. It can be a little bit scary the first time you ride one, but you are welcome to keep holding my hand."

Angela led him to a shaky elevator that made Liam's stomach queasy as it rattled its way up to the unknown. When they reached the ground level in one piece and the doors slid open, Liam noticed tiny bits of light seeping into the building's boarded-up windows.

"Is that ... sunlight?"

Angela nodded.

Liam's heart raced with excitement. "I've read about it in a story."

"There's a lot more of it outside." Angela led Liam to the building's front door.

When she opened the door, light flooded his field of vision. He slipped his hand away from Angela's grip and covered his eyes.

"You just need a little time to adjust," Angela assured him.

When Liam stepped outside, the warmth of the sun on his skin felt like a long-awaited embrace. Angela stood in front of him, shading his eyes from the brightness, then placed her hand over his and eased his hand away.

Liam blinked, squinting in the sun.

"You're all right." She grinned down at him. "See?"

"I never want to be inside again!" Liam declared as his eyes adjusted. Sure, the little bit of grass he saw was dark brown instead of green, the streets were littered with trash, and the buildings were mostly dilapidated ... but there was grass, streets, buildings, sunlight, and fresh air. It was something out of a fairy tale.

Angela laughed. "Well, I can't promise that, but we can spend as much time outside as we can muster."

Liam skipped ahead as his worry dissipated. The sunlight felt so hopeful.

Many of the buildings in the Chicago Settlement had patched and boarded windows, and the roads were full of craters and debris. The city had skyscrapers that stretched toward the clouds in various states of disrepair, yet he could see evidence that some things were being rebuilt and restored, as some areas of the settlement looked more occupied than others.

He read tattered posters and flyers taped to buildings as they walked down the sidewalk.

"'The cure for the future.'" Liam read aloud. The poster had a picture of a sad-looking man with tentacles for arms on the left, and the same man with human arms and a bright smile on the right.

Angela's mouth fell open. "You can read that?"

Liam nodded.

"I think you'll be top of your class at school."

"But what does the poster mean? A cure?"

"I wouldn't worry about it now. There has been talk of a drug that could cure mutations, but it likely will not be available for years to come. President Kane has been working on all kinds of things and making drugs for humans that mimic mutant powers." Angela shook her head. "The Wardens kill mutants for having the same powers that they are trying to copy."

"So, if they make a cure, my family could live up here with me?"

"That's a big if, but maybe," said Angela.

"That's what I'm going to do when I grow up," Liam said. "I can help them figure out a cure for mutants so my parents can live with me."

"So, you want to be a scientist?"

"Yes."

"Trust me, I know the feeling of wanting to help," said Angela. "At the Resistance, all we do is try to help. Over time, I've learned that sometimes we have to focus on helping ourselves first. Deciding to move here is a big change and will take some adjustment, so let's take things one step at a time. I think you are going to have a great first day of school."

Liam nodded in agreement. "The best first day!"

THE SCHOOLHOUSE WAS A LARGE BRICK BUILDING WITH SHATTERED windows. Though the grass was dark brown instead of green, the large field and barren trees surrounding the structure reminded Liam of the illustrations in his book.

"Usually there are other kids out here," Angela said as they entered a pair of large gray doors. "We are a little late. They are already inside."

Liam raced ahead and pushed open the door, then scampered down an empty hallway, his footsteps creating a rhythmic "thunk, thunk." He smiled up at the colorful drawings and painting kids had taped to the walls.

As Liam and Angela approached the classroom, he could hear giggles, chatter, and laughter coming from behind the closed class-room door.

Angela let go of his hand and placed her hand on his back, giving him a small nudge toward the door as she offered a grin that filled him with warmth.

"Everything is going to be okay." Her voice a soft, comforting embrace that reminded Liam of his mother's. "You are going to have such a great day. And after it's over, I'll be here to take you home."

Liam's eyes grew wide, and his pulse sped up. "Home?"

"To the Resistance." Angela corrected herself.

"Oh, right." Liam frowned.

Angela ruffled his hair playfully and once again nudged him to the classroom door.

Liam stared up at the door, listening to the laughter and conversa-tion on the other side. Angela knocked, and Liam, suddenly unsure, hid behind Angela's leg as the door swung open. A short woman with long black hair looked from him to Angela.

Fear seized Liam as he looked at the teacher, and then looked past her into the room full of young children. Liam wasn't so sure how he would fare spending all day in a room full of people without mutations. They looked so different from the kids in The City Below whom he played with. The only experience he'd had with people without mutations was when the Wardens came to The City Below to terrify mutants with raids. Freedom was the only kind person without mutations he had known.

"You must be Liam," the teacher said. She extended her hand, but Liam didn't shake it. "I'm Miss Reed."

Liam continued to hide behind Angela's leg and burrowed his face into the back of her knee.

"He's a little shy." Angela offered the teacher an apologetic smile.

"That's okay." She chuckled. "Liam, how about you have a seat on the carpet? We are having circle time, and I was just about to read a book."

At the mention of a story, Liam's eyes lit up. "A book?"

"He likes books," Angela said to the teacher with a wink, then turned back to Liam. "I'll be back to pick you up in no time."

Liam nodded, and Angela hugged him. "You are such a brave kid," she said before taking her leave.

Liam took a tentative step into the large and colorful classroom. Tiny brown desks sat atop bright green carpet that resembled story-book grass. The desks were clustered together in groups of four to create small tables. Many of the items in the room looked like they had once been broken but had since been repaired with love. There was a shelf against the back wall with books, games, toys, and other materials stacked neatly on it. Across the room from the shelf was a green chalkboard, the true focal point of the room. About eight children sat in a circle in front of the chalkboard, squirming about and talking amongst themselves.

There were words on the board. Liam read them aloud. "Have a happy Monday."

The teacher's eyes shot up in surprise. "You can read that?"

Liam nodded as he looked around at the kids in a circle, trying to figure out where he should sit. While most played and talked with each other, he noticed one girl who wasn't moving. She sat by herself quietly in a corner, her nose tucked into a book. Excitement coursed through him at the sight of "Fairy Tales" by Hans Christian Andersen. He raced over to the girl, sat beside her, and smiled.

She glanced up at him, but only for a second, before looking back down at the beautiful illustrations on the pages.

He peered over her shoulder and saw that she was looking at a picture of a mermaid. "Hi. What's your name?"

"Fable," she said.

"I'm Liam."

Fable nodded without looking up at him.

"May I see the book?"

Fable frowned. "I'm looking at it."

Liam scooted closer to her. "I can read it to you if you would like."

She looked skeptical. "You can read this? This is a big-kid book."

Liam nodded as she handed him the book. As their hands brushed together, Liam noticed a tiny red spot on her wrist. It almost looked like a bruise, but the texture was off. The scaly spot reminded him of his mother's blue skin.

"Why is your arm red?" Liam asked.

The girl tugged her sleeve forward, covering the spot. "I fell. It's a bruise."

"That's a funny-looking bruise."

Fable's shoulders sloped, and she lowered her head. She turned away from Liam, an annoyed expression on her face.

The teacher rang a bell. Fable put her book down. All the students except Liam quickly sat on their hands and gave her their full attention. Liam looked around the room, confused.

"Good." The teacher pulled a stuffed wolf out of her bright red bag. "Today, we are going to read a story about a big bad wolf. Does anyone know which sound a wolf makes?"

The class barked, growled, and howled.

"Correct!" she said. "Now, let's quiet down. We don't want the wolves to hear us. Before we read the book, I want us to introduce ourselves. We have a new student today, so we are going to pass this wolf around. When the wolf gets to you, say your name and one fun thing that you did this week. We will get to know our new friend's name and a little bit about him."

Liam thought hard about his week. For the most part, he'd sat in the dark, smelly confines of The City Below. But today, he left the only family and home he'd ever known. He'd learned what a camera and an elevator were, and he saw the sun for the first time. He knew better than to talk about that, or about moving to the Resistance.

"I went to the park with Mommy," a boy said.

His brain raced as he watched the kids pass the toy wolf around and talk about places he knew nothing about and things he had never done. He tried to think of something interesting to say.

"I played with the big kids who live next door," a girl said.

Liam decided to talk about the mermaid story he'd read just as a redheaded boy with broken glasses held the wolf out to him. Liam flashed the boy a smile, then took the wolf. As his finger brushed against his classmate's, he felt an unfamiliar chilling sensation coursing through his veins toward his fingertips. It was as if the blood flowing through his arm had turned to ice, but somehow it didn't feel bad. It felt invigorating and powerful.

Liam gasped, gripping his classmate's wrist as if holding on for dear life while the room blurred around him. His vision became hazy, as if he had spun around and around and suddenly stopped.

"What … is happening?" Liam asked the class. It was like nothing he'd felt before—exhilarating, but terrifying. He tried to look at his classmate to see if he could feel it, too, but he was so dizzy it looked like his classmate had two heads.

His classmate's four eyes widened in surprise and his two faces looked as if they were on the verge of screaming, but the scream never escaped his lips. Liam blinked in confusion, and the word came into partial focus. Liam screamed instead, in shock from the terror on his classmate's face but unable or unwilling to pull his hand away. The other kids in the classroom covered their ears. Liam could sense his panic and fear, but he didn't know exactly what was happening or what was wrong. His vision snapped back to normal, and he could see the full extent of the terror on everyone's face.

"Are you okay?" Liam asked the classmate whose wrist he held. The boy gasped loudly and grabbed at his chest with his free hand. Finally, Liam let go as the boy collapsed to the ground. A vacant gaze filled his green eyes.

"Wake up." Liam tried to shake his classmate, but he didn't respond.

"Teacher, help him!" Liam looked up at the teacher. "Something is wrong."

Miss Reed raced over. "Excuse me, love." she put a hand on Liam's shoulder. When the teacher's hand touched his shoulder, the cool sensation moved from his fingertips toward the place where her fingers met the fabric of his shirt. He felt as if the room was spinning again, though he didn't feel as dizzy as the first time. His vision stayed in focus as the teacher froze then fell back, her hand gripping her own chest. Liam tried to help the teacher by pulling her upright.

"No!" Miss Reed gasped, crawling away from Liam and grasping her chest. "Get away!"

"What's wrong?" he asked.

Miss Reed collapsed to the ground, her eyes vacant and still. All the kids screamed and ran away from Liam.

Liam looked around the room, confused, then he looked at the two motionless bodies at his feet. The kids were looking at him with fear, as if he had hurt his teacher and classmate.

That wasn't possible, was it?

Had he hurt them?

If so, how?

He'd touched them … but that was all he had done, and he'd touched many people before. People like his parents, his friends, and Angela, but, he realized, never anyone without mutations.

Not until today.

"I didn't do anything!" Liam screamed at the class. Panic and fear welled up inside him as he realized the gravity of the situation.

Liam knew what death was. It happened often in The City Below. But to have two people die right in front of him, by his own hands, was another story altogether. He wanted to go home to his mom and dad … but at the same time, he didn't.

What if he had done this? What would his parents think? They thought he was normal. No, they thought he was perfect. He was supposed to grow up and help them someday. But they were wrong. He was a killer, the worst kind of mutant.

Kids started screaming at each other. "Go get the teacher," someone yelled.

"I wanna go home," another child cried.

"Call the Wardens!" screamed another.

Liam knew if the Wardens came, he would not make it back to the Resistance or to his parents alive. Wardens killed mutants without remorse, even mutant children, and it was clear that his parents had been incorrect in assuming he had no mutations.

Liam shut his eyes and covered his ears, trying to block out the external screams and the internal confusion and guilt. Two hands seized his shoulder. He was surprised someone was brave enough to touch him. He opened his eyes in terror, expecting to see another classmate fall to the ground.

"Look at me." Fable's voice was steady and sure, a beacon of peace in the storm as she held him still. To his relief, she was not hurt, and she was not afraid. "It's all right. Breathe. You're all right."

So Liam focused on her eyes and held her tightly. In that moment, her eyes looked brighter than the sunlight.

"You need to come with me now," she said. "It's not safe for you here."

He nodded in agreement, never wanting to let her go.

# FABLE

*F*able moved stealthily through the shadowy woods, her coily black-and-red hair hidden by a scarlet shawl and hood. Skeletal tree branches rasped against her garments as she crept through the dense forest, looking over her shoulder to make sure she was alone.

The sound of barren branches rustling and snapping behind her caused the hair on the back of her neck to prickle. She couldn't push aside the feeling that she was the target of someone's—or something's —watchful gaze.

*Turn back, you idiot,* Fable thought to herself. She didn't want to risk anyone figuring out where she was going. She didn't want anyone to know that the cabin in the woods existed, or for anyone to find the boy she'd hidden inside of it. Even though 11 years had passed since Liam had accidentally killed two people in class, Wardens were known to hold grudges. His life depended on her stealth and secrecy.

Fable scanned the woods, noticing a lone wolf lurking a few miles in the distance, its yellow eyes a pop of color in the dull forest as it watched her, its body partially shielded by brown, dry shrubbery. She felt a hint of comfort that there was an animal following her rather than a Warden. Wolves tended to congregate around these parts—

maybe due to the fact that her her late grandmother treated them like cherished pets, feeding them as if they were her own.

The wolf looked normal, but with all the experiments that had been done on humans and animals during the Bio Wars, she had no way of truly knowing what she was up against. Mutant animals could hide lethal supernatural abilities. Fable knew better than to run. Nothing good could come from making herself look like prey.

*Why can't I have a helpful mutation, like super strength or fire breath?* Fable thought to herself. *Why can't I stop hearts with my touch, like Liam?* She wanted a power that could put any rabid wolf in its place. Instead, she had useless scaly red patches on her skin that she kept hidden under makeup and oversized clothes to save her own life.

As a child, her skin and hair were both brown, with only a few red spots on her arm and leg. The spots had been inconspicuous enough to pass as bruises. Now that she was 16, the spots had spread and didn't look much like bruises anymore. She covered her face daily with heavy makeup, and she hid her skin under baggy, oversized clothes. She didn't let anyone touch her or get too close. Not her friends from school. Not even the boy in the cabin whom she loved dearly. If the red marks overtook her body and she could no longer hide them, she'd be killed by the Wardens in town.

The wolf took off and disappeared into the forest, and Fable heaved a sigh of relief. She was alone as she ventured deeper into the woods, the ancient trees that loomed overhead giving her a feeling of shelter despite the eerie shadows their gnarled branches cast as they clawed at the darkened sky. Though the wolf had left, she still felt as if she were not alone. She forced herself to brush aside the unsettling feeling.

Among the trees, Fable spotted the hidden cabin, its timeworn logs covered in moss and ivy. The cabin had once belonged to her grandmother before she disappeared. Grandmother had been a mutant fond of exploring, and Fable guessed a Warden had found and captured her. As Fable pushed open the door, the warm, rustic scent of wood and herbs enveloped her. With a glance at the pot on the kitchen table, she immediately noticed the delicate aroma wafting from its contents and could see that he'd made some type of sweet-smelling herbal tea.

Joy filled her heart at the sight of Liam sitting by the fireplace stirring a hearty bowl of soup atop the fire.

He spun around, his eyes widening in surprise as he saw Fable standing there. His coily hair had been styled into a tapered cut and, at seventeen, he had a stubble from the facial hair he shaved off, but for a guy who lived alone in the forest, Fable thought he definitely kept himself together. She hadn't brought him any clothes or tools during this trip. She'd just wanted to see him.

"Hey, Sunshine!" The crooked grin that spread across his lips made Fable's heart flutter. She loved his smile and his humor. She loved the way he looked at her. Fable thought back to the day they met. After Liam had killed a student and teacher during his first day of school, Fable dragged Liam from the school, down the streets of Chicago, to her big blue two-story house where she enlisted the aid of her parents. They helped her sneak Liam out of the Chicago settlement. Fable's family had then taken him to the cabin, where he was raised by Fable's grandmother until she disappeared.

Liam had been living in Fable's grandmother's cabin for eleven years now. As Fable and Liam grew, they developed a fondness for each other. Playdates turned into actual dates, and Fable looked forward to moments she could sneak away from the settlement to see him. He was the only person, outside of her family, who knew about her mutation. He was the only person who made her feel safe and secure.

"Hey, Heartstopper."

He sauntered past his bed, dashing past the clutter of books adorning his small wooden desk, until he enveloped her in his arms, coaxing a tender kiss from her lips. As his lips met hers, a rush of warmth raced through her veins, his gentle touch sending shivers of delight through her body. She could taste the sweetness of the tea on his lips. He tasted like sugar and honey. She was tired from her walk, but his lips were soft and his embrace was warm. The journey had been more than worth it.

"I didn't know you'd be here tonight," he said. "I've missed you."

Fable glanced over at the food atop the fire. "Where did you get that?"

He looked away, a guilty smile playing on his lips.

"Did you go foraging again?"

"You can't keep me caged up in here, Sunshine; I'm not an animal."

"It's not safe for you outside." Fable said, and he chuckled.

Fable frowned. What was she to do with him? He'd definitely grown into a person with a bit of a defiant streak. He was a risk taker, while she saw herself as more level-headed.

"Roaming the woods alone is dangerous," Fable said. "I don't want you to go missing like my grandmother. The majority of the plants are dead. I can't believe you are even finding much of anything edible."

"I'm careful," Liam promised, pulling her closer. "And I find a few things. You don't need to worry about me."

"I brought you a book." Fable pulled a ripped and worn novel out of a pocket in her shawl and watch Liam's eyes light up. She chuckled to herself. He'd never outgrown his love for a good novel.

Liam took the book from her hands and scanned the back, reading the plot summary.

"It was written before the Bio Wars," Fable said. "It's fantasy. About some guy who finds a magical ring or something. Apparently, it was pretty popular back in its day."

Liam walked over to the table full of books and picked one of the larger books up. "I've been reading through this Encyclopedia of Chicago. It was written before the bio wars, but I think it helps me understand how the city came to be what it is now. I've been learning about some landmarks. There were these abandoned freight tunnels under the Chicago Settlement that I think became The City Below."

"That's interesting." Fable pulled a backpack out from under her shawl, opened it, and let apples and bread fall out onto Liam's bed.

Liam's eyes grew wide. "Where did you get apples?"

Fable shrugged. "We get them in our rations from time to time. It's a rare treat."

The Wardens only offered rations to people who didn't have mutations. They would be out of luck if anyone noticed Fable's red patches.

Liam walked over to his bed, plopped down on it, and looked Fable up and down, a bemused expression on his lips. "Aren't you hot in all of that?" he motioned to her layers of clothing.

"It's not like I have a choice."

They broke bread and shared a meal, their limbs in gentle contact, and Fable was acutely aware of their knees and shoulders touching. He made her feel as if her skin was electric. He locked eyes with her as they ate.

"What?" She laughed and looked down.

"You're beautiful," he said. "Can't I look at you?"

Fable gazed back up at him as their eyes met. She felt a type of comfort and peace that she had only ever felt in his presence. He was her shelter from a harsh and dangerous world.

"Well, you are kinda cute yourself," Fable admitted as her cheeks grew warm.

After they ate, Fable melted into Liam's embrace. Her shawl slipped down from her head, and Liam played with her hair.

Fable's muscles tensed. Her hair was turning red. There was a reason she wore long sleeves, gloves, and hats.

"Liam ..." Fable trailed off.

"I know, I know," he said, moving his hand away. "It's just ... your hair looks pretty."

"The red is spreading," Fable said, lowering her voice to a whisper as if they were not the only people in the cabin. "It's getting on my face, on my hair. I might have to live out here with you sooner than I thought."

"Would that be so bad?"

"Honestly, no. But then I wouldn't be able to bring you food and supplies. I don't want to force my parents to make the dangerous trip out here to keep us alive."

"I admit, having you here with me wouldn't feel like much of a tragedy. It gets lonely out here by myself." His hands moved from her hair to her hands that were hidden inside brown leather gloves. He didn't touch them, just placed his hands near where her hands rested. "Why do you hide your hands from me? I think you are beautiful. You know I don't care about the red."

Fable shrugged. "It's getting worse and spreading all over. Do you want to see how bad it's gotten?"

He grinned, looking her up and down.

"On my hands!" She shook her head at him. "How bad it's gotten *on my hands.*"

"If you'd like me to," Liam said, and Fable slid her gloves off, a grimace on her face as she looked at her scaly, bright-red hands. "The Wardens are starting to question why I dress the way I do, covered from head to toe in all seasons."

Liam moved his hand closer, brushing his finger against her skin. "It's been so long since I've held your hand, Fable."

Fable took his hand, lacing her fingers with his. "I know."

Liam smiled at her. "You know. my mother had a mutation very similar to yours. But even before the Bio Wars, things like this happened. There was something called vitiligo that could do this. There is nothing wrong with you. There is everything wrong with a world that would hurt you for being what you are."

"Liam, have you ever considered moving back to The City Below? Visiting your family again? I have some extended family down there, too."

Liam shook his head. "I like being by myself."

Fable knew that wasn't true, but she suspected he would rather be alone than be abandoned or rejected. His family thought he had no mutations. She doubted he wanted to tell them that his mutation had killed two people. He had no family with whom he was in contact and no friends other than her.

"I'm sure your family would love to see you."

He looked away. "Not after what I've done."

"You did nothing wrong," Fable said. "You were a child. You had no control over what happened."

Liam put a finger on Fable's wrist, sliding up her sleeve to expose more red skin. He caressed her wrist with his thumb.

"And you have no control over this," Liam said, motioning to the red on her hand. "Yet you act as if you are ashamed."

He lifted her hand to his lips and kissed the tiny bit of exposed skin. "Every part of you is beautiful. You are a dream come true. And I'm *so glad* that you are as you are, because if you weren't, I wouldn't be able to hold your hand. A world where I could never touch you would be a sad, sad world." A wicked grin curled across his lips. "I can't wait to help you forget the name of everyone who made you feel there was something wrong with you."

He pounced on top of her to steal a kiss, the two of them falling back onto the bed. He grinned at the surprised expression on her face, and Fable laughed. He laughed with her. Then their lips met, and electricity shot through her body as he kissed her hungrily, moving from her lips to her neck, purposefully kissing every red spot he could find.

A distant sound sent a shiver down Fable's spine—a subtle, persistent rustling, like something or someone moving through the underbrush just beyond the cabin's walls. Her muscles coiled with tension as she tuned into the subtle sound.

"Are you okay?" Liam asked.

She pulled herself away from Liam, her eyes widening in stark fear.

"Liam," she whispered, "did you hear that?"

Liam's brow furrowed as he strained to listen. The rustling grew louder and closer. He nodded, concern etching lines on his face. "It's probably just a wolf. Don't worry, we're safe in here."

Fable wasn't so sure. The loud, rhythmic rustling didn't sound like a wolf's stealthy steps. If she didn't know better, she would have guessed there were human's outside. Her heart raced as she listened intently. But now there was silence.

Then, with a sudden, deafening crash, the cabin door pushed open, splintering inwards. Fable's and Liam's eyes widened in terror as a group of four Wardens stormed into the cabin. They were armed with menacing, gleaming guns, and they moved with ruthless precision, surrounding the bed.

Fable opened her mouth to scream, but her voice caught in her throat as she watched them flood into the room, their boots crunching over the broken door.

*This is my fault*, Fable thought to herself. *I wasn't careful enough.*

Fable crawled to the furthest end of the bed, distancing herself from the Wardens. An apple fell from the bed as she moved. It rolled to one of the wardens toes. The warden scowled at it, as if vexed by the notion that someone of their humble status could possess such luxury.

"Liam!" Fable whispered, hoping he would move away from the armed men. Instead, he moved his body in front of Fable protectively and locked eyes with the Wardens.

Behind them, just outside the door, a wolf crept up to the cabin and peered inside, its lips curled in a snarl as a low growl escaped its mouth.

Liam pulled Fable back to shield her from the intruders as they pointed guns at their heads. Fable couldn't look at the guns or the men, so she focused on the glowing yellow eyes of the wolf as it sneaked into the cabin.

# LIAM

*L*iam moved in front of Fable, using his body as a barrier between his girlfriend and the four Wardens' guns. His muscles tensed beneath his shirt, bracing for pain and death as he locked eyes with the nearest Warden, a beefy 20-something with dark hair and eyes. If the Warden chose to pull the trigger, he'd be dead in an instance.

Unless, of course, he touched them first.

"If you want to walk out of here alive, you're gonna want to put the guns down and get out!" Liam yelled from the bed. He prayed that he sounded braver than he felt.

He assessed the firearms, searching for any clue as to whether they were loaded with the tranquilizer bullets the Wardens sometimes used or lethal rounds. They looked lethal enough. Liam reminded himself that he was lethal, too.

The tallest Warden chuckled. "Why, what a big mouth you have." He moved his gun's muzzle closer to Liam's face. "Kids who talk too damn much make me want to blow it off their faces even more."

Fable reached forward and gave his hand a squeeze. He wasn't sure if she was trying to calm him or to remind him to watch his mouth.

"That wasn't a request," Liam said through gritted teeth, crawling forward on the bed, closer to the Wardens, heart pounding with every inch. He'd spent the entirety of his life in isolation, avoiding people so his touch wouldn't kill them. It had all been for nothing, because he knew if these men even looked at Fable the wrong way, they wouldn't see tomorrow. They would not destroy the one good thing this world had left while his own heart still beat. He hated the thought of using his powers, but he'd do what needed to be done and save both of their lives.

"Get back!" the tall warden said.

"Liam …" Fable whispered from behind him.

"This is my home," Liam said to the Warden as he inched closer. "*You* are the invaders. I will move where I want."

Slowly, Liam hung his feet over the edge of the bed. He hoped his slow movement would make them feel safe enough to delay shooting him. He needed to get closer, needed to make sure he could touch them all before one of them pulled the trigger. He watched the Wardens share quick, confused glances as he allowed his feet to touch the floor.

"When a person with a gun tells you to stay put, you stay put," the tall Warden said. "You got a death wish?"

Liam stood in front of his bed, inches away from the muzzle of a gun. He was close enough to touch the tall Warden now, but then the others would have time to shoot. He needed to find a way to touch them all.

"Say goodbye," the tallest Warden said, stepping even closer to Liam and putting his finger on the trigger.

"That girl!" a skinny Warden said to his beefy colleague. "I've seen her in town."

The tall Warden paused and gazed from Liam to Fable.

The skinniest Warden stepped closer to Fable, his gun moving from Liam's chest to her forehead. "You go to my daughter's school, don't you?"

The tall Warden shook his head. "A mutant in our schools. What is this world coming to?"

"My daughter said she's a weird one. Dresses funny. Hardly talks," the skinny Warden said.

A third Warden cocked his weapon. "Let's just kill them both now. Gotta keep our kids safe."

Liam's blood boiled as he listened to them talk about killing Fable. He needed to keep a level head. He remembered how powerless he felt as a child when his teacher and classmate died because of him. Since that day, he vowed to never feel that powerless again. The time for thinking and analyzing was over. They were distracted by Fable, and he needed to move.

Liam lunged forward, knocking the tall Warden's gun to the ground. An icy feeling raced through his limbs as his hand made contact with the Warden's body. Time seemed to slow down and speed up at once as adrenaline surged through him. He blinked, shaking off the dizziness that threatened to cloud his focus. There was no time to indulge in vertigo or hesitation.

He didn't have time to wait and see if his touch still had the ability to kill because, as the tall Warden fell, the two Wardens standing closest pointed their weapons at his chest. With a swift movement, Liam managed to touch them both ever so slightly before the sound of gunfire caused his heart to skip two beats and his body to stumble and fall to the ground.

The sudden sound had jolted him. For a moment, he feared he had been shot. It took him a heartbeat to realize that he remained unharmed. The warden's gunshot had rung out as Liam's touch has made the warden tumble to the ground. The bullet had crashed through a window.

He was on the ground, but he was not alone. All three Wardens whom he had touched were on the ground, gripping their chests until they stopped moving altogether. Liam heard Fable scream, but he saw the relief on her face when he stood back up, unharmed. Nausea filled his gut at the sight of the three dead Wardens at his feet as his brain flashed back to the worst day of his life—his first day of school.

He reminded himself that he wasn't a child anymore. He was seventeen—practically an adult. There was only one Warden to take down now. If he succeeded, no one from town would know who did this or discover Fable's mutation. Liam lunged at the fourth Warden, but when his hands touched his arm, the Warden grinned at Liam and lifted his weapon to Liam's chest.

Liam's stomach sank. He was touching this Warden, but he did not die. Instead, he shoved Liam backward with the muzzle of his gun, then laughed a too-loud laugh.

Liam shoved the Warden back with force, but he didn't bulge. It was as if he was made of concrete. "What are you!" Liam screamed.

The Warden seized Fable, pulling her up from the bed as she screamed and kicked, and placed the head of his gun to her temple. "Try putting your hands on me again and your little girlfriend's dead."

Liam wanted to fight back, but any move he made could be the end of Fable's life. There was no way to move toward the Warden and get to her without giving him time to pull the trigger. His powers were useless here. He looked at Fable, who was sobbing, and spoke to her directly.

"Look at me, Sunshine," he said as the Warden took a step back, pressing the gun to her temple with force.

Fable looked scared, but Liam knew she was no damsel in distress. These men were monsters, but Fable had never been afraid of monsters. She was the little girl brave enough to meet a monster on his worst day, take him by the hand, and hide him deep in the woods for safe keeping. She'd fallen in love with a monster, and he would go to any lengths to keep her safe.

"You are strong," Liam said. "They wouldn't target you if you weren't. Everything is going to be okay. Breathe."

Fable's breaths were labored as she tried to regain her composure.

"Good," Liam said. "Just keep breathing, baby."

"Enough of this," the Warden said, yanking Fable away from Liam. As the Warden dragged Fable to the cabin door, Liam swung at him, hitting him on the head with a fist.

"You don't want to do that," the Warden growled between clenched teeth, pressing the gun against Fable's temple. Liam felt a jolt of terror as the gun clicked, his own heart seeming to stop in sync. The Warden's grin was wide and menacing as he pulled Fable toward his car, the gun still pointed at her head. Liam suddenly felt just as hopeless as he had as a child. He'd need to be less impulsive if he wanted to successfully help her. For his entire life, she had protected him. Now he needed to protect her.

After the Warden shoved Fable into the backseat, the wolf brushed against Liam's leg as it raced to the Warden's leg and bit his ankle. The Warden shot the wolf. The sound of the gunshot caused Fable to scream and cry even louder, but the wolf refused to let go of the warden's leg. The Warden kicked and swore at the wolf before picking up the angry animal and shoving it in the back of the car beside Fable.

"Now you both can get chopped up alive," the Warden said as he slammed the door shut.

Liam ran from the cabin to the Warden, trying to knock the gun out of the Warden's hand. The Warden lifted Liam and tossed him into the cabin with superhuman force. Liam landed amongst the dead as the Warden opened the back seat of the car and stuck his head in, his butt to the cabin door. It looked like he was doing something to Fable or to the wolf, but Liam couldn't see what. Liam raced back outside, stepping over shattered glass, broken wood, and bodies on his was to Fable. As he approached the car, the Warden hopped back in and swiftly drove away.

# FABLE

The blindfold that the Warden had placed over Fable's eyes pinched her ears and pulled her hair. With her hands tied together, she squirmed in her seat in the back of the Warden's car. The car rattled Fable about as it bounced down the road.

*Where the hell is he taking me?* she questioned. *Will Liam be able to find me?*

The wolf was surprisingly docile, despite being shot and given a muzzle. It cuddled up beside her, its head resting on her lap. Before he had covered her eyes, she'd noticed its foot was bleeding from the gunshot wound, but the bullet seemed to have only grazed the animal. The wolf's presence was somewhat comforting, despite her circumstances. Having the wolf so close reminded Fable of her grandmother, who had a fondness for animals. As the car bounced down the road, she shut her eyes and forced her mind to replay happier times.

Twelve-year-old Fable held her mother's hand tightly as they navigated the dirt road. The path between the Chicago Settlement and her grandmother's cabin had always been dark and scary. She could hear creatures hissing and scurrying about as the cold night air made goosebumps emerge on her skin.

"Why can't we bring a flashlight or something?" Fable whined. "I can't see."

Mother carried a basket full of food, clothes, and supplies. She shifted the heavy basket from one hand to the next before answering Fable. "Too many eyes in the woods. That's why we wear black, keep our heads down, and hurry to where we are going."

"But my feet hurt."

"It's good exercise." Mother reassured her, checking her hip for her weapon with her newly freed hand. Fable's mother was a tall woman with long, black braids pulled back into a ponytail. Loving but protective, she shifted her eyes around the forest as she pulled Fable closer. "We are almost there. How about you sing our song, baby?"

Fable crossed her arms and groaned, but her mother's singing voice filled her with peace.

"*This little light of mine …*" Mother started. It was a song from before the Bio Wars that her mother had sung to her as a baby.

"*I'm gonna let it shine,*" Fable joined in.

"*This little light of mine,*" they sang together. "*I'm gonna let it shine.*"

It didn't take long for Fable to spot the cabin the distance. Her heartbeat sped up a bit at the sight of Liam standing outside of it, looking around the forest with wrinkles on his young forehead. Fable wasn't sure why the sight of Liam filled her with joy, but she forgot about the long journey and her sore feet and picked up her pace to reach him.

His face smoothed and his eyes brightened at the sight of her. "Fable!" he called out, racing over and embracing her. He hugged Mother as well, then the worried expression came back.

"She left again." He looked from Fable to Mother. "She's been gone since early this morning. I was thinking about going to look for her—"

"No!" Mother said quickly. "You are safer here."

"But…" Liam protested.

"My mother knows how to take care of herself. Now let's go inside for the night. I'm sure she will be back by the morning."

Liam laced his fingers through Fable's before following Mother into the cabin. Fable blushed as a wave of warmth spread through her. The touch of Liam's hand in hers sent a flutter of emotions that she was still trying to figure out.

INSIDE THE CABIN, LIAM AND FABLE STAYED UP LATE. THEY USED Grandma's old quilts and wooden chairs to build a blanket fort, which they filled with additional blankets and pillows. Inside, they listened to wolves howl at the moon outside while chatting amongst themselves. Fable could tell Liam was nervous about Grandmother's disappearance, and she tried to distract him, retrieving a book she had stashed inside of Mother's basket.

"What's this?" Liam asked.

"It's about a kid who finds out he's partially a Greek god," Fable said. "I've been reading it at school."

She noticed a hint of sadness flash over Liam's face at the mention of school, and so she wrapped her arms around him and pulled him into a hug. Liam held her longer than she expected. In that embrace, Liam held her hand.

Fable's eyes went from her hand to Liam's eyes.

"You must think I'm being a baby." Liam said, moving his hand away.

"Not at all," Fable said quickly.

"I think I'm just nervous about your grandma. She's been leaving more often, staying away longer." Tears filled his eyes. He turned his head and tried to blink them away before Fable could notice.

"Look at me," Fable said, her voice more confident than usual. "You don't have to hide your pain from me. You can show me how you feel."

He brushed the dampness on his cheek away before fixing his gaze on her. His inquisitive stare left Fable perplexed. Why was he afraid to reveal his emotions? He was her best friend. Didn't he understand that she was a refuge where he could be himself? She had never felt freer than when she was with him and she had assumed he felt the same.

"What if she doesn't come back? I'll be out here all alone."

Fable pulled him back into her arms. "You'll never be alone," she promised.

Uncertainty flickered in his eyes, and Fable continued to hold him. They didn't speak, but their silence was comfortable. She listened to his quick breathing slow down while she listened to wolves and other wild animals shuffle about outside.

"You'll never be alone," she whispered again.

He slipped an arm around her waist and held her close, lacing his fingers between her fingers once again.

Moments passed by, and his eyes were perfectly dry, but he still didn't seem ready to let her go. His hands became warm, and he couldn't seem to stop fidgeting, his thumb brushing against hers in a nervous rhythm. His grip tightened as if he needed the physical connection to ground himself amidst a whirlwind of emotions.

"You okay?" Fable asked. She noticed sweat starting to pool on his forehead even tho the crisp night air had cooled the cabin.

"Y...Yes."

A smile tugged at the corners of Fable's lips. He was cute when he was nervous, and the sight of him caused butterflies to dance in her stomach. But what did he have to be nervous about? It was just the two of them.

"Fable..." he said, but the word trailed off at the end, as if he wasn't sure how to say whatever it was that he wanted to say.

"Yes?"

He leaned forward, a question in his eyes as he looked up at her. As they held each other in the blanket fort, tension seemed to electrify the air around them.

He stole a glance at her lips, his gaze lingering for a heartbeat too long, and she sensed his desire to kiss her. Fable's heart raced in anticipation as she offered a subtle nod and a shy but hopeful smile.

He closed the distance between them and his lips met hers in a tender, cautious kiss—their first kiss. A warm glow spread through her as his kiss grew more sure and confident. He pulled away, and a shy grin played on his lips. She could sense a shift in their friendship to something that felt like more. He rested his head on her chest, and she held him until he fell asleep as she watched the full moon shine outside of the cabin window.

By morning, Grandma was back, wide-eyed and wild-haired. At five foot two, she was about Fable's height, but plump, with silver hair and clothes that looked too fancy for a simple life living in the woods. She gave Mother a guilty grin before scooping Fable and Liam into a hug.

"How's my beautiful granddaughter?"

THEY STAYED IN THE CABIN TOGETHER FOR THREE DAYS. FABLE, LIAM, Mother, and Grandmother cooked together, shared stories, and played in the woods. Fable helped her grandmother leave food out for the wolves and woodland animals. This time spent outside of the settlements was one of her fondest childhood memories.

Fable knew her grandmother had a mutation that made it unsafe for her to live in the city, and Grandmother preferred the woods to The City Below. Fable had never been told exactly what her grand-mother's mutation was, but she wondered if it led her to run off and abandon Liam from time to time. Though Liam lived with her grand-mother, he was just as clueless. He said she would often disappear into the forest and come back looking weak, tired, and wild. Eventually, Grandma never came back.

Fable had tried to convince Liam to return to The City Below and reunite with his family, but he insisted he was capable enough to manage the cabin on his own. She suspected he harbored some sense of shame about his abilities that kept him away from his family.

As the Warden's car bounced down the woodland road, Fable

thought about her childhood promise to Liam that he would never be alone.

She'd find a way to keep that promise.

# LIAM

The tall dead Warden's clothes were much too big, but the other dead Wardens' clothes were a touch too small. The pants that fit the best revealed his muddy socks and ankles. The button-up top clung to Liam's chest, squeezing him so tightly he felt as if he could not breathe.

Maybe, Liam thought to himself, the shirt was not the cause of his asphyxiation. Maybe it was the city. His only human interaction had been with Fable for so long, and while she was more than enough, the Chicago settlement was a nightmarish distant memory from the worst day of his life. It felt odd to be back in the city, and wrong to be back without Fable.

No matter the reason, he felt as if the air was being squeezed from his lungs and his organs were being twisted and harvested from within. He thought about his books that detailed Chicago's history, trying to picture the maps inside of them and figure out where he was going. He looked for familiar landmarks from his books, his memories, or from Fable's stories, but didn't find any. His heart drummed a furious rhythm against his ribs as anger and fear swirled within. Damn his nerves. He was doing well to still be standing upright and walking in a straight line at this rate. He straightened his back and relaxed his clenched jaw as he approached a couple of young Wardens walking down a fragmented sidewalk.

He thought of how quickly he could end them with just one touch, how nice it would feel to have a small bit of revenge. But revenge couldn't bring Fable back. Playing it cool could.

Liam took a deep breath and let it out slowly before rushing over to the pair.

"Hello," Liam waved. He kept his free hand in his pocket. He'd have to be careful not to touch anyone while out and about, or his secret would be exposed.

The two Wardens didn't look a day older than 18. The teenage girl offered Liam a wide-eyed smile while the teen boy eyed him suspiciously.

"Need something?" the boy asked.

"Excuse me," Liam said. "There has been an emergency, and I'm a bit lost."

"Why are you wearing our uniform?" the boy asked, looking Liam up and down.

"This is my uniform," Liam said.

"Haven't seen you around before."

"Oh, well, you wouldn't have." Liam lied. "I've been transferred over from the Indianapolis settlement."

The girl smiled at him, and he noticed dark freckles on her cheeks. "Ah, I'm from Indianapolis, too."

Liam bit his lip, then tried to hide his panic under a blasé expression.

"I moved here with my dad when I was just a toddler. He was a Warden, and now I'm following in his footsteps."

A relieved chuckle escaped Liam's lips. "That's wonderful. Looks like he led you to an honorable profession." Liam wanted to gag on his own words.

"Honorable, indeed," the boy said, taking a step closer to Liam. He looked over his uniform with scrutiny, noticing the wrinkles, dirt stains, and small size. "Funny thing is, typically new recruits are flown in or escorted into town by a member of our city's Watch. I've never heard of a Warden making the trip from Indiana to Chicago alone."

"I wasn't alone," Liam said quickly. "That's why I mentioned the emergency. We came across some … trouble … out there."

The girl's eyes grew wide and her lips parted in shock. "Is everything okay?"

"Afraid not. Came across some powerful mutants out in the wilds. Trashed our car. We ran. Got separated. He's still out there, I hope."

"Who?" The male Warden's eyes narrowed. "Which one of our Wardens were you with?"

Liam blinked, unsure of what to say. He tried to think of something generic enough.

"There was more than one. I don't remember everyone's names. First day of meeting them, and then everything blew up. But I think there was someone named Smith. You know him?"

The male Warden pursed his lips but said nothing.

"I need to report what happened. There may still be time to find him."

The girl's eyes shot to her coworker for guidance. "Matty, we can help him."

Matty gritted his teeth and locked his eyes on Liam. Liam prayed he looked calm and casual.

"Come with us," Matty finally said. "I'll take you to Melissa to get you checked in."

As the two Wardens led Liam through the city, he did his best not to gawk at the buildings, cars, and people. While the city was still in a state of ruin, it was much busier than he remembered it. So much had changed in eleven years. As he looked around at the people of the settlement, he thought about the fact that while these people were living in houses, driving cars, and going to work and school, there were people with mutations starving underground in The City Below. He wondered if his parents were okay.

"So, back in the Indiana settlement, did you happen to know a girl named Kat Grey?" the female Warden asked Liam as they approached a large building near an even larger body of water. Liam's parents had told them that Chicago was near a big lake as a child, but he'd never seen it himself before. The lake was beautiful.

"Oh, yeah, Kat!" Liam exclaimed. "We weren't super close, but we went to the same settlement school. Nice girl."

"Kat's my cousin," the girl said. "I don't remember her very much. Someday, I'd love to go back and meet my extended family."

Liam looked over at a few boats that had seen better days floating in Lake Michigan and contemplated trying to use one to escape the settlement as Matty opened the door to the building. There were hundreds of Wardens in the building. Sweat built up on Liam's forehead.

"Eventually, we plan to rebuild Navy Pier. It was a huge attraction in Chicago before the Bio Wars. We are temporarily using this building as a makeshift home for recruits and a place to plan a few upcoming projects here in the city," he said.

"Oh, really. What kind of projects?" Liam asked.

"Shouldn't you know? You were recruited." Matty's eyes gleamed with a victorious spark, silently saying, 'Caught you, didn't I?'

"I was recruited to join The Watch," Liam clarified. "I was never briefed about any special projects."

The girl sighed and rolled her eyes at her coworker. "Matty, you know they don't tell them details until they are here." She turned to Liam, sympathy in her eyes. "We're planning to redevelop the city, envisioning the transformation of spaces like Navy Pier. We're working on medications to benefit both humans and mutants. By harnessing mutant abilities, we aim to assist humans. And there's progress toward creating a safe cure for mutations."

Liam's ears perked up. "A cure for mutations?"

The girl nodded. "We used to do raids in The City Below to find mutants to experiment on. The early attempts at a cure proved fatal for every mutant. However, the Watch has since assembled a dedicated team of scientists tirelessly working on the cure. Although it hasn't been made public, two mutants have officially survived the drug and it is successfully suppressing their mutations."

"Mera, that's classified information," Matty said.

Mera turned up her nose. "He's a Warden. It's something all Wardens should know by now."

"We don't know if he's a Warden yet." He nodded at Liam. "Melissa's office is this way."

Lian followed Matty and Mera down the hall. Liam eyed the door that they were quickly approaching. Once he stepped inside the door, the jig would be up. Melissa would have no clue who he was, and they'd probably be ordered to kill him for impersonating a Warden.

Mera continued to chat.

"I'm excited the cure finally worked," she said. "I mean, it sucks that so many mutants died, but now we can help the rest live a normal life! We are one step closer to making our world the way it once was, the way it could be again if humans and mutants work together."

Liam frowned. He'd never expected a Warden to speak about humans and mutants working together.

Matty, on the other hand, scoffed. "Giving out free cures to mutants for doing nothing doesn't sit right with me. We became Wardens to protect people, not help killers."

"Well, not all mutants are killers." Liam tried to keep his voice casual, but he couldn't help himself. Fable was considered a mutant just for having unusual patches on her skin. His mother and father had never hurt a fly. But he had a feeling that Matty wasn't the type of Warden who was willing to listen, nor was Liam in a position to try to explain.

Matty opened his mouth to respond, but before he could get any words out, the door burst open, and Liam was shocked to see a familiar face.

The Warden who'd kidnapped Fable looked at him with wide eyes, taking in his uniform with confusion. At first, Liam started to sweat, but he realized he could use this Warden to his advantage. Liam was the only person in the room who knew this Warden was a mutant. He could force this Warden to be his saving grace.

"Hey!" Liam declared, waving at the Warden. He turned to Matty and Mera. "He was with me! In the forest! He was out there with me and Smith. Weren't you?"

The Warden's expression filled with rage.

"Don't you remember?" Liam continued before he could speak.

"You told me your secret out there in the forest. You know, your *big* secret." Liam winked. "Would you like me to tell your friends here?"

His lips parted, but no words came out.

"Because I was just telling them about the attack in the forest … when those mutants attacked our car. Wasn't that scary?" Liam asked.

Slowly, to Liam's relief, he nodded.

"Thank you for your help, Mera and Matty," Liam said, "but because he was part of the team assigned to get me started here, I'll let him help me now. He'll be able to help me explain everything that's happened in the forest."

"Of course!" Mera said. "I hope everything works out."

Matty looked surprised, but eventually sighed and nodded. "Let's go get some lunch, Mera."

As Mera followed Matty away, Liam leaned closer to the mutant Warden so no one else could hear his next words.

"Look around," Liam said.

"At what?" the Warden growled.

"All of these people here. Armed people, just waiting to attack any mutants they find.

If you try anything here, I'll yell out to all of the Wardens around us and tell everyone your secret. You will die with me here. Now help me get Fable back."

# FABLE

*F*able huddled in the corner of a cage, ignoring the cool metal bars pressing into her back. The room was cold, and the Wardens had stripped her of her oversized clothes, leaving the red patches on her legs and arms exposed. In shorts and a tank top, she felt naked. She was sure that every living thing in the room was repulsed by her existence. Her only solace was the large black wolf nuzzled against her hand. As she tenderly stroked its fur, she cuddled closer to the beast, allowing its warmth to distract her from her nightmarish reality.

The sounds of animals shuffling about and crying out from within dozens of cages throughout the room gave her a sense of collective distress, and the musty scents of fur and animal waste made Fable gag. There were a couple of other prisoners in the room, too—a woman with long red hair in a cage with a dozen birds, and a bearded man in a cage by himself. They stared blankly into the distance, their minds elsewhere. Fable feared for her mind if she didn't find a way out of this place.

There was a black door in the distance with a tiny glass window. Through the window, she could see a Warden working in a lab. He hovered over test tubes, occasionally glancing over his shoulder to monitor the prisoners. He would see if she tried to escape.

As Fable and the wolf comforted each other, the faint and distant sound of footsteps approached the chamber. Fable held her breath when she heard someone fiddling with keys outside of the metal door. Was a Warden sent to torture her, perhaps? When the door swung open, the pale glow of overhead lights revealed Liam's unmistakable silhouette. Pure joy bubbled to the surface of Fable's tired heart. She wanted to call out to Liam, but he wasn't alone. There was a Warden at his side. Her eyes grew wide as she realized that Liam was with the Warden from the woods. Had Liam been caught, too?

It only took Liam a split second to spot her. When he did, he ran over to her with the swiftness of a river finding its course.

Fable took in Liam's uniform. Her eyes shot open in alarm. It was illegal to dress up as a Warden. Granted, it was illegal for him to simply exist.

"What are you doing, Liam?" She gestured to his uniform. "We are being watched." Her eyes shot to the lab.

"Bringing you home." He looked Fable up and down smiled. "You really are beautiful, red patches and all."

Fable, suddenly aware of her lack of clothes, tried to hide her lean legs behind the large wolf. "Did you have a plan to get me out of here?"

Liam turned to the Warden at his side. "Give me the key."

The Warden's hands trembled as he handed the key over. He hadn't made eye contact with either of them since entering the room.

Liam unlocked the cage, eager to have Fable back in his arms. With a final, echoing click, the lock surrendered. Fable crawled out of the cage and wrapped her arms around Liam. The wolf followed.

"So, how are we getting out of here?" She studied Liam's face to see if he had a plan. Liam's eyes fell on the Warden.

"I suggest invisibility," the Warden said. "The drug hasn't been released to the public yet, but it is safe. Wardens use it all the time to sneak out. Our lab is right through that black door. I can go grab the drug right now."

"We're coming with you," said Liam. They followed him to the door and peered through the glass panel. The man inside wearing a white lab coat was refilling a storage unit with drugs.

"You can't come with me. You are supposed to be a new recruit, so you would not have access to this lab. And how could I explain why we are bringing a mutant into this room? If you want the invisibility drug, you'll have to let me go in and bring it out."

Without waiting for Liam or Fable to respond, the Warden reached for the door.

"Don't even think about trying anything or everyone here is dead, including you," Liam growled through gritted teeth before the Warden rushed into the lab. Fable detected a hint of relief and even amusement in the Warden's eyes. Her hope dissipated. Whatever the Warden was trying to do in the lab, he wasn't planning to help them.

The moment the Warden left, Fable buried her head against Liam's chest. Tears crept down her cheeks.

"Everything's going to be okay."

"I don't see how it's possible for everything to be okay. We are trusting our lives to a Warden."

"I didn't see how that was possible when you told me I'd be okay so many years ago, yet we are both here today. We will both be here tomorrow."

Despite his words, Fable could see doubt in Liam's eyes. He turned away, trying to hide his fear.

"Do you remember when we were kids, and my grandmother ran off, and I promised you would never be alone in this world," Fable said. "I aim to keep that promise."

The wolf limped over to Fable's side.

"That wolf seems to really like you," Liam said as the Warden came back with two pills in his hand. He held out his open palm, offering one to Liam and one to Fable.

"You guys got lucky," the Warden said. "These are our last two invisibility pills. Take these and you'll be able to walk right out of here alive."

Liam picked up a tiny yellow pill and examined it. "You try it first."

"But there are only two," the Warden said swiftly. "And I'm not the one who needs to get out of here alive."

"Yes you are," Fable spoke up. "If you didn't need to get out of here alive you would not be helping us."

"Why do you work for them?" Liam asked, looking from the pills to the Warden.

"It's a job."

"Your job is to kill mutants,"

He frowned. "My job is to protect the settlement."

"From mutants," Liam clarified. "Often, by killing us. But you are a mutant, too. Aren't you?"

The warden said nothing.

"When you are ready to see the conditions you and your Wardens cause the mutants to live in, when you are ready to see that mutants are people, or when you are forced to see it because of what you are, you'll know where to find us," Liam said. "The Resistance isn't fond of turning anyone away. Though I'm sure they make exceptions."

Liam opened the door to the lab so the Warden inside could see him and hear him. He lowered his voice to a whisper. "Take the pill, or I'll say that you just stole drugs for a couple of mutants."

"If you tell them you're a mutant, they will kill you," the Warden pointed out in a whisper.

"But they'll kill you, too," Liam said,

The Warden's lips pressed into a tight line. "I should just shoot you both."

"But you just told two Wardens that I'm a Warden. How will you explain your lie?"

He gritted his teeth. "It's a tranquilizer," the Warden admitted, his voice a whisper. "The pill I gave you. I was not trying to hurt you. I was trying to knock you out."

Liam sighed. "Well, isn't that thoughtful of you? And what did you plan to do with a knocked out Warden and mutant? Throw a party for us?"

"Go get what we need, Liam," Fable said. "I'll stay here with him."

Liam hesitated. "How. They don't know me."

"There's only one Warden in there. If you can't talk your way out of this, I'm sure you can utilize your other skills."

Liam looked from Fable to the Warden.

"I can handle him," Fable said. "Trust me."

Fable rushed forward, planting a kiss on his lips. "Go."

He nodded and rushed into the lab.

FABLE WAITED ON PINS ON NEEDLES, ONE EYE ON THE WARDEN AT HER side and one eye peeking through the glass door as Liam chatted with the Warden inside of the lab. He showed Liam around, pointing out various pieces of equipment and storage areas. Maybe they would get out of this place without having to kill anyone.

"You live in the settlement, don't you?" the Warden asked.

Fable ignored his question, continuing to watch Liam through the glass.

"So you are like me," he continued. "A mutant pretending to be human."

"Mutant's are human," Fable snapped. "And I'm nothing like you."

He looked Fable up and down. "How did you hide all of those ugly red scales?"

Normally, a comment like that would have made Fable want to disappear, but for some reason, it emboldened her.

"I only turn red when I'm poisonous," she lied with a grin, stepping closer to the Warden.

His eyes grew wide, and his lips parted as he took a step away, unsure if he should believe her.

When Liam finally slipped out of the lab, he grinned and opened his palm. She heaved a sigh of relief at the sight of the four tiny green pills in his hand.

"Invisibility pills," he announced. "If they can make this, I believe they could make a cure."

"If they had a safe cure, I would have taken it." The Warden huffed. "The cures they have tried to make are like poison."

"And the invisibility pills?" Fable asked.

"Safe enough," the Warden shrugged. "But why should I let you walk out of here alive?"

"Someday, I suspect you'll need us," Fable said. "Until then, better stay on our good side."

Then Fable turned back to Liam. "Where is the first pill? The one he said was a tranquilizer."

Liam handed it to her, and she shoved it into the Warden's palm. Her voice was forceful when she spoke. "Take it."

The Warden in the lab glanced over at them, so she lowered her voice and let the door shut. "Take the drug you offered us."

"What? Why?" the Warden asked.

"Because you can't follow us if you are knocked out cold."

"But that's really strong. It's for animals."

Fable shrugged. "You had no issue trying to give it to us."

"Because you shouldn't even be here," the Warden growled. "I should pick you both and toss you right out of this room."

"And if you use your powers here, I'm sure the Warden in the lab will come running and find out you threw us with your super strength. Do you plan to die here with us?"

The Warden huffed, then placed the pill on his tongue.

"Swallow," Fable said as the door to the lab swung open.

The Warden in the lab coat stared at them. "Hey, what exactly are you all doing?" he asked. "Why is that mutant out of her cage?"

"Swallow." Fable mouthed, then turned to the Warden in the lab coat. "He was just telling me about his special power ..."

A panicked look filled their new friend's face as he swallowed the pill in one big gulp. It only took a few moments for his eyes to flutter, his knees to weaken, and for him to wobble forward and pass out on the ground.

The lab-coat-wearing Warden shook his head, his straight, shiny black hair falling over his brows. "He's playing with drugs. I'll have to report him for that." He pulled his gun out and pointed it at Fable. "You need to get back in your cage."

Fable's heart skipped a beat as Liam reached out, placing a hand on the Warden's shoulder. The warden let out a loud gasp, dropped his weapon in shock, and clutched his chest until he collapsed atop his slumbering friend.

Fable knelt and examined the two fallen Wardens. "That pill really was a tranquilizer. One of them is still breathing."

"So are we, for now." Liam said. "Let's get out of here before that changes."

"But how?" Fable motioned to her exposed body.

Liam looked down at the Wardens. "Which one do you think is closer to your size?"

# LIAM

*L*iam peered over Freedom's shoulder as she opened the trapdoor in the Resistance headquarters that led down to The City Below. Walking into The City Below dressed like a Warden wouldn't have been the safest or smartest choice, so Freedom and Angela had offered them new clothes. He sighed and wiped the sweat from his palms onto his jeans. His hands trembled with nerves.

Fable took Liam's hand and held it steady as they peered down a ladder that seemed to lead to nothing but darkness. The wolf stood at Fable's side, waving its tail joyfully at the ominous tunnel. "Ready to go home?" Fable asked.

"The cabin is my home," Liam said.

"Was your home. It's not safe anymore," Fable reminded him.

He took a deep breath and let it out slowly.

'Everything will be fine." Fable offered a reassuring smile.

He noticed she still wasn't wearing gloves and, for once, didn't seem bothered by it. Maybe she was distracted by everything that had happened to her, but she looked so beautiful in her simple tank top and shorts.

She took off down the ladder. Liam followed behind her, and Angela helped the wolf down before shutting the door and locking them all in. Liam petted the wolf as he looked around The City Below.

There wasn't much to see. Human voices and animal sounds echoed through the dark tunnels and bounced against the damp walls. The City Below was stickier and smellier than Liam remembered. In his memory, this place was no cozy cabin in the woods, but it was safe and warm. Maybe it was the people he'd been surrounded by as a child who made it feel that way.

"This way," Liam said, leading Fable through the darkness. Muscle memory kicked in as he looked for the area his parents called home. Lanterns and candlelights from other family units illuminated their way.

The wolf raced ahead, as if searching for something, too, yet always looking back to check on Fable and make sure she was still all right. They walked past family units cooking with makeshift fire pits, past giggling toddlers and crying babies, and past the wildest of pets.

"I think I might be lost," Liam admitted. "I thought my unit was somewhere around here ..."

"Liam, maybe we should go back," Fable suggested.

"Liam?" a familiar voice called out. "Did someone say Liam? Liam! Is that you?"

Liam turned to see a woman with blue skin, long brown hair, and bright green eyes.

"Liam!" she screamed, pulling him into an embrace and sobbing into his shoulder. "You came back! You came back."

A sense of peace overcame Liam as he hugged his mother. She led him over to his father, Rose, and Hanna, and they all had a tearful reunion as Liam explained what had happened on his first day of school.

"I didn't want you to know what I had done, so I never came back," Liam admitted. "But I decided to not let fear keep me from love. Remember when you told me not to do that?"

Liam noticed Fable was off by herself, petting the excitable wolf. He took Fable's hand and led her over to his unit.

"This is Fable," Liam introduced her. "She saved my life many years ago, and so many times over after that. When I thought I was a monster, she reminded me that I am human, that all of us are human. Even if they say we are not."

Liam noticed Fable looking at his mother's scaly blue skin in awe.

"You're beautiful," Fable eventually said.

"You are, too," Liam's mother said.

The wolf barked uncontrollably, leaping about excitedly as an old gray-haired woman strolled by. The wolf rushed over to the woman and nuzzled her knees until she bent down and allowed him to lick her face—wrinkles, gray hair, and all.

'Settle down!" Fable said, rushing over to the old lady. "I'm sorry, Ma'am."

"Gloria?" the old woman whispered to the wolf. "Gloria? Is that you?"

"Gloria?" Fable repeated, confused. "That's my grandmother's name."

The woman kissed the wolf's nose, then used the wolf to steady herself as she tried to stand back up. She walked over to Fable and put a hand on Fable's chin to study her face. "Ah, yes. Fable. Why, you were a wee one when I last saw ya. I thought you and your mother and father were living above ground."

"Who are you?" Fable asked.

Liam moved to her side. "You okay, Sunshine?"

Fable nodded.

"I'm Daya, Gloria's sister and your great auntie. What brings you to The City Below?"

"I'm just visiting," Fable said.

"She's with me," Liam interjected. "I wanted her to meet my family."

Daya looked Fable up and down. "Ah, yes. Well, I don't see how the Chicago Settlement would be safe for a girl like you."

Liam noticed Fable cross her arms over her chest, remembering the patches on her skin. He put an arm around her waist.

"Are you saying my grandmother is this wolf?"

"Oh, yes. It happened to her a few times when we were children, see. I remember those big, yellow eyes. That mutation runs in our family. It was one of the mutations made back when they did experiments on people. The Watch loved playing around with science, trying to create the myths and legends of old. Werewolves, I think they were called in the pre-Bio Wars stories. They were people who could shift into animal form under the light of a full moon. For us, no full moon was needed. Just time."

"My mom never told me about any of that." Fable frowned.

"They tried to turn people into all types of things. mermaids, werewolves, witches, vampires, living ghosts. Most people just died from those experiments. But some survived, and these abilities passed down from generation to generation."

"So will I change into something like that?"

"Hell if I know. I've never changed into anything but an old woman. I mean, I do have acidic blood, which lets the Wardens know I'm a mutant, but that's not nearly as fun as being a Werewolf."

"Can Grandma change back?"

"That's the thing. In our family, usually after a while, people permanently stay as whatever they changed into. Your great-great-grandpa spent his golden years as an ant. Your great-great-grandma was always concerned someone would step on him."

"I've been trying to find a safe place for me and Liam to live. I'm not sure if it's the forest, or if it's The City Below. I admit, I'm fond of the forest, but it didn't turn out to be safe. Do you feel safe down here?"

"I don't think any place in this world was made to keep us safe, but here we can protect each other."

"I remember that the most," Liam said. "Everyone helped each other out in The City Below."

His heart ached with sadness as he thought about all the time he had spent away, alone. Why hadn't he come back? He had told himself he didn't need people, aside from Fable, but perhaps she had been right. Being around others could be beneficial for him. He left home with the dream of being a hero and helping his family someday. Sure, he couldn't fix their mutations, but just being with them mattered.

"Well, we definitely need some help right now. There is a Warden who knows about Liam's abilities, so we need to lie low for a bit." Fable sighed. "I'm not sure where we will eventually end up, but maybe this is where I'm supposed to be for now. I could use some community, and it would be nice to get to know my family who lives down here."

Mother turned to Daya. "Would your unit like to come have dinner with our unit?"

Daya looked away. "My unit is just me right now. Has been for a while. But I can bring over the rations Freedom left me."

"It's settled then." Mother cupped her hand together. "You're joining us for dinner. We are all family over here, and everyone's welcome at the table."

Liam took Fable's hand and led her to the small fire pit. Father started the fire, and they split rations and continued to chat long after the food was gone.

"One day, they will find a cure," Fable whispered to Liam. "You and your family will have a big house in the Chicago Settlement, and you'll be safe. Everyone will be safe someday."

Liam didn't respond. Maybe she was right, and maybe she was wrong. He held Fable close, stealing a tender kiss and enjoying the warmth of the fire. The City Below was far from perfect, and their living conditions were far from good, but he'd seen firsthand that the world above could be even nastier than the world down here. As he held Fable in front of the fire, he realized, for the first time, that there could be light in The City Below, too. The world was not a fairy tale, but having the right people around seemed to infuse the broken earth with a touch of magic. No matter where he lived, as long as Fable was at his side, he knew he'd have his happily ever after.

# ABOUT THE AUTHOR

K. R. S. McEntire is from the generation that dashed through platform 9 ¾, fell in love with vegetarian vampires and motorcycle-riding werewolves, and took down a corrupt government during the Hunger Games. Her sorting hat placed her in Gryffinpuff (she's convinced it's a thing).

McEntire remembers how magical it felt to follow wardrobes into unimaginable worlds, and she hopes to bring that same joy to the next generation. Her earliest introduction to swords, dragons, and mythical kingdoms was playing RPG games alongside her father, and she's glad that writing allows her to build her own epic worlds.

She runs the Facebook page Diverse Books with Magic, where she promotes diversity in speculative fiction. McEntire lives in Indianapolis with her husband and her two sons, Justus and Kaden.

Want more of this dystopian world? Be sure to explore the author's complete trilogy, *The Eden Saga* by K. R. S. McEntire, which includes the books *Saving Eden, Finding Eden,* and *Making Eden.* If you've had your dystopian fix check out her Upper YA / New Adult Fae fantasy *A Dance of Blood and Destiny.*

MONTREZ

SHADOW AND SONG

She has a bright future.
He has a dark past.
When two wayward souls collide, sparks fly, and fate calls …

A contemporary YA fantasy set in the world of *The Selah Tales,* loosely
inspired by *Peter Pan.*

# SUNFLOWERS AND
# SNICKERDOODLES

*"Would you like an adventure now, or would you like to have your tea first?" – Peter Pan*

LYRIC MASTERSON HAD A WAY WITH WORDS. SHE WAS NO GREAT ORATOR like her grandfather, and she didn't have her cousin Maya's knack for storytelling, but she was her namesake. She could pen a song. Her talent was undeniable. She brought a smile to broken hearts and energized the sluggish. She soothed the restless. She made even the toughest critic cry like a newborn just by sharing her songs. But with all the power of her gift, she had one problem. Whether she was in front of an expectant crowd or in the company of her supportive family, she could never sing the words how she felt them. She tried many times, but the words would get trapped in her throat or wouldn't come at all.

So, instead, she filled notebook after notebook, pouring her songs out on paper, infusing those pages with the beautiful words she couldn't voice herself. If she couldn't sing the words, maybe she could capture the words and find others who could. Lyric would put on her headphones, crank up the tunes that inspired her most, and get to work, lost in her world of music from sunup to sundown. Sometimes even into the wee hours of the morning.

It was in those moments of unguarded musical joy that her family would catch the sweet whispers of her songs, though they didn't mention it for fear that her nerves would bury her budding gift altogether. You see, it was those little random snatches of song that held their frayed family together. When arguments brewed and tempers flared, when melancholy loomed and bitterness tried to plant its ugly roots, her melodic voice would sing a note, bringing sunshine to their increasingly rainy days.

Lost in her musical world, she didn't realize her family was falling apart. At least, not until it was almost too late …

Grandpa Selah wasn't well. The spry septuagenarian, who didn't look a day over 40, suddenly looked very much his 74 years, if not older. Always chatty and full of stories about the good old days, he barely said a word to his neighbors, if he was even to be seen beyond looking through the blinds of his bedroom window. He didn't leave the house anymore. He didn't answer the phone or respond to friendly visits. He barely bothered with the groceries and the cooked meals they left on his porch. His concerned neighbors tried to look after his lawn and the neglected garden he loved so much. They knew something was very wrong. The man who had always been a pillar in their community needed help now more than ever. He needed his family.

That summer, Lyric and her family packed their bags, leaving the hustle and bustle of Chicago for the quaint, somewhat dilapidated charm of Old Glory East, Ohio. It sat just outside the Greater Columbus downtown area, a small urban suburb, fighting and losing its battle against gentrification. The local small businesses were disappearing, but the residents refused to be moved from their homes, homes that had belonged to their families for several generations. They didn't build homes like that anymore, houses carved in sturdy, brick layers and stone, with large porches held by thick Grecian-style columns, full of cozy rooms, grand fireplaces, and hidden nooks and crannies to explore.

Grandpa's house was always a welcoming haven. Lyric and her

siblings looked forward to visiting him during their breaks from school. His house held the aroma of spices and the promise of hearty meals from sizzling, hickory bacon, eggs fried hard, and buttery biscuits in the morning, to his famous meatloaf or slow-cooked pot roast for dinner. Their bellies were always full. But Lyric's favorite part of her stay with Grandpa was his famous hot cocoa topped with Cool Whip and a touch of cinnamon powder.

They would nurse the comfort drink, curled up on his soft, sinking sofa while he sucked on Werther's caramel candies and told them tall tales with the evening news droning in the backdrop. Grandpa's house was warmth and joy wrapped into 2,500 square feet. His house was always home away from home. At least, it used to be.

Butler's Bookstore & Café was Lyric's third place now. It was a cozy joint at the edge of the historic Olde Glory East neighborhood that smelled like dusty pages, buttery pastries, and burnt coffee beans. It was an acquired scent for some, but for Lyric Masterson that smell was more familiar than anything else in her life lately.

Not even home felt like home anymore. New address. Different zip code. Different everything. Lyric's throat tightened as she suppressed the tears. She turned up the volume of her crooning beats. She could drown out her worries with her headphones in and her music turned up until her ears ached more than her heart did.

The soft light in the bookstore café darkened, jolting Lyric from her even darker mood. She stared up at her sister, whose face was identical in most features but uniquely her own in style and attitude. Big bright brown eyes, even bigger smile, she drummed on the table, a beat Lyric could feel more than hear. She frowned, reluctant to leave the comfort of her music for whatever mischief Mel was dreaming up.

Mel wriggled her brows but waited for Lyric to remove her head-phones before she spoke. "I knew you liked your new little dusty hide-out, but now I see why."

She cut her eyes to the café's counter. Lyric, still yearning for music and solitude, struggled to follow her gaze. A short line had formed, and the barista was busy taking orders. He looked up when he saw her, a quick flash of his eyes, before returning his attention back to a gray-haired woman asking about the soup of the day. She frowned at her sister. "Why are you over here bugging me? What happened to that musician you were flirting with?"

Mel slapped a flyer on her table and tapped it with her manicured French tips. "It's like fate! This is your chance to brush off your nerves and embrace the spotlight."

Lyric rolled her eyes even as she tried to shove the mounting panic down. Mel could smell fear like sharks could smell blood in water. Once she caught a whiff of it, she'd make it her personal mission to help her sister get over it. Whatever it was.

Lyric sighed. "They're hosting an open mic here tonight."

"In an hour. Enough time for you to work up the nerve to talk to that cute barista, order us something from the café, and warm up that sultry voice," Mel said with a shimmy.

Lyric balled up the flyer. "I'm not singing."

Mel leaned into the table, her cinnamon-gum breath making Lyric's nose tingle. "Nope. You're just reading, reciting your beautiful lyrics like the poetry they are."

Lyric rolled her eyes. Sometimes her sister could be so dramatic. She thrived in front of a crowd, as bright and warm as sunshine. Lyric wished she had her sister's confidence, but where Mel was constant, Lyric wavered like the moon—going through cycles of highs and lows, doubt and belief, fear and something almost like boldness, but not quite.

"You have a beautiful voice, and you write amazing songs. There's no reason to waste all that talent. For real, sis, trying to sell your music for other people to sing is like selling pieces of your soul. It's just not right."

Lyric sat back in her chair and folded her arms. "Not everyone is made for the spotlight," she grumbled.

She knew her music was good, but she wasn't sure she was good enough for her music. She'd worked up enough nerve to submit her songs to a few indies and even some of the mainstream artists she admired, but they'd all said the same thing.

*It's good. But not for me.*

Mel dismissed her words with a wave of her hand. "If you aren't ready to sing those lyrics, you can recite them. You gotta start some-where, sis."

Lyric groaned, and Mel flicked her forehead, a light censure for her sister to stop whining, before she continued, "Get me a latte with an extra shot of expresso. Something sweet. Not too nutty. And remember ..."

"I'm a sunflower. Not a shrinking violet," Lyric finished with a sigh.

Mel winked. "Selahs are made for the light. You're going to be great."

"What are you? My manager now?" She scoffed, but Mel had already walked away to flirt with the tatted, dreamy-eyed musician setting up his keyboard at the front of the café's dining area.

"You're a sunflower. Not a shrinking violet," she whispered, repeating her sister's mantra. But her hands were already sweating, and her throat felt like it was packed full of cotton.

Lyric surveyed the bookstore, finding some comfort in the small crowd of customers. Maybe she could do this ...

Her sister's talks and friendly, but assertive, nudges always left her feeling pleasantly anxious, somewhere between terror and excite-ment, like waiting in line for a rollercoaster.

She eyed the café's register, her gaze connecting with the curious barista's unapologetic stare. He offered her a quick, crooked smirk before bowing his head to focus on cleaning the counters.

There was no line, and with anxiety making her throat feel drier than a desert, she could use a comfort food to give her a boost. She cleared her throat as she approached the register, her body a ball of trembling nerves.

"What can I get you?" the boy said, his deep brown eyes rising to meet her gaze.

She liked his eyes, how he looked at her so directly, which was odd for her. She *hated* when people stared. Lyric averted her gaze before forcing herself to study the menu. The barista's eyes stayed on her face. She could feel it just as sure as she felt the butterflies gathering in the pit of her stomach. "I'll have a red velvet latte?"

He snorted. "No."

"No?" she echoed.

"You don't want that," he said as their eyes connected again. "I think you're more of a tea kind of girl."

"I'll take that latte and your soup of the day, with a quiche and water," she said, this time more firmly. Just because she let Mel boss her around didn't mean she was a pushover. She wasn't going to let— her eyes found his name tag—Peter tell her what to do. If she wanted a red velvet latte (she didn't), she'd have a red velvet latte.

Barista Peter raised his hands in half-hearted surrender. He offered her a flash of a smile, sporting an annoying boyish dimple in one cheek, before keying in her order. "If you like it, I love it," he said.

She gave him a sour look as she paid, and despite her annoyance, her cheeks went hot when his fingers brushed hers as he dropped the change into her hand. She shoved the money in her pocket while Peter whipped up her order.

He served her latte with a large, droll smile. It seemed almost mischievous. Retreating to her seat, Lyric sipped her sister's drink, tossing him a defiant, deliberate look of her own. But as soon as the warm liquid hit her tongue, she choked, resisting the urge to spit it back into her sister's cup. Her tastebuds had never been so insulted. She nearly gagged, and despite herself, she turned to see Peter watching her, his eyes twinkling with laughter.

"What's in this?" she muttered, prying open the lid to inspect what looked like a cup of warm blood. She shuddered. The red velvet latte definitely didn't suit her taste, though she suspected her sister would love the syrupy flavor.

"Like I said, you strike me as more of a tea kind of girl," came Peter's voice. He gave her one of his dimpled smiles again, setting two hot cups down on her table.

"The latte's for my sister," she admitted.

His eyes flicked to her sister. "That makes more sense," he said as her sister's giggles traveled, filling the air with her levity. Even her laugh was beautiful.

"She signed me up for the open mic event," she said, peering up at Peter and finding his eyes refocused on her. Most guys saw Mel and normally didn't look in her direction again. Not that she minded. She liked being unbothered. She liked her peace, though now with Peter smiling at her, she thought his curious attention wasn't so bad.

At least, not until he sat down across from her. Then her already nervous heart fluttered some more. But the aroma of baked goods and coffee beans became more apparent, soothing some of her initial jitters. Pete didn't smell like a sporty cologne or like all the dreamy boys from her favorite books. He smelled like the *bookstore*. She inhaled the comforting scent with a sigh before she realized what she was doing.

Pete's eyes widened and he sniffed at the air. "What?"

But she didn't need to answer. His cheeks reddened when he smelled his shirt and he chuckled. "Snickerdoodles. I just took a batch out before I made your order. Want one?"

She gestured at the uneaten quiche, but he was already up, retrieving the freshly baked goods from behind the counter.

He returned with a handful of large cookies decorated with sugar flakes, and he offered her one before taking a giant bite out of the one he had snagged for himself. Then he took one of the cups from the table, nudging the other hot drink in her direction.

"I might not be good at much nowadays, but I do have impeccable skills when it comes to customer satisfaction." he said, talking in between chews. "I have this uncanny ability to know what refreshments are just right for each person, just by looking at them."

"So … Snickerdoodles. That's what you think of when you see me," she said.

He gulped his drink down and wiped his mouth. "Fresh out the oven, sweet, buttery and satisfying without doing too much. Who could resist?"

Lyric took a small bite of the treat, and then another, all too aware of Peter's attentive gaze. She nodded. "It's alright."

There was no way she'd tell him he was right, that the sweet treat was just what she needed to soothe her nerves. Her sweaty hands and racing heart were gone, replaced by another kind of feeling, one that was just as uncomfortable but somehow much more pleasant.

"It's my favorite," he said with a smile, before biting another cookie.

Her face warmed, and the gentle heat spread to her chest, sinking deep into her heart. She was sorting out her words, trying to figure out a response, but the moment she couldn't define was gone before she could form a syllable.

Peter pointed at her cup and winked. "A cup of tea before your moment in the spotlight."

Then he was striding back behind the counter like a confident peacock.

Lyric had never felt so annoyed or so seen.

# SHADOW AND SONG

"*All are keeping a sharp look-out in front, but no one suspects that the danger may be creeping up from behind.*" – Peter Pan

"YOU'RE A SUNFLOWER," LYRIC WHISPERED TO HERSELF, THOUGH SHE didn't believe it.

"Sunflower, sunflower," she whispered before taking another quick sip of tea while Peter was distracted. She didn't want him to know how right he was. The boy knew his way around a good cup of tea. She wondered what other things he knew beyond his knack for tea and fondness for baked goods. What did he do when he wasn't behind that counter? Did he smile at everyone the way he smiled at her? Maybe it was all part of his customer service act.

"You ready?"

Mel blocked her view of Peter, though she thought she saw him wink at her a moment before she lost sight of him. Her heart made that weird jump again.

"Lyric?"

Her sister waved her cup. "Good stuff."

Lyric snorted before downing the rest of her tea. On the loud-speaker, someone announced the open mic event.

Lyric had noticed the growing crowd before, but now ... So many voices. So many bodies. All the eyes. Sure they were strangers, but could she really do this? Could she really share her songs?

"You're a sunflower. Not a shrinking violet."

Her sister gripped her hand. "You were made for the light."

She wished her cup of tea wasn't empty. The hint of honey and light citrus still coated her tongue, just enough to make her want another sip. Maybe she could treat herself to a second one after she survived being on the mic.

Mel whistled. "Somebody really is coming out of their shell. Did you see this?" She turned Lyric's cup and pointed at the ten digits scribbled on the generic frame. "The cute barista gave you his number."

Lyric's mouth dropped, her eyes moving from the cup to find Peter, as if one look at him might confirm what she'd seen with her own eyes. She was both grateful and irritated when he didn't give her one of his mischievous, knowing looks. He was busy cleaning his station.

Lyric was vaguely aware of Mel grabbing her phone. She watched her sister's thumbs fly over the keys, pausing only to ask his name. Lyric answered her with a squeaky stutter, which her sister rewarded with a stern look.

"Stop looking so surprised he gave you his number. He knows a good thing when he sees it. You're gorgeous! Trust me, I should know."

Lyric snorted, a little louder than she meant to. Both girls ducked their heads to hide from the onslaught of giggles. Mel nudged her. "You should text him."

As the open mic event started, Lyric felt more nervous to text Peter than she was at the thought of sharing her songs with the crowd. She contemplated what she should say to him rather than what song she should recite. Until the last minute, when the event MC called her to perform, she stood while all eyes were on her. She took her phone and trudged to the front of the crowd. Apart from her sister's smiling face and bright eyes, the rest of the audience was politely disinterested. Strained smiles, a few yawns, and uncomfortable shuffling.

"No one wants to hear you," a nagging thought whispered in her head.

She cleared her throat and stared at her phone, caught between two daring acts. If she didn't text Peter now, she never would. If she didn't open her mouth to sing, she never would. Steadying herself, Lyric let her fingers slide across her keys so fast she was sure her message was littered with typos and bad autocorrects.

"Thanks for the tea," she wrote.

And on a bold whim, she recited the song in her heart, putting her phone away and closing her eyes to recall the words. Her voice came out shaky at first, barely audible beyond her racing heart. For a minute, she didn't hear anything else. The café was nothing more than the darkness behind her eyelids. Then a phone beeped, breaking through the silence. She opened her eyes, finding the source of the distinct sound.

Peter cradled his phone in both hands. His jaw went slack, and that annoyingly cocky charm transformed into something else, before a smile touched his face, a real smile. Not a smirk, but a genuine smile. He looked up. Their eyes met, and her heart pounded some more. But the room was no longer silent, and she wasn't whispering anymore. Mel's musician friend joined Lyric's voice, coloring her words with the swooning chords and keystrokes, adding a rush of courage and joy so much that Lyric was no longer quoting her song. She was singing.

She watched Peter, her eyes wide at the sound of her own voice. His eyes were wide, too, as if pleasantly surprised, and then he shook his head as if trying and failing to shake the moment's hold. He was suddenly awkward behind the counter, as if he didn't know his way around the space, as if he had forgotten how his hands and feet were supposed to work. He grabbed out a few plates and saucers stacked at the edge of the counter. His hand shook, and all of them fell, shattering on the floor.

Lyric jumped at the burst of sound, but pushed through, watching Peter scramble for the broken glass. He jerked, pulling back, clutching his right hand. Her voice pitched when their eyes met again. This time, Peter's eyes weren't bright with mischief or wonder. His eyes were dark, and that darkness engulfed him like a cloud. She'd never seen something so vivid, as if every shadow in the room had flocked to him.

Lyric stopped singing then, unable to find her words. She broke her gaze with Peter, finding her sister. Did she see it too? The growing shadow building over the café? Didn't anyone else see it, stretching, looming like a massive, thick smoke? Peter clutched his hand to his chest, his eyes dark and wild, before he retreated through the doors of the kitchenette.

As soon as it appeared, the shadows rolled away. It followed Peter like a stalking shadow, leaving no hint it existed at all, replaced instead with thunderous applause and a standing ovation.

# ANGELS AND WISHFLOWERS

"*If you cannot teach me to fly, teach me to sing.*" – Peter Pan

IT WAS OFFICIAL. LYRIC WAS NO SHRINKING VIOLET, BUT SHE DIDN'T FEEL like a bright sunflower, either. She felt more like a dandelion, the white, fanciful, and persistent garden pest young children made wishes on. She'd always been fond of dandelions, but feeling like one was something else altogether. She felt dazed and wind-blown.

Her evening had become something between a dream and a nightmare. She had faced her greatest fear, only to be taunted by a new one, one that felt just as terrifyingly surreal as her short-lived victory. She had sung once. Could she do it again? And what were those shadows? It had to be nerves. Just her imagination. Something as wild and vivid as that … How else could she explain it? No one else had seen the black mass of shadows. Except for Peter. Maybe?

She searched for Peter after her performance, but he wasn't in the café's kitchenette or anywhere in the bookstore. He hadn't responded to her text, either. Worst, he'd left her message on read.

"Thanks for the *tea*?" Mel repeated her text for the fifth time. They were back at Grandpa Selah's place, settling in for the night. The rest of the house was silent, everyone else deep in sleep. But Lyric was restless, pacing the wood floors of the room she shared with her twin.

"Okay, I get it. It's not the best line," Lyric grumbled.

Her sister flung herself on the bed. "You think?"

"Well, what would you have said?" Lyric asked, pausing her restless pace in favor of glancing out the open window. She peered outside, leaned over the frame, and breathed in the warm night air. The smell of pinecones and the itchy pollen in the air made her nose tingle.

"I would've asked him out," her sister said.

She could hear the calculation in her sister's voice. Mel could probably smell the anxiety rolling off her, just like she could sense her need to mettle. The small hairs on her arm bristled with alarm.

Mel sat up. "Give me your phone."

Lyric threw up her hands. "Can we forget about *him* for a minute," she said, "And can we talk about the fact that I did it? I sang in public, in front of an entire crowd of people!"

Mel's face softened with a genuine smile, her scheming momentarily forgotten. "I knew you could do it." Mel tilted her head, offering her sister a considerate look. "You're like a person who's photogenic when they don't know the camera is on them. You sound amazing until you know someone's listening. But tonight ..."

Mel broke into song, mimicking Lyric's voice. When her voice cracked at the end of a run, the sisters laughed. Lyric nudged her, repeating the note back with ease. Mel rolled her eyes. "Show off."

Lyric repeated the run, moving her hips to the rhythm.

Mel fanned her like she was on fire. "Ooh, sing it again."

Lyric obliged, repeating a few lines, only stopping when a slow, satisfied smirk spread across her sister's face. That meddlesome look was back. She couldn't figure out just what Mel was up to, but judging by the instinctual discomfort in the pit of her gut, she knew it wasn't good. "What? What did you do?"

Mel's eyes slid past Lyric to the window behind her, and she scrambled up and toward the door. "Nothing. Love you. Bye!"

Mel fled from the room so fast, Lyric could barely get a word out, but her heart pounded so hard in her chest, she could feel it in her ears. Her sister was gone, but she wasn't alone.

She felt invisible eyes on her, like static prickling against her back. Lyric spun on her heel to face the open window. Just outside, perched on the branches of the tall evergreen, was a boy. He was dressed in a black tee and dark jeans. His curly fro was captured haphazardly under his matching beanie cap, a few strands obscuring the view of his bright brown eyes. Lyric yelped when she saw him, but instead of slamming the window down, she stumbled back in surprise.

"You!"

Peter put a finger to his lips, his eyes darting around the yard before he edged closer toward her. As nimble as a cat on the limb, he almost looked at home there, staring up at her. "Well if it isn't the legend herself. I should've known it was you …"

"What are you talking about?"

"The Angel of Olde Glory East," he explained without explaining much at all.

Lyric glared at him, not at all charmed by the admiration in his tone or that same look of wonder he'd shown when she sang at the bookstore before he ghosted her.

"You going to let me up?"

She snorted. "Not unless you can fly."

He had the nerve to sigh. Not in an irritated way, but in a thoughtful, dreamy kind of way she never imagined a boy might. At least, not when it came to her. "Sing for me and I might," he said.

Her cheeks grew hot, and she fought the smile tugging at the corners of her mouth. "I think you should go."

She moved to shut her window, but Peter shot up so fast she paused.

"Wait! Please," he said.

Lyric hesitated. "Why did you disappear back at the bookstore?" she asked. "And what are you doing here? Did you follow me?"

He looked insulted. "No! I'm staying with my aunt next door. And I can explain."

She blinked. "You're related to Miss Nova?"

She stopped short of asking how many cats her grandfather's neighbor actually had, and if she was really dating Mr. Hill from down the street. The retired accountant was infamous for thrifting in neighborhood trash bins and repurposing unwanted curb items into odd homemade gadgets. Mel swore she saw him leave Miss Nova's house at odd hours. But confirming the Olde Glory East rumors should be the least of her concerns, a thought that echoed with Peter's flash of irritation.

"I don't have all night, Snickerdoodle. The neighborhood is in trouble, and you're our only hope."

# TALL TALES AND TRUTHS

*"The moment you doubt whether you can fly, you cease forever to be able to do it."* – Peter Pan

LYRIC TIPTOED BAREFOOT OUT OF HER ROOM, PIVOTING AROUND ALL THE known noisy floorboards she'd discovered over the years. Her mother's snores and little brother's sleep talking sounded from their rooms, while Grandpa Selah's door loomed more silent and sullener than she would have liked. She paused at his door, tempted to crack it open to check in on him. Resisting the urge, she made her way to the stairs, descending them as quickly and lightly as she could.

Mel was lounging, drooling on the couch as old reruns of her favorite reality show echoed from Grandpa Selah's ancient television. Lyric flitted past her sister and unlocked the front door to find Peter sitting on the porch stairs. His shoulders were slumped, but when the front door shut, he stood straight.

"I didn't think you were coming," he admitted, his light brown eyes wide and earnest in the dark.

"You wanted to talk?" she whispered as they both sat side by side on the porch swing.

Lyric couldn't help but appreciate the summer night. The air felt just right, snug like a fleece blanket across her skin, though the heavy smell of pollen and pine made her nose itch. Fireflies lit up the night, tiny pockets of green and yellow. While she admired the beauty of the historic neighborhood, with its grand, old, weathered houses and quaint landscape, she could feel Peter's eyes on her.

"Everyone knows your family is something special. My aunt says that wherever there's a Selah, mayhem and miracles are sure to follow," he said after a while.

Lyric smiled at that. Her family did have a reputation for good trouble.

"I used to visit here and there over the years," he continued, "before my parents died."

He cut her a look, somewhere between panic and suspicion, but rushed on before Lyric had time to fully process what he'd said. He leaned forward on his knees, his voice hushed and so soft she found herself leaning closer to hear him.

"Everyone knows your grandpa's a storyteller, but we have our own urban legend around these parts. Aunt Nova would tell me about the 'Angel of Olde Glory East'. She said the angel would fly in every summer, and if you kept your windows open and had an ear to hear, her song could lift your spirits." His eyes twinkled with fondness and a soft smile lit his face. "I always thought it was just a story. Until tonight."

Lyric didn't know what to say to any of that. Her family was rich in storytelling and exaggerated tall tales they claimed as family history. From royalty and rebels to inventors and creative revolutionaries, her mother's side of the family had a hard name to live up to. She never once imagined there would be a story about her, whispered like some grand myth. There had to be a mistake.

"My family is something else," she said, "but I'm no angel, and I'm definitely no legend."

"No, you're not," Peter agreed, and even though she already knew it, the words still hurt. But before she could feel too sorry for herself, he continued. "You're the real thing."

A black cat crossed the lawn just then, peering up at them with glittering yellow eyes. It sauntered up the porch and jumped into

Peter's lap. He welcomed the cat, sitting back in the swing to cradle it in his arms. "One of Aunt Nova's foster pets. She's a retired veterinarian, you know. Likes to rescue strays from the pound and find them good homes," he explained.

Lyric's mouth fell open, and Peter laughed. "Yeah, I've heard the rumors, but she's no crazy cat lady. She's just got a heart for lost boys like Jet here."

"I guess you can't believe everything you hear," she murmured.

"Not everything," he agreed, "But *some* things."

Lyric rolled her eyes. "I'm a songwriter. Not a singer. Tonight was just a fluke, some lucky accident. My sister is the star. She's going to acting school this summer and studying theater, and ..."

Her voice trailed off as Peter shook his head. "Don't give me that, Snickerdoodle. If you can inspire an entire neighborhood from your bedroom window, you can win over a measly crowd."

His words triggered an unexpected burst of irritation. They'd only just met and he was already lecturing her, discounting her fears and insecurities. "Don't call me that. That's a horrible nickname! Besides, what do you know?" she snapped.

He flinched and his bright eyes darkened. "I know that it would be a waste to bury your gift, to hide yourself from the world. Don't take it for granted, Lyric. Some of us don't have the luxury of dreaming. Some people never will."

Jet, who had been purring before, suddenly hissed, jumping out of Peter's arms. He frowned, clutching the arm he'd injured earlier that night. "Are you okay?"

"None of us are okay. Olde Glory East is a mess," he said with a scowl. "There's a darkness here like I've never seen before, and it's spreading. If you hadn't worked up the nerve to sing, tonight ..."

He let the words hang, but she pressed. "Peter?"

His eyes locked with hers, all hints of cheer and laughter gone. "You saw it. You saw the shadows. Your song saved my life, and it's the only thing that can save your grandpa. Don't lose your newfound nerve, now."

# HOPE AND TERROR

*"Sometimes, though not often, he had dreams, and they were more painful than the dreams of other boys. For hours he could not be separated from these dreams, though he wailed piteously in them. They had to do, I think, with the riddle of his existence."* - Peter Pan

PETER HADN'T DROPPED BY HER HOUSE TO ASK HER ON A DATE. THERE'D been no first kisses or anything else one might expect during a late-night visit. He'd come to whisper about the kind of things you find in bedtime stories.

Lyric was no stranger to myths and tall tales. She was related to legends, acquainted with very real fairy tale love stories. But she never imagined she'd have her own story to tell, or that someone was already telling stories about her. It felt almost silly to even consider, but the longer she tossed and turned that night, the more real it seemed.

But Lyric was no angel. There was no way her voice could chase away the shadows that had crept into Olde Glory East, not when she couldn't remove them from her own life.

Peter claimed her song had pushed back the shadows, but there was still a lingering darkness. Now that she knew it wasn't just a figment of her imagination, she could see it everywhere. Stretching across the floorboards, hovering in the dark corners of her room, even in the flickering lamppost outside her window.

Grandpa Selah's house was no longer her summer retreat. It felt as strange and as foreboding as everything else in her life lately. Like her father not being with them. Or the way her heart felt half crushed with panic at the thought of her sister leaving her behind. Her song writing was going nowhere, but Mel was going places. More specifically, Juilliard. From there, anything was possible.

Lyric was happy for her sister, but frightened for herself. She didn't have a backup dream, but once her sister left, she knew her mom had more sensible plans waiting for her after senior year. Something reliable. Something safe and stable and more grown up. She shivered, burrowing deeper in her sheets and blankets. As if that could stop her impending doom.

Light spilled into her room, reflected from the glass window next door. Ms. Nova's house. She didn't have to look to know it was Peter's light, Peter's window. She traded her anxious thoughts of shadows and unwanted change for daydreams about a boy she barely knew who believed in her more than she believed in herself. A boy who smelled like cookies and books and coffee. She smiled at the thought of dimpled, crooked grins, ridiculous nicknames, and warm brown eyes.

The glow was like a comforting nightlight. Lyric found herself able to rest knowing she wasn't the only one who saw the shadows, who had been touched by their malevolence. She wasn't alone.

Though she had managed to fall asleep, Lyric was far from rested the next morning. She woke to the scent of bacon and biscuits, and it was enough to get her out of bed. She found her sister snoring, buried under a mass of blankets. She must have crawled into bed in the wee hours of the morning, the few hours Lyric had managed to sleep. Lyric nudged her sister awake, and after a moment of delayed grogginess, Mel shot up out of bed. Her eyes widened. "It smells like a Selah breakfast," she said, and both girls scrambled for the door.

They raced down the stairs in time to see their mother fanning a smoking oven while their five-year-old brother Louis eyed a platter of burnt biscuits. Lyric opened the kitchen windows to clear out the building smoke while Mel surveyed the rest of the chaos in the kitchen. Lyric breathed in the fresh outside air before taking in the tainted smell of breakfast gone wrong.

"We thought Grandpa was down here ..." Mel's voice trailed off.

Their mother wiped flour from her face with the back of her hand and swiped at strands of wayward hair that managed to escape her messy updo. The stove was littered with cracked eggs, splotches of pancake batter and an empty burnt pot.

Their mother didn't meet their eyes as she spoke. "I got distracted. Your father called, and I—"

"It's okay, Mommy," Louis said, "I'm not hungry, anyway."

Lyric's heart twisted. Louis was normally the bane of her peaceful existence. He was a constant nuisance who loved playing pranks on the family. But his laughter always made up for the trouble he caused. Lately, he'd been less of a lovable bugaboo and more quiet and withdrawn.

Lyric, Mel, and their mother shared a look.

"How about we all go out for breakfast and stop at that bookstore your sister likes to hide away at?" their mother suggested.

"No!" The objection came out much louder and squeakier than Lyric intended, nearly drowning out her family's unanimous support of the idea. Now all eyes were on her. "You go. I'll stay here with Grandpa."

Her mother frowned, but Louis pulled on her, his eyes light again. "Let's go! I want hot chocolate from the bookstore. He made it just right!"

Lyric couldn't help wondering if Louis was talking about Peter. He sure knew how to leave a lasting impression.

Mel gave her a knowing look. "I'll help Lyric clean the kitchen. Why don't you and Lou get some fresh air?"

Their mother looked relieved. "Do you want us to bring you back anything special?"

"Surprise us," Mel said, shooing them out the door in a way only she could get away with. With their mom and little brother gone, Mel herded Lyric to the kitchen table. "Judging by the bags under your eyes and the way you blush when you're thinking about who I think you're thinking of, last night either went extremely well or extremely wrong. Which is it?"

Lyric sighed and her sister rolled her eyes, shushing her before she could get a word out. "Before you tell me *everything*, there are some things you might want to know. Your barista boy has quite the reputation."

Lyric groaned, and Mel slapped her hand. "Apparently, he was a track star at his old school. He was planning to go to some Ivy League on a track scholarship. But his family got into a car accident during a really bad storm. Their car hydroplaned. His parents died at the scene, and he injured his spine."

Lyric went still, her chest aching a little more with every word her sister whispered. Her eyes grew hot with pressure as her heart squeezed, its beat echoing, the pulsing blood rushing to heat her face.

*"Some of us don't have the luxury of dreaming. Some people never will."*

She hadn't been able to understand him then. She was too busy worrying about her own problems, about her own fears. She'd seen his pain, but she hadn't asked about it. Didn't think he wanted to talk about it. He could talk about shadows stalking the neighborhood, but he braced himself every time he showed a little piece of himself that wasn't happy or likable.

"He learned to walk again, but he'll never be able to run like he did before," her sister continued. "He was in a bad place for a while. But Grandpa helped him get through it. R-right before Grandpa started to … well, you know."

Right before their grandpa got stuck in his own rut. No one knew what triggered it, but now that she knew about Peter, she knew the shadows were connected.

Had her barista boy brought the shadows with him to Olde Glory East? Were they like a virus? Did they infect their victims? Did they feed on their sorrow?

Grandpa had always been such a light to everyone else. He had always been the one everyone came to with problems, the one who always had answers or an excuse to laugh and smile. How had the shadows come? Did they cling to him the way they had to Peter? Were they following anyone else?

"Lyric?" She looked up to find her sister frowning at her. Her brows were creased with worry. Lyric looked over her shoulders, wondering if the shadows were back, if they were coming for her now. But there was nothing. "Sis, what's wrong?"

Lyric sighed, looking at the mess around the kitchen. "Besides everything?"

Mel rolled her eyes. "And you say I'm dramatic. You aren't wrong, though. Stuff is messed up. But nothing's too hard for a Selah. We'll turn a depression into a renaissance," she said, breaking into her best Grandpa Selah's pep talk voice.

"Our songs can inspire revolutions and charm boys out of enchanted wolf skins!" Lyric chimed in, giving her own best impression.

"If we can build fashion empires in our slippers ..." Mel declared.

"And beat the sandman at his own game ..."

"We can sho'nuff clean this kitchen," Mel concluded in her Grandpa Selah best.

He was famous for giving lectures disguised as pep talks. He never let his family or neighbors feel sorry for themselves for too long without a story, a moral, and a plan of action.

Mel snorted. Lyric echoed the sound, and before long, both girls were laughing and cleaning up the chaos in the kitchen.

Twenty minutes later, with a little sweat on their brows and large but tired smiles, the girls had the kitchen looking like it always did.

That small burst of joy and love for her sister felt a lot like the other night in the bookstore. The reminder of their grandpa's rousing speeches and resonant voice stirred something even deeper. It wasn't a heavy shadow, it wasn't anxiety or fear. And though it was touched with a bittersweet tinge of sadness, it was light and butterfly-like and fiery.

It was hope.

# SHADOWS AND SONG

"*One can't leave his shadow lying about and not miss it sooner or later.*" – Peter Pan

LYRIC KNEW HOW TO SAVE GRANDPA SELAH. JUST LIKE ALWAYS, HE HAD given her the solution and the courage to fix her predicament. He had prepared her for this with every story, with every talking to, with every word of affirmation. As much as she and her sister had rolled their eyes behind his back, his words had nestled their way deep inside her soul.

Whether fact or fiction, recounting Grandpa Selah's stories was the spark she needed to light the fire inside. It was time for Grandpa Selah to get a taste of his own medicine, to get the love he'd always given. He'd been strong for everyone else, and now it was her turn to be there for him. No one knew what had started his decline, but there was no way she'd let him wither away without a fight. The shadows couldn't have him.

She was no shrinking violet. She was no sunflower or wishflower, and she definitely wasn't a snickerdoodle. She was a Selah, and the first step to saving her grandpa was to remind him who he was, too.

But she couldn't do it alone.

When her mom and Louis returned armed with breakfast and drinks, she smiled at the warm snickerdoodle and the handcrafted beverage made just for her. There was a note scribbled in black marker on the side. It was hardly legible, but she thought it said something about miracles and mayhem and angels. Mel shook her head at the chicken scratch. "He needs to text that mess."

She cleared her throat and took a long, deep sip of the tea, letting the gentle hint of warmth, citrus, and honey chase away her lingering nerves.

"That nice boy at the café made your grandpa a cup of tea," their mother said, organizing the takeout food. "It was a nice gesture."

Lyric took her grandpa's drink from her mom. "I'll take it to him."

"And I'll get his plate ready," Mel offered.

Lyric drank more of her tea while her sister prepared a small saucer of food. It was his favorite meal from the brunch carryout spot, one of the few remaining local eateries left in Olde Glory East.

"If he doesn't eat the steak and cheese eggs, it's mine," Mel said.

Lyric rolled her eyes before gathering his food and drink and climbing the stairs. Louis followed behind her, knocking politely on the door before opening it for her. "Good luck," he whispered before retreating downstairs.

Lyric took a deep breath and inched her way forward. The old wood floor creaked under the weight of her feet. She could hear her own heavy, shuddered breathing as her arms ached from carrying the tray of food. Her hands were sweaty. Her heart pounded against the stillness of the dark room. She set the tray on her grandfather's nightstand and took in the somber surroundings.

The room was as dark as it was silent. With the floor lamp leaning and unplugged, only a slither of light peaked through the barrier of closed curtains. Grandpa Selah sat upright in his bed like a weathered stone. There was little to no movement beyond the rise and fall of his chest. His face was ashen and hard, freshly shaved only thanks to her mother's care. "I brought you something to eat," she said.

He grimaced. "I'll get to it," he said, his voice no more than a tenored whisper.

"Peter sent you some tea," she countered, reaching for the cup and handing it to him. He took it begrudgingly, cradling it in his strong, wrinkled hands.

Lyric slowly nudged the curtains open. "We've been trying not to disturb you, you know. Tiptoeing around the house. Which is crazy because these floorboards are always so whiny." Her chuckles were met with a weary sigh, but she didn't let it discourage her. "I think we've been going about this the wrong way. You don't need peace and quiet. You have enough of that when we aren't here. And maybe that's the problem?"

"I'm old, is the problem. Tired," he said. "I just want to be alone."

"No," she said, opening his window so some fresh air could circulate through the musty room. "No one wants to be alone."

When he didn't respond, she sat on the large chest at the foot of his bed. "I think Mom and Dad are getting a divorce."

Grandpa Selah shuffled in his bed, but didn't respond. So she continued. "Mel's leaving for her summer theater program in two weeks."

"That's nice," he said, but there was no feeling behind his words.

"I got a response from one of my favorite performers. It was a rejection, but she *responded*. She said my song was beautiful. It made her cry because she wished she could sing it. But it's not for her."

She told him about the open mic event, how she managed to sing that song. Then she found herself humming some of the melody. She looked out the window at the blue sky, but caught movement from the corner of her eye. She paused, knowing that movement wasn't Grandpa Selah. It was coming from his bedside. From underneath the bed. She scrambled to her feet in time to see the shadows snake up in smoky tendrils, expanding into a thick cloud-like mass. It stretched and pulsed, as if it was breathing, filling more of the room with every moment.

The shadows surrounded the sides of the bed, to the ceilings, and stretched out along the walls. Grandpa Selah's voice broke through her paralysis. "Run!"

She wanted to run, but her back was against the open window and the shadows covered the perimeter of the room, still expanding. Lyric dropped to the floor, holding her knees to her chest as the shadows hovered, a sharp contrast against the sunny sky behind her. Some of the light penetrated the shadows, creating a dusted, less corporeal form.

The shadows were persistent. They were hungry. She could feel them licking, biting at her, amplifying every dark and painful part of her life. Every negative thought, all her disappointment, every sad memory sharp and so distinct she thought her heart would break.

Tears flowed freely, stinging her eyes. Her head ached from the sobbing, and still the shadows pushed, dimming down the burgeoning hope, shredding the little bit of confidence she had mustered. She was no match for its visceral nature.

Her song wasn't enough.

But then, she wasn't alone. Grandpa Selah was right there with her. If she couldn't save him from the shadows, maybe they could save each other. And if that wasn't enough ...

No. It was enough. Love was always enough. Love was her family's secret weapon, the special ingredient to their impossible feats. Love gave her ancestors the courage to fight their way out of oppression. Love helped them create something beautiful when the world was nothing but ugliness and chaos, and love would give her strength now.

She didn't have her headphones to drown out the fear of hearing her own voice, but she didn't need it. The shadows had amplified every dark thing, like a roaring sea of despair drowning her in a wave of infinite and unyielding sorrow. But she pushed through the tears, she pushed through the pain, and she sang her heart out.

The shadows might consume her, but she wouldn't go without a fight.

She couldn't form words. She couldn't think beyond the deluge of pain and anguish. So she lifted her voice the only way she knew how. She sang a note in a range she'd never touched before with a clarity and a purity she'd never imagined. It came out so strong and clear it jolted her out of the shadow's hold.

The shadows recoiled, but they didn't run as they had before. But she didn't want them to run. She wanted to destroy them. For Peter. For Grandpa Selah. For her family rushing up the stairs, even as she fought. For the neighborhood. For herself. Her mother and Mel burst into the room and the shadows turned their attention, swirling and stretching, not sure who to latch on to.

"Use that Selah gift," her grandpa urged.

And so she did. She lifted her voice without apology. The shadows drew back. Her grandpa joined after a moment, harmonizing with her. Soon her whole family was singing, their voices rising above the shadow's assault until that oppressive cloud shriveled into a fleeting vapor of dust.

Grandpa Selah coughed, his throat dry from singing. "I think I'll have that tea now," he said, sounding more like himself.

Lyric wanted to laugh, but just as the laughter came, the tears poured out harder.

Her voice was raw from exertion, her vocal cords stretched and burning, which only made her cry more. Louis ran to her, crashing into her legs and wrapping his arms around her waist. Mel followed, and soon they were all crying and hugging one another. The shadows were gone.

# SUNSHINE AND ROSES

"*A*bsence makes the heart grow fonder ... or forgetful." – Peter Pan

THE SELAH HOUSE CARRIED ON AS IF IT WERE ANY ORDINARY DAY, AND not like they just had an epic showdown against soul-sucking shadows. They finished breakfast before heading outside to enjoy the sunshine and fresh air. Mom sat on the porch swing to answer an important call while Mel went bug hunting with Louis.

Lyric joined Grandpa Selah in tending his garden in the backyard. Yard work had never been her favorite summer pastime, but she found she'd missed it this summer. More than anything, she'd missed her grandpa. She rolled up her sleeves and settled beside him to pull out the weeds. Grandpa Selah adjusted his straw hat before handing her an extra pair of garden gloves.

"Thank you," he said, though she wasn't sure what he was thanking her for. Gardening was rarely an option. No one left his house without getting their hands dirty at least a few times over the summer.

"Sure thing, Grandpa," she said softly. Her voice was hoarse from hitting notes she never knew she was capable of, from singing like she

89

never had before. That discomfort was the only real evidence of their earlier fight and triumph.

"Pull the weeds from the root," he said.

She nodded, separating the deeply embedded root from the flower bed soil. The sun felt hot on her bare arms as she worked through the weeds. She welcomed the warmth even as sweat broke across the surface of her skin. The contrast of the sun-soaked outdoors was welcoming to the cold, suffocating grip of those shadows. She'd only endured it for a handful of minutes. Peter and Grandpa Selah had carried that weight for weeks on end. She couldn't imagine how that must have felt, and she didn't want to, either.

"Do you think it'll come back?" she asked. "The shadows?"

She waited for his answer, watching as he twisted, pulled, and cut at a thick root. "Of course they will. It's not something you can really get rid of." He paused to give her a look that said she should know that already. "You can't have sun without a little shade."

Lyric rolled her eyes. "What we just faced is way different from the shade," she countered.

Her grandpa sighed. "All right, well, here's one for you. Where there's a garden, there will always be weeds. It's part of life. When there's weeds, you pull 'em. When life gives you shade, you put your feet up, and stop worrying about stuff you can't control. Life isn't always sunny, and it won't always be a bed of roses."

Lyric wiped her forehead with the back of her arm. "It's always a story or a metaphor with you, but I think I get it."

Her honesty won her a smile. "Yes, the shadows will be back," he answered plainly. "But now you know how to deal with them. We all do."

She didn't like his answer. That feeling the shadows had magnified in her, all those dark thoughts, all the pain all at once … she never wanted to feel that way again. But at least she wasn't alone.

"What were you worried about? What did those shadows have on you?"

"Nothing for us to worry about now."

"How are you always so strong?" she wondered.

"I'm not any stronger than you," he said, gathering the discarded weeds in a paper bag. "It's easier to help lift someone else than deal with our own problems. But there comes a time when we have to pull our own weeds and deal with our own shadows."

"How do you do that? Deal with it?"

Her grandpa's wise eyes softened when he looked at her. "You ask for help."

"Know-it-alls like you need help?" she teased.

He laughed. "Especially us know-it-alls, because we don't know when we need it."

Lyric frowned. "You're always there for us, but we weren't there for you."

He touched her gloved hand with his own. "You're here now. That's what matters."

A piercing scream interrupted their quiet moment. Grandpa Selah was a little slow to rise because of the stiffness in his knees, but soon they were both on their feet, racing to the front of the house.

When Lyric made it to the front of the house, she found her dad standing on the porch with luggage at his feet and Louis in his arms. Louis had his arms wrapped around their dad's neck, his hold so tight their dad could hardly breathe, let alone speak.

Their mother peeled Louis from their dad's arms. "Daddy can't breathe, baby."

But Louis was already hugging him again, this time wrapping his arms around his side and squeezing just as hard. "Sorry, daddy! I'm just glad you're here. What took you so long? Are you staying?"

Her father's eyes locked with their mother's, and he smiled. "I don't know, but I'm not going anywhere."

Soon, Louis wasn't the only one holding on tightly to him. The entire family surrounded him.

"Welcome home, love," her mother said.

# EPILOGUE

"*H*ow about a cup of tea before your next adventure?" Peter said, setting Lyric's favorite drink in front of her. She sighed. "I think I'm adventured out."

He helped himself to a chair at her table, straddling it backwards and leaning forward to take one of her cookies. "If the stories are true, you won't be able to help yourself. The Selah brand is mayhem and miracles, remember?"

Lyric rolled her eyes. "How is it you know all about me, and I don't know your last name?"

He munched on a cookie. "It's Darling."

She choked on her tea, spitting in his face. "You're kidding!"

He wiped his face with one of the café's napkins but seemed otherwise unfazed by her outburst. "I'd never lie to you, Snickerdoodle."

She groaned. "Stop calling me that."

"Would you rather me call you 'Darling'?"

She balled up a piece of paper and threw it at him. "In your dreams."

"Maybe," he said, his warm brown eyes searching her face before stuffing his mouth with more treats.

"Do you ever eat anything else?" she wondered.

He gave her a dimpled smile. "It depends. You asking me out to dinner?"

Her face flushed red and hot. "N-no!"

Peter clutched his chest, feigning disappointment, before retrieving a paper from his jean pocket. "I do have another proposal for you."

Lyric glared at him, even though her heart fluttered, and she leaned closer to him to scan the paper.

"Since you're over your singing phobia, I was thinking we could go on tour."

Her eyes widened. "Are you crazy? We just met, and do you even know how to sing or play an instrument?"

He shrugged. "I have a few friends that tinker around. I can manage the team. You can write the songs, provide the vocals."

"You're seriously thinking about starting a band?"

His eyes flashed and he leaned in closer. The severity of his tone was at odds with the strong scent of sugar and coffee beans wafting from his work uniform. "Even better. Let's go hunting. Your grandpa said those shadows are everywhere. I don't want to wait for them to show up to get me. I want to be the thing those shadows are afraid of. Besides, those shadow creatures aren't the only things that go bump in the night."

Lyric rubbed her temples. "What are you talking about?"

His face darkened, almost making her question if the shadows were already back. "Let's just say my family has stories of our own. It's a lot less fairy tale, more horror anthology type stuff."

She had barely processed what he said when he stood and gave her a wink. "Think about it. But don't keep me waiting. The first gig's next Saturday."

Some tall tales are true. Lyric's story is proof of that. But as she ate her snickerdoodles and drank her tea, she mulled over Peter's offer. It made her think of all the family's stories her grandpa had shared. Maybe they weren't as made up as she thought. And if those stories were true, what else was out there?

Did she really want to know?

Would you?

# ABOUT THE AUTHOR

Montrez is an urban fantasy and romantasy author who lives in the moody Midwest with her husband and three sons. Inspired by super-heroes, anime, and an eclectic mix of literature, she is passionate about creating fantastical worlds full of heart, heroics, and Black Girl Power.

When she's not writing her own whimsical and super-powered worlds, she enjoys her work as Co-Editor-In-Chief of Konkret Comics, a Glyph Award-winning, Black-owned comic book publishing company.

Power up fiction!

Join her Novel Creature Community to recharge for your own real life adventures for her books, diverse speculative fiction recom-mendations, and more.

authormontrez.com/links

ALICIA ELLIS

Gia and Harlan stand on the edge of homelessness. The tech revolution robbed their father of everything—health, career, hope—leaving the teens to work odd jobs after school. Now, the newest AI rips even that away. Machines do the work faster and cheaper.

Desperate, Gia volunteers them to test CyberCorp's experimental computer-brain interface. The test derails, trapping Harlan and Gia in a virtual forest with a hacker poised to shatter their minds.

Can they escape this neuro-nightmare, or will their digital prison become their tomb?

*Circuits and Nerve* is a retelling of the classic fairy tale *Hansel and Gretel*, set in the universe of the *Flesh and Metal* trilogy.

# GIA

*I* sat on the couch in our apartment, slack faced as I watched the ads that paid our rent.

*"Meet LifeTrack. Your LifeTrack jewelry records every aspect of your life in audio and video,"* came a cheerful female voice from the forty-inch vid on the wall. *"Its advanced artificial intelligence steers you toward your every dream."*

It was the third advert today for this high-tech accessory, designed for people who could afford jewelry that told them what to do. By now, I could have quoted it by heart.

"Look at this." My twin brother Harlan pointed to his hand-screen propped on the stained coffee table.

The voice of Lena Hayes burst from it, raw and clear despite the tinny speaker. "CyberCorp Technology *will* recover from the recent tragedies, which—I remind everyone—were the fault of humans and not our technology. If you continue to trust us, I assure you …"

It was easy to be passionate when you were born with a silver spoon stuck up your butt.

I shot a look at Harlan, who stared at the hand-screen as if it was the holy grail.

My mouth was a millimeter from a quip about how, if we had as much money as her, the last thing I'd do with it was revive a company whose reputation was on the fast track to the sewer. But Harlan listened with awe carved into his face, so I let him have his joy.

Only a year older than us, Lena Hayes steered the world's most advanced tech firm. On the display, she sat in a minimalist office. Pearlescent white walls backed her and her metal desk. Her fists clenched on the desk's top—one flesh and one a metal prosthetic.

I could resent her privilege, but I also admired that she had suffered devastating setbacks and emerged with purpose.

Meanwhile, I'd be lucky to keep this household limping forward.

The ad on the wall continued. *"With LifeTrack, your dreams become reality."*

If I had to choose between the ad parade and Lena's narcissistic video blog, I'd pick Lena every time. It wasn't even a close call.

"Volume down," I shouted at the vid.

*"Volume is on the lowest setting,"* came the vid's computerized response. The ad paused for a fraction of a second and restarted from the beginning.

I groaned.

Harlan squinted at me from a tattered armchair. "You okay, Gia? It's always on low."

"I can hope."

He graced me with a grin or a grimace—maybe a little of both.

"That reminds me." Harlan snatched the hand-screen from the coffee table and navigated to a web page. Lena's impassioned voice abruptly cut off as he left her stream.

Harlan angled it toward me. "Someone in this forum says we can trick the vid into thinking we're watching to get credit when we're not around."

While the hand-screen was a luxury for which I was grateful—one of the few we'd managed to keep after our father's accident—the wall-mounted vid and its incessant adverts were torture.

Necessary torture.

"Really?" I peered over his shoulder as he scrolled.

"Yeah, we would need . . ." He frowned and navigated away from the page, back to Lena's stream. "Forget it."

"No. What?"

"We can't afford it."

"*Get your life on track with LifeTrack,*" the vid continued in the cheerful voice of someone who'd never met adversity a day in their life.

I groaned. "Vid off."

It went silent, leaving Lena's voice to fill the room. "The board won't let me test my computer-brain interface even though I know it would make a difference—not just to CyberCorp, to *everyone.* This tech could touch the lives of so many who don't have full control of their bodies and want that to change. Improved prosthetics." She waved her left arm, and the overhead lights glinted off the metal that spanned from her fingertips to her shoulder. "Even the potential to bring people back from vegetative states."

I willed myself not to look across the room at my father in his hospital-style bed. Harlan looked, though, and my resolve melted into a puddle.

Dad was as unconscious as he had been for the past two years.

Thanks to artificial intelligence integrated into the latest building equipment, his contractor jobs had dried up. In a desperate attempt to stay relevant, he took increasingly dangerous work with increasingly strict time constraints and increasingly lax safety standards.

It cost him everything.

His monitoring equipment beeped every three seconds as if demanding attention. I squeezed my eyes shut and refused to cry. That would be giving up my little remaining power.

"So I'm going to test it myself," Lena continued from my brother's hand-screen. She paused, and her fingers trembled until she pressed them flat against her desktop.

Her gaze flicked to one side, and her irises scanned back and forth, reading something.

"Some are asking about the board's hold on testing new products." Her gaze returned straight forward. She stared right at us. "I don't need the board's money or permission to test *my* invention on *my* body."

Harlan's attention was laser-focused on me. "Gia?"

We both knew that the peace from the vid's ads was temporary, but I loved him for giving me this one minute of solace. The vid's service providers subsidized our rent based on how many minutes per month we watched. If we turned it off or left the room, that meant fewer dollars we could dedicate to Dad's rented medical equipment.

We needed *every* dollar.

"Can't we keep it off for an hour?" My whine irritated even me. I should have been stronger, better. I had to be for us to survive.

"If you want."

Lena's stream ended, and the beeping of my father's life support filled the space left by the now-quiet vid. His eyes remained closed, his wasted body unmoving under the faded blanket. A familiar feeling soured my stomach but made me sit taller.

*He* was why we did this.

Harlan closed his hand over mine.

"Vid on," I whispered.

Again, the ad restarted from the beginning. *"Meet LifeTrack. Your LifeTrack jewelry will record every aspect ..."*

"We should go over what money we've made this week," I said, as if I could drown it out with conversation.

Harlan flicked off the hand-screen, blacking out Lena's frozen final expression, leaving us alone with our problems.

"Delivery jobs are gone," he said. "Drones are faster and don't expect tips. The shipping companies are churning them out like water. I had only a couple requests the past two weeks, and none this week."

His expression went flat, cold. That was the best way to deal with this—stay calculating, leave emotion out of it, and find work where possible. He rotated his wrist downward over the hand-screen's scanner. It beeped, and his account balance flashed on the display.

I cringed. "How did you make anything at all?"

His brown skin looked ashen, almost pale. "A few classmates paid me to do their homework."

My heart ached at the shame in his voice. Harlan prized education above all else, yet he sacrificed his principles out of desperation.

I scanned my ID chip and winced as my account total popped up.

"Babysitting helped a little. Luckily, the androids can't do that reliably yet."

The vid finally moved on to a different ad. *"Meals go from freezer to table in three minutes with the HyperOven's patented hyper-excite technology ..."*

"We have to find another income stream," I continued.

Harlan slammed a fist against his armrest, sending stuffing puffing upward from a hole in the fabric. "Jobs are being automated. What are we supposed to do?"

*"The HyperOven should not be used near medical or other critical equipment due to electrical interference."* The ad ended with a scrolling list of its dangers along with disclaimers of liability for death or injury.

The lock on the front door beeped, clicked, and our stepmother Ellen stalked into the room.

Harlan tightened his fingers around the armrest.

Ellen's makeup and hair were flawless, with a smooth and even complexion, perfectly defined eyebrows, and just the right amount of mascara to accentuate her eyes. She took pains to maintain her professional appearance as an interior designer—another job computers hadn't yet perfected. But her costly upkeep left little for the rest of us.

She glared at the vid, which played yet another ad. "Vid off."

The display blanked.

"Let's have it. What did you make this week?"

Harlan turned the hand-screen toward her so she could see the balances in our scrawny accounts.

"There are no more deliveries," he said. "I had to—"

"Don't waste my time. We all live here, and I still manage to work."

"You have a college degree and experience," I said. "If you'd give us the funds to get professional clothing, we might at least be able to compete for—"

"More excuses." Ellen's lips flattened into a hard line as she dropped into the armchair. Despite still being in her thirties, weariness lined her face, and the makeup couldn't hide it.

Ellen didn't acknowledge Dad. As far as she was concerned, he no longer existed except as a drain on this household.

"How much did *you* make?" Harlan asked. "Maybe you could give us a little more this week? The hospital sent a third notice about the increased rental fees for Dad's equipment. We're already behind."

"I cover my own expenses so I can keep clients happy. Maybe if you contributed, I could spare more of my hard-earned cash for your whims."

Our *whims?*

Fury set my temperature boiling. "We don't need money for *whims*, you stupid bi—"

Harlan grabbed my hand and yanked me so hard that the backs of my knees slammed into the couch, and I fell into the seat beside him. "We understand, and we appreciate anything you can give us. You've been so generous."

My fingernails clawed his palm, but he held firm.

Ellen breathed a long, high-pitched sigh. "I'll see what I can set aside." Her voice was generous, but her slitted eyes and thinned lips told the greedy truth.

As much as I hated tiptoeing around her, we needed her contribution. The alternative was to do what the doctors suggested—and Ellen supported—unplug Dad and let him die.

Ellen flounced to her feet. "Vid on."

A meat market ad flashed across the screen, boasting obscene payouts for bodily organs. The practice existed in legal limbo, not explicitly illegal but highly unethical.

Ellen glanced at the screen. "That's an option."

A classmate of ours had died after a procedure negotiated there went wrong. Her family couldn't afford to pay a lawyer, and no lawyers volunteered to take the case pro bono because of the rocky legal footing. I shuddered.

"People die because of those places," Harlan said in a voice more level than I could have offered.

"Then they didn't do adequate research about the clinic they used."

"Desperate people don't have time or money for research." I tried to keep my voice calm and professional, something Ellen respected, but emotion made my words tremble. "Research is a privilege."

"Let's go." The lines on Ellen's face smoothed, leaving her looking younger than her age, energized after having shifted her negative energy to us. "Right now. You aren't motivated to earn your share, so let's go down there and see what you can contribute."

My blood iced. I shot a wild look at Harlan.

"Give us more time," he said.

"No." A scowl contorted her features. She stomped over to Dad's bed and yanked his power cable from the wall.

The beeping stopped.

Harlan jumped to his feet.

"Plug it back in!" I shouted.

I charged at her, but she held the end of the cable over her head. I grabbed a section that dangled below and yanked.

Dad's bed shuddered under the tension.

I dropped it and raised my hands high, palm out. The worst-case scenario would be to break something. She stared at me with a challenge written all over her face.

Harlan fell to his knees, grabbed Ellen's legs, and pressed his face into them. "Please. We'll get the money."

"It's too late." She leaned forward, soaking up every bit of the attention. "They're coming tomorrow." She reached into her pocket and withdrew a pink piece of paper.

My stomach clenched, threatened to catapult its contents. When people sent physical paper, they meant business.

Ellen read from the page. "Your landlord has been ordered to allow us access to your home on Thursday—that's tomorrow—to retrieve our property."

"Can you plug it back in, please?" I asked.

My dad's machines weren't beeping, which meant nothing was keeping his heart beating or his lungs pumping. Panic pressed against my chest, expanding larger and larger by the second.

"We can divert the apartment rent," Harlan said.

"We're thirty days overdue already. If we skip it again, we'll be evicted in a month."

"We made rent last month!"

Ellen shrugged. "I needed my share to entertain potential clients."

"What happened to the money we contributed?" I asked.

She shrugged again.

Only the look on Harlan's face kept me from strangling her.

"Please," I said again, "plug it back in." My hands shook. How long until he suffered brain damage from lack of oxygen? I tasted wet salt on my lips before I noticed I was crying.

"It's your father or this apartment," Ellen said. "We can't keep both."

Harlan released her legs and looked up at her from the floor. "There has to be another way."

"There is." She made her voice singsong sweet. "The meat market."

"We need more time," he said. "We can fix this."

"In a day?" She laughed. "Even if you could, it would be temporary. You refuse to work full time—"

Harlan rose to his feet. "We have school."

"Plug him back in!" I shouted. I couldn't breathe. My body vibrated like a live wire.

That earned a scornful look from my stepmother, who waved the unplugged cable like a banner. "You're incapable of supporting yourselves with odd jobs. This is the end of your laziness. The meat market is the answer."

"No." Harlan tensed beside me. "We stay in school. Education is our only chance at a decent future, and going to the meat market could destroy that. We stay the course."

Ellen's free hand cracked across Harlan's cheek. "You're as delusional as your father."

A red handprint stood out on his brown skin, and his eyes watered. I jumped between them before Harlan could retaliate, but he didn't even try.

Ellen straightened to her full height, a couple inches shorter than Harlan. She shouldered past me and leaned close to his face as if daring him to strike back. "I said *get in the car.*"

"I won't." His voice came out lower than usual, controlled but with danger under the surface.

A new ad started on the vid. *"CyberCorp Technology's newest embedded micro-comm takes a huge leap into the future ..."*

I grabbed Harlan's hand. "No, let's get in the car."

"Gia, we can't—"

"It's okay. I have an idea." To Ellen, I said, "We'll go with you. Plug him back in."

She pressed the plug into its socket.

I waited for the beeping to start. It did, and his vitals rolled across the small display by his head. The tension in my chest loosened, and I could breathe again.

Her head held high, Ellen strode to the door with me at her heels. Harlan trailed behind us. His expression mirrored the horror clenched in my gut, but I had a plan. We just needed a ride.

Somewhere we could make money. Anywhere but the meat market.

# LENA

$\mathcal{T}$he hum of reporters gathered outside, in front of CyberCorp Tower, filled my ears and shocked my pulse to accelerate.

I straightened my fitted white blouse and tailored jeans for the third time. I looked fine. It was a great outfit, casual yet professional, not trying to be something it wasn't. Not trying to be something *I* wasn't.

My mother's assistant, Missy, fussed over me with a critical eye. "Really, Lena." She buttoned the neck of my blouse. "We could have found something more formal for your first presser."

Meeting her eyes dead on, I unhooked the button so I could breathe. I didn't have a lot of leeway these days as CyberCorp's newest owner and spokesperson, but I drew the line at people dressing me.

The two of us stood just behind a raised platform in the circular drive of gleaming CyberCorp Tower. Behind us, the building's sleek rose stone and glass exterior towered seventy-two stories into the sky, a testament to innovation and progress. Engraved above the entrance was the iconic CyberCorp logo in blocky red letters.

A crowd of reporters and onlookers had gathered on the other side of the platform, a sea of people peppered with floating drones armed with cameras recording every move.

Missy licked her hand and reached out to slick a stray curl that had escaped my hairband.

I ducked. "No. Absolutely not."

With my robotic left hand, I pulled the hairband from my hair until it popped and let my wild dark curls fly free. The wind whipped it against my face, and I grinned at Missy's scowl.

Lena Hayes—score one.

Missy Matherson—zero.

Okay, that was a lie. She'd scored more than her fair share of blows over the past month since I'd risen to this role.

"At least wear the blazer your mother picked." She held out a royal-purple jacket that, if I was honest, I might have picked myself if given a choice of business wear.

I slipped my arms into the sleeves and kept my tongue in my mouth. This was my life now—compromising for the good of everyone. Representing CyberCorp was bigger than me.

Missy Matherson—score one hundred.

She froze, then held up a finger and tapped the micro-comm stuck behind her ear. "Marissa, what can I—" She nodded at whatever my mother was saying into her ear.

A call from my mom ten seconds before my first press conference could only be bad news. Tension started in my toes and squirmed upward.

"Marissa, I'm sure Lena—" More nodding. To me, she whispered, "She's canceling your computer-brain interface test."

"She can't do that!" The tension clawed up my calves and burrowed in my knees.

"If you could just allow her to—" Missy's nodding had reached a velocity where her head might shoot off her neck.

"What's she saying?" I asked when the tension reached my big fat mouth. "Did you tell her she can't do that?"

Missy shook her head and pointed at her micro, as if I couldn't see she was on a call.

"Give her to me," I said. When Missy didn't react, I repeated, "Transfer the call."

"Marissa," she said. "Lena wants to talk." She tapped her micro and swiped in the direction of my own, which, like hers, was stuck to the side of my head.

A second later, my mother was in my ear. "Lena, you don't have time to chat. Never make the press wait without a good reason."

"You can't cancel my test. I don't need the board's funds. It's my decision."

"I cannot allow you to be the first test subject for a technology that links into the brain."

"How can we create positive change if we let the board tie our hands? The whole point of going public was to generate public trust, and the board wants to throw that away by putting money above the public good."

"The public *cares* about money, Lena. More importantly, though, it's too dangerous. I wouldn't allow you to test that thing on yourself even if the board okayed it."

"Why can't I just—"

"I see you from my window, and your reporters are losing interest. This is the job. I'm sorry."

The audience was indeed getting restless. Their murmurs grew louder by the second.

"This isn't over," I said.

"Have a good press conference, dear." She disconnected.

My tension had locked into every joint, so I closed my eyes and inhaled for six seconds, opened my eyes, and exhaled for eight more. It didn't relax me, but at least my fists uncurled.

I started toward the platform to meet the reporters.

Missy clasped my arm. "Stick to the script. Your mother trusts you."

I fidgeted with the edge of my blazer as Missy went over the rules —again.

"Read the speech they're streaming to your EyeNet connection. When reporters ask questions, talk about CyberCorp's reorganization, not the legal troubles. Focus on the Model Two androids, not the recalled Model Ones. Play up the new micro-comm implants, but steer clear of research projects still in limbo." She paused for a breath.

I didn't object. If I didn't get on that stage in the next ten seconds, the nervous simmer in my stomach might come to a boil.

"Say nothing negative about CyberCorp's new governing board. You know—"

"I got it. I'll be a good little soldier."

She searched my face and then released my arm. "You've got this."

The moment I stepped onto the platform, the sea of faces stunned me to freezing. Sunlight glinted off my cybernetic arm. A camera flashed and left me blinking spots before everything slammed back into focus.

I closed my eyes for a long second to activate my EyeNet connection. Most people needed specialized lenses to see virtual objects in the net, but my interface was a chip embedded at the base of my skull. It connected my left arm to my brain and allowed me to access the EyeNet at will.

When I opened my eyes, the words of my speech floated in front of me.

"Thank you all for coming to see CyberCorp Technology reborn as a public company worthy of the public trust." I cleared my throat. "As of last month, I own twenty-five percent of CyberCorp. My mother, Marissa Hayes, and I together retain fifty percent ownership. The other half belongs to others, members of the public who will work with us to direct the company toward a high-tech future that will benefit us all."

The words were carefully crafted, polished to a shine, but lacking raw honesty, lacking heart.

"Technology isn't going away. It's here to stay, so we must guide it, leverage it into a future that works for the common good." My voice steadied, and the little remaining chatter in the audience subsided.

I delivered the rest of the speech with my head high and my tone confident, buoyed by the respectful silence. "Any questions?" I finished.

A reporter, a man with salt-and-pepper hair and a well-worn jacket, raised his hand. "Can you say anything about the recall of Model One androids? It's been months. When do you expect to re-release them?"

Missy's gaze snared me as I sidestepped the question. "Our focus is now on the Model Twos, which have shown impeccable promise in their learning capabilities and obedience."

I tried to keep my voice steady despite the unease gnawing at me. This wasn't the transparency I wanted to bring to CyberCorp, but I had to play the game.

Another reporter spoke up next, a woman with vibrant red hair and an emerald-green blouse that stood out against the sea of muted colors. "What new products are coming soon?"

This was a softball question, and I gave it the expected answer. "Our new micro-comm implants will revolutionize communications."

A massive, three-dimensional hologram of the device appeared above our heads.

In real life, the micro-comm implant was mere millimeters in size, but the hologram extended six feet on each side. A night-black rectangular device held a reflective etching of the CyberCorp logo. The device shrank, and a human head appeared. The device disappeared into the side of the head just behind the ear.

The crowd *ooh*ed and *ah*ed.

I resisted the urge to roll my eyes.

"Just like our external micros," I continued, "these facilitate a seamless audio connection. These, however, are embedded under the skin to make them even more convenient. No more chargers. No more losing them. You are connected anywhere, everywhere, anytime. You can hold a conversation as if that other person is right in the room with you, without carrying or wearing a device."

To my left, Missy beamed. Before now, I had only seen that look on her face when she spoke to my mother.

My smile faltered. I didn't want her looking at me that way. I didn't want to be my mother.

More words spilled out. "In the near future, I also hope to release my computer-brain interface."

Missy stiffened.

"Like our micro update, it will be an implant." My voice grew stronger. "It will render all other interface devices obsolete. No more micro-comms, no more EyeNet lenses. The computer-brain interface seamlessly connects you to any adaptable device. More important-ly"—I sucked in a breath—"the human brain is the most important device we have, and my interface can connect it to the body."

A hush fell over the audience. Anticipation sizzled through me like an electric shock.

"My interface can reconnect people to paralyzed limbs. Its potential for healing the human body is boundless. This is what technology is about—helping humanity."

The words poured from me, and I felt alive, authentic. As the reporters nodded, I dared to hope that the world might believe in my invention too.

Missy covered her face with her hands. She was probably thinking about how to explain this to my mother.

I'd have to answer for it too—but not right now. Right now, I was floating.

"Miss Hayes," shouted a man near the front of the crowd, "when will the interface be ready?" His words knocked me back to Earth.

"I'm honestly not sure. The board hesitates to invest in a new project of this size, so I'll need to find test subjects without using CyberCorp funds."

Without my mother's support, the board would never back my invention. And without a successful test, I'd never get her support. I wasn't prepared to give up hope, but this project could be in limbo indefinitely.

If I could convince the public, maybe I could get her on my side …

A beat-up car screeched to a halt at the curb of CyberCorp Tower, its rusted exterior a stark contrast to the gleaming building behind me. The side door slid upward with a metallic whine, and a teenage girl tumbled out of the passenger seat as if shoved. A boy sprang from the backseat and helped her up.

Lean, sullen, and dark-skinned, the boy slouched his shoulders as if trying to disappear. His closely cropped black hair framed a face with sharp cheekbones. A faded black T-shirt hung loosely on his frame.

He wiped dirt off the girl's clothing. She straightened up, and her long brown locs tumbled down her back.

"The interface will …" I tried to win back my audience, but every gaze locked on the odd pair.

The car's door slammed down, and it peeled away from the curb with a screech that left black marks on the white pavement.

My metal fingers balled at my side. This was *my* audience.

The girl shouted curses after the car until the boy tapped her shoulder and jerked his head toward the crowd. She shut up.

He cleared his throat and gestured toward me as if returning my audience. "Sorry."

I cleared my throat. "With testing, I believe … this technology …"

I'd lost them. The reporters mumbled among themselves.

"That's it," I snapped out.

A few reporters squinted at me, but others still gawked at the new arrivals or pointed fingers at the hologram.

"Thank you for coming," I added in a more measured tone, transitioning back to the business version of me. "We look forward to your continued support."

As the confused press dispersed, I waited for a clear path.

When one appeared, I hopped off the dais and strode to the curb. The two teens watched me with wide, nervous eyes like prey waiting for the inevitable. The girl shifted behind her brother as I barreled down on them.

"What the hell was that?" When two departing reporters looked my way, I lowered my voice. "This was an important press conference."

"Your first one," the boy said.

I blinked, unsure whether to be irritated or pleased that he followed my news.

He stuck out his right hand. "I'm Harlan Mercer. This is my sister. She had the idea to …" He glanced at her. "It was Gia's idea, so I'll let her tell you."

Gia stared at me through suspicious, slitted eyes while her brother clasped and pumped my hand. Since he seemed in no hurry to release my right hand, I extended my left to the girl.

The metal prosthetic, a gift from a car accident that had been partly my fault and partly the fault of tech gone awry—mostly my fault—extended from fingertips to shoulder. The silver metal glittered under the bright sun. Gia stared at it like it was a poisonous snake.

I sighed, extracted my right hand from her brother, and extended it to Gia. She shook it.

"What can I do for you?" I said in a tone that still had wisps of irritation beneath its professional facade. I missed the days when I could throw a temper tantrum when things didn't go my way.

Harlan grabbed his sister's shoulder and pushed her forward.

"We want to be your test subjects," she said, looking at him instead of me. "We don't trust you, but our options are limited."

"That's not helping." He shoved her aside. "For your computer-brain interface. We volunteer."

"You understand that it's an experimental technology that will directly interact with your brain?" I tapped my temple. "You would have an untested device inside your head."

He nodded.

"Why?" I turned to the girl. "Especially since you don't trust me?"

The original plan was to test the interface on myself. Then eventually, I'd test it on someone already on the verge of death, someone who could afford to risk their life because their cause was already lost.

But this? No way was I drafting some kids—only a year or two younger than myself, by my best guess.

"Why?" I asked again, this time posing it as a demand.

"Our backup plan is the meat market," Gia said. "Our stepmother expects us to support the household because our dad is … He can't and … and …" She shot wide eyes at her brother.

Harlan finished for her. "A friend of ours died at the meat market. If we're going to risk our lives, we'd rather do it for something useful."

So it was life or death, after all. "Come with me."

# GIA

*L*ena led us into CyberCorp Tower. I'd only ever *dreamed* of going inside.

Nightmares counted as dreams, right?

Harlan followed close behind Lena while I took up the rear. His wide eyes marveled at the soaring atrium, the reflective tile floors, and the shining globe-like lighting system hanging from the ceiling tens of floors above. The lobby came to life with every step as virtual displays of CyberCorp tech appeared and disappeared.

Electricity hummed like the beating heart of this building.

"Wow." Harlan gaped at the ceiling and at the lobby, where a new set of holograms blipped into existence.

This place was better than the meat market.

It still might kill us.

As we passed reception, a cheerful brunette waved from behind the long black desk. "Lena! How are you?"

"Getting better." She stopped walking and turned. "Your mom okay?"

"She's good. Thanks for asking."

Lena stopped walking for a second and then hurried over to the receptionist. The woman nodded as Lena spoke in her ear.

"Sorry about that," she said as she hurried back to us.

She led us toward the elevator bay and scanned her left wrist at a scanner embedded into the wall. A pair of sleek elevator doors slid open, revealing a spacious cabin lined with padded light-gray walls.

"Seventy-two," Lena announced as we stepped inside.

Harlan and I inched past her to the back.

The doors closed, and the giant floating letter *L* appeared on each side wall. A moment later, it changed to the number *two*, then *three*. The numbers climbed.

Harlan nudged me with an elbow. "Even the elevators are ridiculous."

I shushed him. If we had any bargaining power, the best way to keep it intact was to act unimpressed ... even if we were, at least a little.

The numbers on the walls accelerated, rushing upward so fast they blurred together, even though I felt no movement.

They stopped at *seventy-two*, and the doors opened.

Lena stepped out as Harlan and I gaped. This was the highest level of CyberCorp Tower. The penthouse of the most advanced tech company in the country, maybe even the world. How many people had been welcomed on this floor?

The hallway before us had one door on the left and one on the right. The floors of the building narrowed toward the top, and apparently, this one was reserved for the most executive of executive offices.

As Lena approached the door on the right, a tiny green light blinked from the wall beside it. The door slid open and disappeared into the wall.

Beyond it stood a humongous office, a masterpiece of modern design. The floor-to-ceiling windows offered a view of the daytime city, where digital billboards flashed colorful advertisements against the backdrop of gleaming skyscrapers, all shorter than this one.

A giant vid acted as the front wall, a hundred feet from where we stood. Images and text slid across the surface, occasionally pausing and then gliding away to a folder icon in the bottom-right corner.

"It's just running a program," Lena said in my ear after I must have stared at the eye-popping display for too long. "Not nearly as cool as it looks."

It looked pretty cool.

"Welcome to my office," she said with her arms wide.

From her video blog, I thought she had a small, plain space. Now, I noted the position of her desk in a far, undecorated corner. She must stream from there with the camera facing away from most of the room.

So she was a private person. I wouldn't have guessed.

In the center of the room stood a large table, twenty feet long but surrounded by only four chairs, two occupied. The table's six legs were powdered white metal, topped by a long steel tabletop.

The two people seated popped to their feet.

"Who's this?" asked the man, tall and lanky and squinting at us like we were bugs under his microscope.

"Guys, meet Harlan and Gia," Lena said. She pointed at her team members one at a time. "Meet Jarret and Katie."

Jarret's short brown hair stuck up at odd angles, and as he ran a hand through it, it became immediately clear why.

The woman, Katie, looked only a few years older than us. Her graphic T-shirt sported the word *Skynet* in a stylized font that looked suspiciously like the one used in the CyberCorp logo. Below wide brown eyes, her warm smile welcomed us. Her jet-black hair swayed as she pulled out two chairs and gestured for us to sit.

"Jarret has worked here since he graduated college six years ago," Lena continued, "and Katie was my first hire."

"I started a few months ago, and I've been entirely focused on the computer-brain interface, which is"—she waved her arms in every direction—"going to change everything."

Lena grinned. "I love the enthusiasm."

"This project *deserves* enthusiasm," Jarret added. He shot a look at Lena and said, in a poor attempt at a whisper, "Your mother called and forbade us from running any tests on you. She threatened our jobs. Katie can't afford to be unemployed."

"It's fine." Lena patted his shoulder. "Harlan and Gia are our test subjects."

He leaned closer. "Security will be up to secure the prototypes. They want to make sure we don't do it anyway."

"How long do we have?"

Jarret's irises shifted upward a fraction, where networked contact lenses displayed the time. "Five minutes ago, she told us to be packed up in fifteen."

"Then we'd better get moving."

Both engineers grinned so widely I almost got burned by the beam.

"All right then." Lena's attention flicked between Harlan and me. "Let's get down to business." She hesitated, and for the first time, her face betrayed nervousness, probably a foreign expression for her. "Let's introduce you to the world's first operational computer-brain interface."

Jarret walked over to a long, narrow counter on one side of the room and brought back two shiny devices—if *device* was even the right word for them.

Each was a stack of black circuit boards connected by too-visible wires and held in place by duct tape wrapped around the whole thing. From each one, an inch-wide silver square extended from the mass of boards. Small connectors with short metal points stuck out from one side of the square.

I tensed. This was a computer-*brain* interface, so where were those needles supposed to go?

Harlan shot a panicked look in my direction, but when I gestured toward the door, he shook his head.

Lena took one from Jarret's outstretched hand. "Please don't be alarmed by its appearance. This is a prototype, and looks aren't everything. Once the board approves our funds, we'll pretty it up a bit more."

A bit *more*? Did she think it was *at all* pretty right now?

Lena held the device out for us to examine. When neither of us took it, she reached for my hand and set it on my palm. "You should look closer, understand what you're getting into."

She might not be my first choice for addressing our family problems—my first choice was to go back in time and stop the technical revolution—but Lena wasn't uncaring.

"The final version will be smaller and wire-free, suitable for in-skull installation." She touched the back of her head, just above the neck.

I cringed.

I vaguely recalled hearing somewhere that she had a chip installed in her head to operate her prosthetic arm. At least this wasn't brand-new territory.

"Once connected," Lena continued, "it will act as an interface between your brain and our proprietary computer system. This will allow us to test various sensory inputs and ensure proper functionality."

Without prompting, Katie passed a hand-screen to Harlan. "Read it." She looked him straight in the eye. "Seriously. Chat between yourselves. Then sign."

She lifted the device from my hand and pushed me toward a chair. Jarret gestured for Harlan to sit as well.

The three of them walked to another spot in the massive space, not-so-subtly giving us a moment to regroup. They bent their heads together and talked in low voices I couldn't understand.

I pointed at the hand-screen. "What is it?"

Harlan set it on the table between us. He touched the display to scroll to the top and then the bottom. "It looks like a consent form."

I cracked a grin without humor. "To warn us of the chances of death and dismemberment?"

He pressed his lips together.

We sat in silence as we read together. After a minute, I tapped him on the shoulder and gestured for him to scroll downward. After we'd read the thing from top to bottom twice, Harlan raised his finger to digitally sign.

I grabbed his hand and called across the room, "One more thing."

Lena, Jarret, and Katie looked in our direction at the same time, and I suspected whatever they were discussing was only meant to bide their time until we were ready.

Staring at the three pairs of eyes now was like staring down the tunnel of fate. And I didn't know what lay at the end.

"We want our father to be your first real patient." I pulled in a long breath and tumbled into the speech I'd been practicing in my head since we got into Ellen's car an hour ago. "He's been in a vegetative state for almost two years. If this thing is everything you claim it is, it can help—"

"Done," Lena said.

"Done?" I asked. She'd interrupted before I reached the kicker—the part where we threatened to walk out if she refused.

"I had Vanessa downstairs make a few calls about your background. She got back to me, and I think I can help him." She gestured at the hand-screen both Harlan and I gripped in our hands. "Swipe to the right."

Harlan swiped, and another document popped up. This one was short and already signed—by Lena. A promise to pay us for our time and care for our father to the best of her abilities, including but not limited to using this technology.

I swiped back to our informed consent and signed with my finger. Harlan did the same and passed the hand-screen to Lena, who passed it to Katie.

Katie took a quick look and strode toward the front of the room. She raised both arms, and the giant vid wall blanked. When she flicked a wrist, new data scrolled across the screen. The code accompanied images of this office without any furniture except the table and two chairs Harlan and I occupied.

"Jarret," Lena said, "can you get Dr. Fisher here as soon as possible?"

I froze.

"It's nothing to worry about. I'd like to have her monitor you as a precaution." To Harlan and me, she added, "A couple more things before we start."

"Shouldn't all the warnings be in the informed consent?" I asked.

Harlan put a hand on my arm as if to hold me back.

Lena laughed. "You're the skeptical one. I appreciate a healthy amount of skepticism. I like to carry some around myself."

Her smile put me more at ease than I appreciated, and I struggled to keep from tossing all my reservations aside. Harlan idolized her, so one of us had to stay focused.

"These aren't warnings, just information." She nodded toward Jarret. "He designed the breadcrumbs, so he can explain them best."

"Dr. Fisher is finishing a surgery, but she'll be here." He looked up at his time display again. "We may not have time to wait."

He and Lena stared at Harlan and me.

"She's coming, though?" Harlan asked.

"She will be here no more than *minutes* after you are plugged up," Jarret promised.

Harlan and I exchanged a look, and I nodded.

Jarret picked up where Lena left off. "When we plug you in, you'll be inside a digital construct. Most of what you'll see is software, but two things are hardwired into each device." Jarret tapped the pile of circuit boards in his hand. "First are the breadcrumbs. These only exist in the prototype and will be gone when we finalize the design. They—"

Lena cut him off. "They're markers you can use to note anything about the construct that seems off." She bounced her knees as she spoke, her excitement too big to be contained in stationary space.

"I thought *I* was explaining," Jarret said, holding back a grin.

She gestured him forward as she stepped back.

"Each breadcrumb is designed to record its surroundings for only a second or two," he continued. "That's enough for it to send us data describing the location in the construct's coordinate space as well as what exactly is wrong at that location."

"So if we see something weird," I said, "we use a breadcrumb."

"Exactly. They'll look like tiny little computer chips in your pocket. All you have to do is drop one on the floor, and it will record its surroundings and send us a message automatically."

"What's the other hardware thing?" I asked.

"The exit," Lena said. "It will always look like a door, and we'll keep it in plain sight for this test. If you feel distressed and want to leave the construct, you can use the door."

"You can't just end the construct?"

"We can, but it's good to have redundant safeguards. Exiting through the door initiates the shutdown process, which safely removes all software threads from your brain to ensure nothing is left running when we unplug you."

"Because leftover threads would be bad?"

"It's just like any program running on a computer. If threads keep running after a program is done, they are unpredictable because their ancestor program no longer exists to end them. In this case, the program is running in your brain. Any leftover threads could cause confusion."

"Confusion, as in …"

Jarret and Lena exchanged a look.

"Split realities. Hallucinations. Early dementia. Etcetera, etcetera," Katie added without looking away from the vid wall.

"But"—Lena glared at her back—"none of that is going to happen because we can initiate the shutdown process ourselves, or *you* can do it by using the exit door. You never have to worry about being powerless. You can unilaterally leave the construct at any time. That's why we have the hardwired exit."

"To make us feel better?" Harlan asked.

The door might have been designed for our comfort, but this conversation was *not*.

"As a redundant safeguard," Lena confirmed. "Ready to go?"

I inhaled and tried to exhale all my fears. "As much as we'll ever be."

"Here we go." Lena called Katie over to us before handing her one of the makeshift devices and the other to Jarret.

Jarret dragged a chair behind mine, as if to sit, but instead stood in front of it, hovering over me. He stared down at me with a somber look.

Katie stood behind Harlan.

"Second thoughts?" I asked my brother.

"There's nothing to worry about."

Lena inspected each of us and the devices one last time. The weight of her intensity hurried my pulse, and I shifted in my seat.

Despite the safeguards, this thing would have full access to my brain. No part of that was *nothing to worry about.*

Lena met my eyes with an unasked question. Despite the consent form, she wouldn't fight me if I wanted to grab my brother and run out the door.

I sat straighter. "Let's go."

# GIA

"We're going to connect to the back of your heads now." Lena's voice was clear and steady, and I tried to absorb her confidence.

A knot expanded in my stomach, growing arms and legs that wrapped around my nerves and pulled taut.

"This is going to hurt," Jarret said from behind me.

I faced forward and squeezed my eyes shut. "Do it."

"We'll do it at the same time," Katie said from behind Harlan. "No need for one of you to anticipate it after the other is already—"

A sharp pain pierced the back of my head. I gasped at the same time Harlan shrieked and jumped to his feet. The wires of his device dangled from his head down the stack of connected circuits in Katie's hand.

"So much for a warning." He eased back into his seat.

I cringed even as the pain dissipated into sharp tingles. "No, it was good. Better not to know."

Katie offered a self-congratulatory smile.

Lena faced the giant vid wall and raised both arms as if preparing to direct an orchestra. It blanked except for my name on the top left and Harlan's on the right. An instant later, numbers and code filled both sides under our names.

"Everything looks great!" Lena grinned at us. "Let's do this."

"What should we expect to—" The world flexed around me.

Lena disappeared. The wall of data faded into pure white. Jarret, Katie, and everything in the office melted into a white void except the chairs and table in front of me. Even the white door disappeared, as if this room were the entire world.

A new door popped into existence in the middle of the space where the vid had been. Unlike the white one, this was utilitarian steel lacking any decor.

My chest tightened, and my breathing shallowed. My stomach was on a roller coaster through the knots that had taken up residence. The coaster plunged down at a blistering speed. A low hum came from the back of my head, but when I reached back, the wires were gone.

I jumped to my feet.

Harlan appeared beside me, also on his feet with his chair knocked over behind him.

It was the same office with the same shape and structure, but he and I were alone.

"It's fine," Harlan said, seeing my panic. "I'm here. We're okay."

"Lena?" I whispered in a tone about as steady as an earthquake.

"I'm here." Her voice came from inside my head. "Nobody has moved. Your perception has changed."

"Please sit down," said a voice I vaguely recognized as Jarret's. "Everything is fine. There is no cause for panic."

"I'm not panicked," I said through gritted teeth.

"Your numbers say otherwise," Katie said, her tone too cheerful.

"Gia, Harlan," Lena said. "Please sit so we can continue."

I sucked in three deep breaths, each one steadier than the last. Harlan's presence was a soothing balm on my frayed nerves.

I sat. "Right."

"It's just a test," Harlan said as he set his chair upright and sat himself in it. "For Dad."

"For Dad," I repeated.

"Good." Lena's voice reverberated through my skull. "Can we proceed?"

"Please do," I said with more confidence than I felt.

"Both of you, please imagine your favorite foods."

Steak. Our family hadn't been able to afford it for years. It was the only food I missed from when I was small.

"Medium-rare steak," Harlan chimed in as if reading my mind.

I looked down to see two plates materialize on the table. A giant slab of ribeye steak nearly hid the white porcelain underneath. A pad of butter appeared on top, half melted, and oozed over the meat and down its side.

My mouth watered.

A fork and knife appeared on either side.

"Eat," Lena urged.

Harlan dug in. He sliced off a small piece, revealing the juicy red inside. The smell nearly set me on fire.

I couldn't hold back, so I grabbed my fork and knife and sliced off a piece. The knife slid through the steak as if the meat itself were butter. The moment it touched my tongue, rich flavor exploded in my mouth.

I groaned. "Oh my God."

Harlan swallowed. "That's incredible."

"Please describe your experience," said Lena's disembodied voice.

I cut off another piece and stuffed it in my mouth before speaking, mouth full. "Amazing. Taste, texture, smell—the whole experience is better than I remember."

"Does it feel like a simulation?"

"Not at all," Harlan said. "I can feel myself chewing, my teeth mashing into the meat." He touched his neck as he swallowed. "I can feel the steak going down my throat. It's a completely believable experience."

"Flawless," I added, surprised by my enthusiasm. "Just like the real thing."

I'd been wrong. There was nothing to worry about. Lena was a genius, this would go smoothly, and we'd be back home in no time with help for Dad.

We heard Lena celebrating with her team in excited, disembodied voices. They stood in the same room with us, but as far as we could see, Harlan and I were alone.

Their cheers subsided, and the gravity of all this slammed into me like a brick wall.

This was one step in a much larger process. There was no telling what challenges lay ahead. A chasm existed between virtual steak and bringing a man back from the edge of death.

"How is this going to help our dad?" I asked, keeping my tone respectful. Lena and her team held my fate in their palms in more ways than one.

"Good question," Lena said. "This is the first step. If we can connect people's brains with sensations, we can also connect those sensations with people's bodies. So basically, this device acts as an interface between brain and body. But we can't do any of that until we confirm the basics are operational."

"What's next?" Harlan asked.

"We're going to try something a little harder." Lena mumbled words to her team, and the sound came out muffled, not meant for our ears.

My nervousness stirred as the knots that had begun to loosen retightened in my gut.

"We built a forest construct that simulates all five senses," she said. "Sight, sound, smell, taste, and touch. We're loading it now. It will feel like you're being teleported, which might be uncomfortable."

"It *will* be uncomfortable," Katie chimed in.

Harlan glanced at me for confirmation.

I shrugged. We came this far. Why quit now?

"Will we be together in the forest?" Harlan asked.

"Every second."

I shot another look at Harlan, and he squeezed my shoulder.

"Okay," I said.

A pause of about twenty seconds followed, and then Lena's voice came again. "The transition may be a bit jarring."

"It *will* be a *lot* jarring," Katie corrected.

I chewed my lower lip. I appreciated Katie's honesty, but Lena's positivity would work better without the clarifications.

I clutched Harlan's hand and held my breath.

"Don't hold your breath," Katie said. "That will make it worse."

"Ten ... nine ..." a monotone voice began the countdown in a unisex tenor.

Harlan squeezed my hand, and my shoulders relaxed a millimeter.

"Eight ... seven ..."

My heart rate quickened, and I focused on keeping my breaths slow and steady and definitely not holding them.

"Six ... five ..."

My body tightened, not by my own reaction but by something external. My stomach curled on the inside as if twisting into itself, finding those knots and folding into them. My throat tightened as sour saliva filled my mouth.

"Four ..."

I squeezed my eyes shut and fought the urge to vomit. *Might* be uncomfortable, Lena had said. A *bit* jarring. Ugh.

"Three ..."

I clutched my skull. Why was that voice so loud, and why was there an entire year between each endless number in this count?

"Two ..."

Was my head on fire?

"One."

The white room flashed red. An alarm clanked. Everything went black except the pain, which was the brightest thing I'd ever felt.

"Something's wrong. Stop." I reached for Harlan's hand, but my fingers hit air. "Stop!"

Like a light switch, the pain went out.

I opened my eyes.

I was in a forest. Tall trees towered overhead. Their leaves rustled in a light breeze. Sunlight filtered through the canopy, casting dappled shadows on the ground. The smell of damp earth and fresh greenery filled my nose.

My tension melted away. We made it. The forest construct was here, and the pain was gone. I glanced at Harlan.

He wasn't there.

"Harlan?"

I spun a circle in one direction and then back in the other, but I saw not even a glimpse of his dark hair or kind eyes that calmed my storm.

"Lena!"

Nothing.

"Jarret? Katie?"

I was alone.

# GIA

"*H*arlan!"

My voice echoed through the towering trees and faded into nothing.

"Harlan." This time a whisper, and no echo—or maybe it was smothered by the panicked sound of my pulse rushing, quickening, trampling.

The green extended forever in every direction. An endless forest.

Panic hurled me into motion, and I ran. My feet stomped the forest floor, kicking up the scent of damp earth. Nothing but trees lay this way. Endless trees with a cloudless blue sky overhead and pine-colored earth beneath.

I spun a one-eighty and sprinted in the other direction.

"Harlan! Lena!" Nothing. No one.

My sneaker caught a root. I tumbled to the ground. My hands hit dirt and stung.

When I turned them over and examined my palms, there were no scrapes, no blood, just the burn.

The digital construct extended around me in all directions, its perfect beauty mocking me. When I screamed, the only reply was the echo of my voice and the rustle of pine needles.

Think. Breathe.

I pulled myself to a sitting position and tried to calm my heart. I wiped tears from my face, and my hand came away smudged with mud. I wasn't going to appear back in that gorgeous office with Harlan, Lena, and her team, or that would have happened already.

I had to save myself.

Lena said there would always be an exit. It would start the exit process and get me out of here. I shoved to my feet and spun a slow circle, squinting into the thick trees.

They'd rendered every leaf, pine needle, and blade of grass with stunning detail. Sunlight streamed through the canopy to create shadow patterns that shifted with each gust of wind. But there was no door, no exit as Lena had promised. Nothing except . . .

I froze.

Was that a glitch in this otherwise flawless construct? Straight ahead, the air shimmered and warped like heat waves distorting the trees. It flickered in and out of existence, a tear in the fabric of the digital reality.

As I held my breath, I reached into my pocket—and celebrated as my fingers touched tiny metal chips that must be the breadcrumbs the team had promised. At least something had gone right.

I extracted one, dropped it at my feet, and moved toward the glitch.

A beep sounded in my head. A unisex computerized voice said, "Recording captured," and went silent.

Right, Jarret had said each breadcrumb would capture a short recording.

I pulled another metal chip from my pocket and dropped it. "Something went wrong—"

"Recording captured," interrupted the voice.

I stuffed my hand in my pocket, yanked out all the breadcrumbs, and used my other hand to spread them across my palm. Only five more. One second of recording each didn't give me much time in total.

After slipping the crumbs back into my pocket, I started my journey toward the glitch. It was the only oddity in this forest, so it could be my way out.

Occasionally, I dropped another breadcrumb and left a message.

"Lost."

"Recording captured," confirmed the voice.

"Alone. Walking."

"Recording captured."

"Toward a glitch."

"Recording captured."

I hoped Lena and her team could piece it together and find me. Most of all, I needed Harlan to be safe. Wherever he was, maybe he was headed to the glitch too.

Maybe it was our salvation.

# LENA

"What the hell just happened?" I shouted at the vid on my office wall.

I gestured to initiate the exit process for both test subjects. Nothing happened. The software had been rewritten. My commands didn't work.

My design had been twisted, corrupted. "Get them out!" I screamed at Jarret and Katie.

When I waved my arms, images of the forest, vital signs, and digital locations hurtled across the display. I slowed them enough so I could read the data.

Gia was dropping her breadcrumbs, but the images and audio they pinpointed didn't help. She was walking toward a glitch, she said. I didn't care about a stupid *glitch* right now. I cared only about getting her out.

Behind me, the unconscious bodies of Harlan and Gia slumped at the table, where they'd been since the test began. Their eyes stayed closed and their breaths steady, but their consciousnesses were elsewhere.

If I couldn't get them back, they'd be vegetative—like their father.

"Where's Dr. Fisher?" I shouted.

"She's wrapping up her surgery," Jarret said. "She'll be here."

I cursed.

My team scrambled into action. Katie gestured at the vid with both arms in a practiced motion, like directing an orchestra. The vid shoved my data to the left and gave her control of the right.

"I don't know what happened," Jarret said from behind us, where he bent over our test subjects. "Everything was fine. I don't know what happened … I don't know …"

"None of us knows!" Katie shouted.

"Just stay with them," I said without turning. "Keep an eye on their vitals."

I kept my gaze locked on the vid. Any bit of data could be the key to getting Harlan and Gia out of this neuro-nightmare.

The sound of something knocking against the steel table yanked my attention, and I looked. Jarret was shaking Gia's body.

"Don't!" I tripped over my feet to get to him and yanked his arms away.

He screeched as my metal fingers bit into his wrist.

"Sorry." I stepped back and showed my palms in surrender. "Please don't do that."

"You're right." Jarret looked down at his own hands as though they'd betrayed him. "We can't wake them without the exit process."

"You could rip them in two."

Jarret clutched his head as if imagining it. "No touching. Definitely no unplugging."

I spun back to the vid and sorted and filtered, even though I didn't know what I was looking for. Katie and I flung data across the giant display in silence broken only by our rapid breaths.

The door beeped and flew open, revealing two suited security guards on the other side. They barged into the room.

I blocked their path. "The prototypes are already in use." I made a point to fist my metal hand at my side. I didn't intend to hit anyone with it, but I wanted them to know I could.

"We have orders to confiscate them," one of the guards said.

I stepped aside to reveal Harlan's and Gia's unconscious bodies slumped in their chairs. "Are you going to rip them out of our test subjects' heads?"

The guard on the left stuttered a half step forward before the other held her back.

"No?" I gestured toward the door. "Then get out of our way so this doesn't turn into a disaster." It already was one, but they didn't need to report that to my mother and the board.

They hesitated, exchanged hissed whispers, and backed out of the room. The automated door slammed shut behind them.

When Jarret spoke again, his tone was calmer than before. "You need to approach this from the other direction. Instead of figuring out what's wrong, find out what *went* wrong and work forward."

"Good idea." I swiped in the air, and everything on the left side of the vid disappeared. "We need to find the source."

Katie continued to fling her arms, directing traffic on her side of the display.

"Keep at it." I steadied my voice. My team would fall apart if I looked as panicked as I felt. "We'll approach this from both directions."

Jarret said, "I think we can all agree we have a hack."

"We find the hacker. Kick their ass."

"Make them stop," Jarret said.

I grunted my assent. "*Stop* them. *Then* kick their ass."

"You can't solve every problem by beating someone up," Katie said, never slowing in her manipulations of the vid.

I cleared my throat and said to the vid, "Load cybersecurity bot."

An animated image of a boxy robot appeared on the left side of the display, leaving Katie control of the right. In a chirpy voice, it prompted, "Whose ass are we kicking today?"

Katie looked at me.

"What? I customized it a little." To the screen, I added, "Bot, we need to identify a hacker. Collect all data since we activated the computer-brain interface prototypes. For the first five minutes, the test went perfectly. Use that as your control."

The boxy robot danced across the screen, each movement punctuated by a kick or karate chop. It returned to attention. "Collected. Do you have a sample of the anomalous data?"

"Use the last five minutes for that. Can you compare the two, determine precisely when the anomaly started, identify the injected data, and then match the injected data to signatures of known hackers?"

"Processing." The animated robot returned to kickbox grooving.

Katie stared.

"Maybe I went a little overboard with the customization." I waved at her side of the screen. "Worry about your end."

The robot stilled. "I have ninety-two percent certainty that the Web Witch performed this hack."

"Web Witch?" Katie's movements momentarily dampened. "Never heard of him."

"*Her,*" the robot said. "Here is everything we know about the Web Witch."

The robot faded into the black screen, replaced by text and images arranged in neat, labeled groups: known hacks, web posts, motivations, IP addresses.

"Katie," I said, "a little help?"

The room went silent as she and I scanned through the information. I started with the IP addresses, but there was no pattern.

"She's routing her connections through multiple servers," I said. "Different servers each time. She's smart."

"I've got something," Katie said. "She keeps coming back to this forum to brag about her exploits. Looks like she's online now."

"Call her."

"Creating an account … Done. Now, I'm requesting a video call."

A series of low, steady beeps filled the room as we waited. After the sixth beep, the call connected, pushing all the other data aside to fill the screen.

An image of a hag digitally masked the person's face. The hag's skin looked like cracked leather, stretched taut over sharp cheekbones and a hooked nose. Dark, bottomless pits filled her eye sockets. Her mouth twisted into a sinister grin. Wispy strands of white hair framed the grotesque face.

"Miss Hayes," came the computer-disguised voice. The mouth opened and closed, and the inside was an empty black hole. "What took so long?"

"Cut the theatrics," I said. "What do you want from me to release what you stole?"

"What I stole?" The voice was slow, taunting. "You mean your test subjects? I have Harlan right here. If I don't get what I want, I could just ... end him."

"This isn't about murder," I shot back. "You want something, or you wouldn't have answered my call."

"Technically, it would just be shutting down a consciousness in a virtual space."

Killing Harlan's consciousness would sever the connection to his body. A body without its mind is an empty shell. That was the same as murder in my book.

The hag's image flickered, replaced by a video clip of Gia stumbling through the forest. Dirt streaks trailed down her cheeks. She tripped, collapsed, and sobbed as she struggled back to her feet.

My breath stilled.

The footage was from a high angle, recorded from above—as if she were being stalked.

"Is it ransom you want?" I asked in a steady voice that wasn't my own. The last month of practicing to be Business Lena was finally paying off.

"Patience, Miss Hayes." The image shifted back to the hag, now wearing a mocking pout.

"What do you want for Harlan and Gia's safe return?"

"Ah, better." The hag's grin widened, stretching the inky black mouth. "I want what every civic-minded, intelligent member of society wants."

Impatience roiled in my stomach. I clenched my metal fist by my side and stayed silent.

"Control of CyberCorp Technology," she finished.

Despite myself, I guffawed. "I couldn't give you that if I wanted to. Every idiot who can watch a press conference knows I own only twenty-five percent."

The grin tightened. "Then deliver that. I'll worry about the rest."

My laughter died. I could see how this would go. First, my quarter share. Then she'd come for the other significant owners. Maybe not my mother, but the others would fall like glass soldiers. None of them truly believed that CyberCorp could survive without my fresh perspective.

I was the keystone—one of the few who would fight the world to keep CyberCorp running and preserve its ability to do good in this world.

If this witch squeezed in the right spots, she could get her controlling interest. If I let her win now, no one would be left to fight.

"It's a simple trade," the hag continued. "Your shares for two innocent lives."

Katie's face mirrored my horror, but Jarret remained focused on Harlan and Gia. He touched their foreheads and pressed his fingers into their wrists. That couldn't be a good sign.

"Give me time to figure out how to do the transfer to an anonymous recipient." Before she could answer, I gestured with my right hand, closing it into a fist, and the call disconnected.

The display blanked, and silence pressed in on all sides.

"How are they?" I asked Jarret.

"Pulses are slow. We should get Dr. Fisher."

Fear clutched my heart and squeezed. I nodded, and he tapped his micro-comm to make the call.

"What's the plan?" Katie asked me.

"We pray Harlan and Gia find the hardware exit to initiate safe extraction," I said. "And we stall."

# GIA

*E*xhaustion clung to me like a second skin.

I reached the glitch.

It shimmered and flickered, but I could see it for what it was. A single rustic cabin sat in these endless woods. Judging by how it behaved like a tear in the fabric of this construct, I knew it wasn't supposed to be here.

The door refused to budge, so I moved to the window.

The tiny building had a single-room interior with a cozy sitting area and quaint kitchen. Even odder than the cabin-that-shouldn't-exist was the *door*-that-shouldn't-exist. A solid steel door stood in the middle of the room, connected to nothing.

It defied gravity. Its matte, industrial metal contrasted with everything else in this reality. It looked exactly like the exit in our first construct.

It was my way out, hard-coded and ever-present, just like Lena and her team had promised. The door was part of Lena's construct. The *cabin* wasn't.

Someone had put it in this precise spot to hide the exit.

I reached into my pocket and pulled out another cool metal breadcrumb. I would have one—maybe two—seconds to explain this development.

As I dropped the breadcrumb, I shoved as many words as possible into one breath. "Glitch is a cabin. Exit—"

"Recording captured," the robotic voice interrupted.

That would have to be enough. I had one breadcrumb left, and I needed to save it for something important.

Inside the cabin, a worn wooden table stood near the window, adorned with mismatched chairs. Faded paintings of forests and animals decorated the walls, along with framed photos of families of numerous races with too-perfect features that could only have been AI-generated.

The kitchen was a throwback to days I'd only heard about, with its hand-pump sink, stovetop teakettle, and hanging copper pots that gleamed as if freshly shined. In complete contrast to all that, a Hyper-Oven sat on the counter.

The curved outer shell of the high-tech cooker wore a glossy, mirrored look with a broad base that narrowed to the top. An oval-shaped glass door took up most of the front, with a slight blue tint that gave it a futuristic look.

According to the ads, which I'd seen a hundred times, it could cook a compressed meal pod for a family of eight in less than three minutes.

"Hot and fresh in a fraction, HyperOven perfection in rapid action," I muttered, quoting its advertisements.

The cabin had no doors except the front one and the steel one floating in the center. That meant no bedroom, no bathroom—just a bizarrely detailed living space.

I tried the door again, but it clicked against the lock.

"Come on!" I rattled the handle.

An orb-like drone zipped across my eyeline and hovered above, graceful as a hummingbird.

If I remembered correctly from *its* advertisements, this was a surveillance drone—an expensive one. Why would Lena need surveillance inside her construct?

This cabin didn't mesh with what I knew of her. She was all about realism and attention to detail. She wouldn't create this place with no bathroom or bedroom, with a HyperOven next to a pump-action sink, a random door in the middle, and a fancy drone outside.

Maybe a member of her team built it as a bad joke.

"Hilarious." I stuck my middle finger up at the drone.

I slammed my elbow into the window. Pain throbbed up my arm, but the glass didn't give. Not even a crack.

The effort left me gasping. I bent at the waist and put my hands on my knees. My walk couldn't have been more than an hour, yet I felt utterly drained. The breeze chilled my forehead, already damp with sweat.

I let myself collapse to the earth.

My body wouldn't be this tired from just walking, but this *wasn't* my body. This was some virtual version of me walking around an imaginary forest-scape CyberCorp had built inside my head.

If I didn't escape this place, Harlan would be inconsolable.

Worse, Ellen would send him to the meat market.

I shoved to my feet, fighting against fatigue that pressed me down like a lead weight on every limb. My life could depend on getting inside this cabin.

The windows on this side had no locks, no latches. They hadn't been designed to open. Trees pressed against the structure's outer walls, so I'd have to squeeze past them to get to the back.

Branches scratched and clawed as I shoved them aside until I reached the opposite side. Two more windows marked the back of the cabin. Like the ones in front, these had no latches.

They offered a different view of the interior. Against the wall beside the front door stood a massive wood-burning oven, large enough to fit an entire hog. A stack of logs sat beside it, piled almost to the ceiling.

The surveillance drone buzzed close to my face, and I swatted. It zoomed out of reach but hovered nearby. I turned back to the window.

Across the cabin, the front door slammed open, and Harlan stumbled through.

Someone strode through behind him and snuffed out my hope just as quickly.

The other person's leather-like skin was taut over sharp cheek-bones and a long nose. Wispy strands of white hair framed a thin face. Narrow eye slits, filled with malice, emanated a cold so great I shivered, even from a window away.

The hag shoved him forward, and he tumbled to the ground. His forehead hit the floor with a thud that made me cringe. I slammed my palm against the window, but neither looked up.

Rope kept his hands locked in front of him.

"Look what you made me do." Her voice was nails scratching a chalkboard.

As he struggled to stand, she shoved him with her foot. He toppled to the side. He scrambled to a sitting position and scooted backward until he hit the couch.

"Harlan!" I slammed a fist against the window and screamed.

Neither of them noticed. I could hear them but not the other way around.

The witch hummed a discordant tune as she screeched open the door to the giant wood-burning oven and tossed in a log.

"Please, listen to me." Harlan's voice cracked. "I don't know what you want, but Lena Hayes will give it to you if you let me go."

The hag threw more logs into the fire. Her wild tune grew louder with each toss.

Harlan scrambled to his feet.

The witch spun on him. When she touched his chest and shoved, Harlan's form flickered where they touched. His face contorted. His horrific scream flickered in and out like an audio device on the fritz.

I slammed both fists against the window, but my voice dried up. A silent scream caught the salt tears streaming down my face.

"Stop it!" I shouted. I slammed my elbow against the glass, and pain shot through my arm. I howled.

Harlan's body twisted and distorted beneath the witch's touch. All the while, she caught my eye and her gaze skewered me.

The doors and windows were locked and unbreakable, at least as far as I was concerned. Harlan couldn't hear me … but the witch could. This cabin was *her* construct.

I ripped my final breadcrumb from my pocket. The metal cooled my hot fingertips and my nerves.

If I used it, my recording needed to be perfect. None of my other breadcrumbs had saved us. If Lena and her team received my messages, the content I'd given them hadn't been enough to set Harlan and me free.

This one had to be better.

I rubbed the metal between my fingertips.

"Time's up," the witch screeched in a voice that could sear metal. "The CyberCorp Princess doesn't care about your life."

The witch grabbed and shoved him toward the oven. Fire roared upward like a rocket. I couldn't feel the heat from my spot outside, but the air shimmered as it met the cooler temperature of the cabin.

A scream grappled up my throat and hurled itself into the air.

Despite his trembling, Harlan's eyes went wild. He clawed at the witch's face, but her grip was unbreakable. The orange light of the fire reflected off the HyperOven only feet away.

The HyperOven. That was it!

"HyperOven interference," I shouted as I let my final breadcrumb slip from my fingers and drop to the dirt.

"Recording captured," came the electronic voice.

# LENA

Gia's voice sounded from the vid-screen. With it, the display shifted to display her position with pinpoint precision in the digital construct.

Not that knowing her position had done us any good so far.

"HyperOven interference?" Katie repeated. "What's that supposed to mean?"

I held my palms together and then widened the space between them. The image on the left side of the display zoomed through the cabin wall to show the interior. I magnified the image until the HyperOven filled the frame.

"It's a HyperOven," Jarret said in a flat tone. "So what?"

I shook my head. Every second counted, but we were chasing black holes with no hope of catching them.

Behind me, the steady beep of Gia's and Harlan's life support equipment pulled at my nerves. "Any improvement?"

"If there were, I would tell you." Dr. Fisher said, her voice sharp and commanding, as always when she worked.

In the time since we'd met the Web Witch, Dr. Fisher had finished her surgery and barreled into the room out of breath. Although she and I had started our relationship at odds—when my parents yanked her off her dream project to build my cybernetic arm—we'd grown to rely on each other.

She was the only person I trusted to care for Gia and Harlan right now.

"There's nothing I can do except keep their bodies viable until their minds return." She jerked her chin at the vid. "You do your job, and I'll do mine."

The large blonde woman had a presence bigger than her six-foot frame. She exuded authority and competence. Her team had already lugged two ice baths into the room, and Harlan and Gia each occupied one, fully clothed. Monitors beeped their vital signs.

The beeps stretched further and further apart. Soon, there would be a gulf between them.

If they got too far apart, it would be time to negotiate with this hacker.

Jarret manipulated the vid to put Gia back on the screen, still peering through the cabin window. In 32K resolution, every pine needle and notch of wood stood out like a distinct entity. Gia's shirt was now dirt-covered and torn. A small circular orb floated nearby.

I pointed. "Is that a surveillance drone?"

Jarret nodded. "A new model, designed to be difficult for intruders to disable."

"That explains the footage the Web Witch sent us of Gia walking through the woods."

He mumbled his agreement.

"A fully operational surveillance drone inside my construct," I said. "Hovering outside a cabin, which is also inside my construct. This Web Witch doesn't like to go small, does she?"

"Definitely not," Jarret agreed as he zoomed in on the cabin's interior.

The inside was a mishmash of eras, with copper pots hanging from hooks and an imposing wood-burning oven that dominated the small space. The HyperOven sat only a foot away from what looked like a pump-action sink that predated my parents.

For her digital representation, the Web Witch had stuck with the hag she'd presented during our call. Despite a face undefinably ancient, her back remained rod straight rather than bent over by years.

On the vid, she pulled Harlan's face close to hers. They were planted in front of the oven. The open door revealed a blaze inside. Her bony fingers dug into his cheeks as she teased him closer to the fire.

She seemed in no hurry. A smile twisted her mouth.

She enjoyed this.

"If she throws him in there ..." The implications were too terrifying to articulate.

"He'll never be able to exit the construct," Jarret finished for me.

Harlan's mind would die. Without the mind, the body is an empty shell. He would be unable to return to reality, and it would be my fault. My creation, my responsibility.

"How did she get in my construct?" I shouted. My heart pounded in my chest as panic threatened to take over. "Do we have any idea?"

"Got it," Katie said. Her arms waved at the air in front of her, manipulating data that slid across the vid. "There was an opportunity for code injection when we switched constructs without initiating a full exit."

"Code injection from *where*? We're on a closed network. You can't just inject code into a CyberCorp device without ..."

Jarret, Katie, and I all froze at the same time.

A split second later, Jarret scrambled into motion. "I'm calling security." He tapped his micro-comm even as he moved to the corner of the room to make the call in private. "Get me security at the request of Lena Hayes. There's a hacker ..."

"How could I let this happen?" I stared slack-jawed at the Web Witch and Harlan on the display.

"It's not unexpected," Katie said. "The point of prototypes is to discover issues."

"This is a huge damn issue," I snapped. I pulled in deep breaths and let my focus narrow on all the facts. "What do you think she meant about the HyperOven?"

Off to the side, Jarret screamed at security through his micro-comm, telling them the hack had come from inside the building. It was the only explanation.

"I'm not sure," Katie said. To the vid, she added, "Run a search for HyperOven interference."

New data came flying onto the vid.

Jared returned from making his call, his face red. "They're searching the premises. It shouldn't take long since all ID chips in the building are logged. The hacker will be one of the few without one. Security will need to cross-reference their motion detectors with anyone chipless and find who doesn't belong."

"Ten minutes?" I guessed.

Jarret cringed. "They said thirty. It's a full house today."

"These two might not have that long," Dr. Fisher called from behind us.

The beeps marking Harlan's and Gia's vitals were so far apart that, after each one, I wondered if it was the last. Despite the ice bath, sweat rolled down Gia's forehead. Her brother's face looked just as ashen despite his brown skin.

"Remember," Fisher said grimly. Her gaze found mine and locked. "You do your job."

"And you'll do yours," I muttered. I returned my attention to Katie. "What have you got?"

"Here." She blew up two documents side by side on the display.

They looked like court filings. Lots of legal jargon, but it was clear enough that the HyperOven's manufacturer had paid an ungodly amount of money to two plaintiffs related to electrical interference.

"Give me the condensed version," I said.

"The HyperOven causes an unexpectedly large electrical interference," Katie said. As she spoke, lines in the documents lit up yellow to draw my attention. "There have been numerous lawsuits. In these two cases, medical devices running nearby experienced issues due to the interference. It didn't end well."

"Ouch." An epiphany hit me. "Can we send a message to Harlan?"

"Sure," Jarret said. "He hasn't dropped any of his breadcrumbs. We can reverse their functionality and use them to send a message to him.

We would get less than a second for each, though, since part of the recording time for each one has to be used up for the reversal itself."

"He has seven breadcrumbs," I said. "Seven seconds."

Jarret nodded. "*Less* than seven seconds. Make it count."

On the left side of the vid, the hag and Harlan were close enough to the fire that orange-yellow flames reflected in Harlan's terrified eyes.

I stood straighter. "Send this message …"

# HARLAN

*H*eat licked my face as the witch held me only inches from the giant oven. Sweat stung my eyes and pooled above my lip.

If I died in this construct, that would be okay—as long as Gia was safe. Gia would hold Lena to her promise, and my family could survive. I could be the sacrifice.

It wasn't my first choice, but it would do as a backup.

My pocket vibrated. A voice from nowhere followed. "Get the Hyper—" It cut off abruptly. I'd barely processed that when another vibration pulsed, and the voice continued, "Oven to the—"

The words clipped off.

The hag stared at me with soulless, empty eyes. "What is that? Is something vibrating?"

"How should I know?" I said.

More vibrations came in succession, each accompanied by a burst of words. "Wall to the—"

"Right of the—"

"Counter un—"

"Der the win—"

"Your life de—" said a synthesized voice inside my brain.

Technically, *all* of this was inside my brain. The voice was the least odd and terrifying thing about today.

The witch didn't appear to hear the words, just the vibration of the breadcrumbs.

"What is that? Answer me!" she screeched. Her eye sockets bored into me as if they might suck me into their void. "What is that infernal buzzing?"

I held my breath, waiting for more.

The hag's face reddened, and her thin body shook. Her fingers tightened around my jaw as she pulled my face closer. "I built this cabin to exact specifications." Her voice trembled. "Nothing in here buzzes!"

Her breath smelled of rotting meat. My instincts screamed to pull away, but her clawed fingers held me still.

No more vibrations, no more words.

There were exactly seven brief messages. Jarret had given me seven breadcrumbs, so the messages must have come from the team. Altogether, they said, *Get the HyperOven to the wall to the right of the counter under the window. Your life de ...*

My life depended on it?

"Speak!" The witch shook me so hard my head lolled on my shoulders.

"It's just my stomach." The lie came smoothly. "I've never been this terrified before, and I think I might vomit." I gagged and raised my bound hands to my face.

"Not in my construct!" The witch released my face and stepped back. "It's all in your head. If you ruin this gorgeous construct with your ridiculous biological ..." She made a retching sound and flung me toward the kitchen.

The heat of the fire receded as I tripped toward the sink—and the HyperOven beside it.

I hit the counter hard and bent over it.

My hands were still bound, but years of playing sports had given me excellent hand-eye coordination. I swung my fists like a bat. I connected with the HyperOven, and with a satisfying crunch, the machine sailed through the air.

It hit the floor with a thud, bounced, and landed against the cabin wall, directly under the window.

The wall flickered.

# GIA

The wall flickered.

It glitched like a faulty hologram. It couldn't separate me from my brother anymore.

The HyperOven lay on the floor at my feet, on the other side of the failing wall. Harlan hunched against the kitchen counter, wearing a triumphant smile.

The witch's empty dark eye sockets widened as she, too, recognized the frailty of her cabin. She lunged at Harlan, grabbed his shoulders, and hauled him toward the person-sized wood-burning oven that stood wide open.

Before, she was teasing. Now, her muscles strained as she dragged him. His feet lost purchase on the beaten hardwood floor, and his legs flailed behind him.

"No!" I screamed.

A sturdy branch lay to my right, and I snatched it up. I barreled forward and swung it at her head. My arms vibrated as it cracked against her skull.

She released her grasp on my brother and stumbled to the side.

I clasped his wrist and yanked him toward the steel door in the center of the room. As if on command, the door clicked and flung open. Beyond it, bright light beckoned.

The witch recovered and lunged for Harlan's arm. He flinched as her nails bit into his flesh, but he kept moving. I reached the door first and had one foot over the threshold when the witch released Harlan.

He locked his feet in place. I tugged, but his eyes slitted at the hag who'd kept him captive.

"What are you doing?" I shouted. "Move!"

"They're going to use this same technology on Dad."

It took me a split second to catch up. When Dad was connected, would the hag be there? Would she find a way to trap him in his own head, kill him?

Harlan closed his eyes for a second as if asking forgiveness, wrapped his hands around the witch's wrist, and pulled her after us. Her face contorted in horror as she toppled through the doorway.

# GIA

$\mathcal{I}$ opened my eyes and gasped.

"It's okay. It's okay." A tall blonde woman bent over me.

Except for my head, I was submerged in an ice bath. "It's freezing!" My feet slipped against the inside of the tub.

"I know. Sorry." Her voice was steady and soothing, and her hand over mine was comforting. "Try to relax."

I stopped kicking.

"I'm Dr. Athena Fisher. The ice was to keep your body from burning up. You can get out now, but you'll be groggy. Go slowly."

On the other side of her, Harlan awoke in his own tub.

"What the hell?" he shouted.

The blonde woman stilled him with the same look and soothing voice she'd used on me. "Harlan, you are fine. Take a moment before you stand. Hold the sides of the tub when you do."

I laid my head back and settled in. My body did indeed feel like a cooling fire on the inside. A little longer in cold water wouldn't hurt.

I tossed a tired smile at my brother, and he returned it.

"Hey," he said in a voice that was both exhausted and content.

"Hey," I returned.

WHEN I WAVED MY WRIST, THE FRONT DOOR OF OUR APARTMENT clicked and shot open to one side, disappearing into the wall. Harlan and I led Lena and Dr. Fisher into our apartment. The scent of stale air and burnt food greeted us.

A month had passed since we first tested the computer-brain interface. Since that date, my hopes had alternately dived and soared a thousand times. Yet here we were. Finally.

The vid on the wall powered itself on, and the ads started. *"Introducing the Micro-Dome, a revolutionary wristband that provides a personalized microclimate for its wearer . . ."*

Lena marched straight to my father's bed on the far side of the room, unbothered by the patched walls and mismatched furniture.

"You must be Mr. Mercer." She squeezed his right hand as if by introduction. "I'm Lena Hayes, and this is Dr. Athena Fisher."

In ten seconds, Lena had shown more respect to my dad than I'd ever seen from my stepmother. I let hope bloom in my stomach where dread had multiplied for years.

"Your kids brought us here to help you," she continued. "We're going to start by examining your equipment to ensure we understand how everything works."

Dad didn't move, but his machines kept beeping.

Dr. Fisher got to work inspecting all of Dad's devices. She crawled under the bed to follow the wires from one machine to the next.

When she reappeared, Lena passed her a hand-screen. The two of them bent over it, swiping across the display. Every once in a while, one of them would point and murmur words I couldn't hear.

The vid rambled in the background. *"The patented wristband checks your temperature and heart rate and aligns your personal climate dome to deliver the most comfortable—"*

"Vid off," I said, with more smugness in my tone than I'd ever used while talking to an electronic device. We wouldn't need those ads anymore.

Harlan and I settled on the couch.

Lena and Dr. Fisher finished prepping and came over to us. Lena sat on the coffee table facing us. Dr. Fisher stood at her side.

"We should chat before we begin," Lena said, "since things went a bit sideways during our first test."

Dr. Fisher guffawed.

Lena glared at her. "The data we gathered during that test and the later ones—not just from your feedback but also from the security loopholes—taught us a lot about improving the computer-brain interface. *You* taught us a lot, and—"

"You're still going to do it, right?" Harlan sat on the edge of his cushion. "He's in a vegetative state. You can't make that worse. You might as well try."

Lena held up a fist.

He shut his mouth.

"We're going to install the device." She opened her hand to reveal a small chip, barely larger than a micro-comm, in a clear box. "We used the body of our new embeddable micro-comm as a casing for the tech. The entire computer-brain interface is here."

My hand trembled as stretched it out, palm up. Lena dropped the box into my palm. It was no heavier than a feather, but it held the weight of Dad's future.

"Take it back," I whispered.

She lifted it from my hand and held it out to Harlan.

He shook his head.

"Do you trust me?" Lena asked.

She had allowed a security loophole that almost got my brother and me killed. She'd also done everything in her power to save us. More importantly, she was the only one in the world offering to save our dad when every medical center had turned him away.

"With our lives," I said.

Lena looked down at the device in her hand.

"Is there a problem?"

"I'm just not good at speeches." She licked her lips. "*When* this works, it will be because of you. If we save one person or a million, it will be because you took a chance. Technology isn't good or evil, but the people who wield it can change everything."

A month ago, I would have disagreed. Technology had put Dad out of work and caused his condition. Technology kept Harlan and me from supporting this household. Yet technology was also going to save us.

"When this works," Lena continued, "*you* are your dad's heroes. Not me. Not this interface."

Words of thanks choked in my throat, so I just nodded.

"One more thing." She paused. "The team is trying to get permission for our second patient to be the Web Witch. I thought you should know."

Harlan looked down at his hands.

"You have nothing to be ashamed of," she said. "She's in a vegetative state because you were defending yourself. It was my invention that broke her. It's my responsibility to fix her so she can get the prison time she deserves."

Lena and Dr. Fisher regrouped at our father's bed. They moved with practiced precision. Lena entered commands into the handscreen. Dr. Fisher pulled out her scalpel and cut into the back of Dad's head with steady, focused fingers.

I squeezed Harlan's hand.

The front door slid open, and Ellen breezed into the room.

Her self-satisfied grin withered on her painted lips. "What the hell is this?"

Harlan met her at the door. "Don't interfere. Lena Hayes and Dr. Fisher are trying to wake Dad."

"Lena …" She shoved him aside so she could see past him. "Hayes? From CyberCorp Technology?"

When she tried to move past him, he slid into her path. "Do *not* interfere."

I usually separated them when things got heated because Ellen had controlled our fates. Today, I rooted for Harlan from my seat.

"Sit." He gestured toward her bedroom. "Or go to your room, but stay out of this."

Ellen chewed her lower lip. Then she raised her chin and flounced toward the main bedroom. "I have reading to do for work anyway. When I'm done, I'm making a smoothie in the kitchen whether you're finished here or not."

She disappeared into her room and slammed the door so hard the walls shook.

With Ellen out of sight, the tension in the room dropped. Lena and Dr. Fisher never paused their work. Busy and precise, the two moved around each other as if they'd done this a hundred times.

"Almost there." With a soft click, Lena snapped the chip into place at the base of Dad's skull.

Dr. Fisher dove in, executed a few quick stitches, and applied a healing balm to secure it.

Without looking down, Lena tapped a sequence on her hand-screen. "That should do it."

The room held its breath. Even the beeping of my dad's machines seemed to suspend in anticipation. Harlan's grip on my hand tightened so hard his pulse beat against mine. Two hearts intertwined.

Our hopes hinged on this moment.

Our fate rested on this moment.

Our lives depended on this moment.

Dad opened his eyes.

# ABOUT THE AUTHOR

Alicia Ellis decided to write books about ten minutes before graduating from law school. She's now an Atlanta attorney moonlighting as an author, electronics junkie, and secret superhero. With two degrees in computer science and an MFA in Writing Popular Fiction, she loves creative problem-solving, especially as it relates to high-tech things. She writes mysteries, sometimes for young adults, sometimes in fantasy or science fiction settings, and sometimes in the real world.

Her debut novel, Girl of Flesh and Metal, a young adult sci-fi mystery, was the first self-published book ever to make the American Library Association's LITA Excellence in Children's and Young Adult Science Fiction Notable Lists.

E.M. LACEY

The Toltec has dreamed of being a god, and with the guidance of his magic obsidian mirror, he has become the voice of the Aztec king. As the Aztec calendar ends, he seizes the perfect moment to fulfill his ambition. To attain godhood, he needs a god to ordain it, so he turns to a child with a divine mark.

Little Cuicatl bears the mark of the sun god, yet it feels more like a prison than an honor. Torn from her family to fulfill the Toltec's plans, she is forced to recite a false prophecy at the New Fire Ceremony. If she doesn't, her family will die.

Under a bloodstained sun, Cuicatl speaks, unleashing a prophecy that twists fate, altering destinies for herself, the Aztec Nation, and the Toltec.

A *Bloodstained Sun* is a retelling of fairytale *Snow White*, set in the universe of Biggs and Myer. This is Alba's story and how she came to be in Covenant, Illinois. It takes place in the Aztec nation. Throughout the book, Aztec names and places are incorporated, and there is a glossary and pronunciation guide.

*He who possesses the white hummingbird holds the power of the sun.*

*But a prophecy delivered through mortal means earns the wrath of a god.*

# GLOSSARY AND PRONUNCIATION GUIDE

## A BLOODSTAINED SUN

**Cuicatl.** *kah - ihk - aetl.* means song.

**Chicahua.** *chs- hay - kaa - waa.* means shield/strong.

**Atlacoya.** *atlah - koy - ah.* means storm.

**Huitzilin.** *wiy - tziy - lihn.* means hummingbird.

**Tenochtitlán.** *teh - noch - tee - tlahn.* Aztec capital

**Ilhicamina.** *Il - huicam - in - na.* means the one who shoots arrows.

**Eztli.** *ez - tli - ez - li.* (gender neutral) means blood.

**Cuallea.** *kwah - lee.* means good.

**Ahuatzi.** *aa - weyt - ziy.* means small oak.

**Guatemoc.** *kwaụ - ṭe - mok.* means falling eagle.

**Huipil.** *ẉI - pil.* means a long shift-like blouse.

**Mictlan.** *meek - tlan.* Aztec underworld

**Macuahuitl.** *mak - wa - hwee - til.* a weapon, a wooden club with several embedded obsidian blades.

**Huipil.** *wee - peel.* It is a boxy colorful embroidered blouse.

**Huitzilopochtli.** *wee - tsee - loh - poch' –'tlee.* means sun god.

**Tezcatlipoca.** *tez - kuht - luh - pow - kuh.* is a king/chief.

**Xoloitzcuintli.** *show - low - itz - queent - ly.* Mexican hairless dog, also known as **Xolo.** *show - low.* Known to guide humans to the afterlife.

# ONE

*1* *519 – Mexica-Tenochtitlán*
*Los Años Vinculantes*
*trans. The Binding Years*

"AGAIN," THE TOLTEC DEMANDED IN NAHUATL AS HE STOMPED TOWARD the girl. She flinched, clutching her dirty huipil as the sharp bitter stench of piss stained the air. Her thin arms squeezed her middle. Stopping him in his tracks.

The girl was young, maybe eight years old. Her golden skin gleamed under the torchlight. He stretched his hand toward her hair, his fingers itched to touch it. Test it. It was so different from his own smooth black hair. It framed her face like a halo. Under the firelight, it glowed. Two thin braids hung like ropes across her shoulders. Each with three turquoise and three onyx beads. He blinked, pulled his hand back, remembering his purpose.

*Claiming the power of the white hummingbird.*

The Toltec grinned, knowing his bared teeth added to the girl's terror. Most of his teeth lined up in a somewhat normal smile, but he had extras. They jutted through his gums. Cutting the inside of his mouth. It didn't hurt. The flesh inside his between his lips and gums was calloused. Acting more like a sheath for a blade. His grin widened and the girl whined which pleased him.

Terror was a power greater than physical strength. It stunned the mind. A mind unable to think was easy to manipulate. He took a step back making a show of smoothing his robes. As the king's priest he shared power. Over time his words became the king's words. If his plan flowed as the mirror decreed, his voice would be greater than the king's.

He freed an obsidian blade from its sheath, laid it across his palm and cut while meeting the child's eyes. He'd spent years searching for her. Wrapping his hand around the blade, he squeezed. Blood spilled through his fingers and dripped down his wrist. He flicked his hand, showering the girl in crimson. He frowned. It was supposed to sizzle like it did when she was delivered to him.

Fear. He was certain fear activated her power. The simpering cowering thing before him would not do. He needed her to stop whining. If the New Fire Ceremony was to have the impact he designed, she had to speak with confidence. Move like a goddess.

His lip curled.

*Children were such difficult creatures!*

He clicked his tongue before striding away from the girl to the door where he sheathed his blade. He tore a strip from his robe and wrapped his bleeding hand. There had to be a better way to coax the girl's powers to the surface. He brought his freshly wrapped hand to his chin as he considered his options. Children were simple creatures. He chuckled. The act primed his face for its new mask. He faced the girl again. This time, he wore a closed-mouth smile when he approached the girl.

"What is your name, girl?" The Toltec was pleased with the warmth of his tone.

"Cui ... Cui ... Cuitcatl," the girl croaked.

In his head, he sneered at the name. It meant 'song'. Girls were not songs. They were weights that clanged and dragged. The good ones were silent, watchful, and did not have to be told what pleased their masters.

He kneeled before the child, doing his best not to show his revulsion. His lips twitched as he struggled to keep his benevolent facade in place. Breathing deep, he reminded himself of the reward. In a little while, he would stand with the gods. Looking down at the girl, his smile, genuine. He reached for the girl, gently capturing her chin between his palms, guiding her bruised face to meet his slate gray gaze and said, "Your name is Alba."

It was an uncommon name, but it had come to him in a dream. A dream of floating mountains with colorful summits that moved with the wind, graceful as they glided across the water. There was a flock of hummingbirds, each a vibrant color, like a flower. In the dream, he looked down from the heavens on the floating mountains. Men tended the great bodies of land. The mountains were near Mexica-Tenochtitlán, and he would make sure that he was the first priest the strangers met. In the dream, it was his hand that reached out toward the approaching marvel. It was on his hand that a white hummingbird landed. Its wings beat as the name Alba trilled like little bells. The Toltec knew dreams were prophetic. To help it come to pass, he would follow it to the letter. His grip tightened on the girl's face, and he repeated the name.

Her honey-brown brows threaded with gold strands bowed in confusion. "My name is—"

"Alba," the Toltec cut her off.

The girl's mouth hung open. He slid a hand beneath her chin and used a finger to close it.

That same finger slid up the side of her tear-stained face, ending at her forehead where he pressed the telltale birthmark. The mark that should be his. He repeated his instruction slowly. "You are Alba, and I am going to make you a god."

The girl blinked at him.

"They're alive, you know." The Toltec leaned back, savoring the hope he created. It was laughable, the way her mouth moved like a freshly caught fish. Open and shut. Soft rasping puffs of air spewed from her mouth instead of words. Finally, after a noisy swallow of air, she spoke. Her voice reverent.

"They're alive?"

He nodded.

"If you do as I say," he gestured toward the high window. Torch-light gleamed along the edge of the windowsill. It spread along the upper wall, causing the stones to shimmer. Its beauty inspired him. "Some of them may yet survive," he said to the girl.

"But why can't—" the girl began.

A sharp wave of his finger halted her protests.

Rebellion. He would not have it. Not from the girl.

His lips twisted, as stormed over to the corner she occupied. The girl did her best to crawl into the wall which pleased him. He towered over her, though he was not a large man. The girl was small for her age. Thin. Odd looking. He inhaled, pushing his shoulders straight as he looked down his nose at her.

"This is the Year of Fire! You know what that entails, even though you are not from Tenochtitlán."

The girl whimpered, bunching up her huipil as her whining continued.

"The seven men who sheltered you," the Toltec sniffed. "Your uncles ..." He rolled his eyes before glowering at the child. He could see how her pitiful state called to the protective nature in good men. The seven were known along the western border near Lake Texcoco as honest farmers. Good workers. His spies informed him that the men were brothers, four widowers, two married, and one bachelor. Their entire family had been winnowed down to the seven. The widowers had lost not only their wives but their children to either war or sickness. The married pair had no children. The brothers raised the girl between households, treating her like a daughter, providing shelter, food, and affection. Her reaction to the news of their survival pleased him.

"What does it matter if I leave you four, or even one? You will have someone," he said. His proposal sounded reasonable, yet his intent was clear: once the girl was secured in his chambers, their fate was sealed. Two had managed to escape, but his gaze lingered on the pile of skulls nearby, five shiny trophies atop the stand beside his ceremonial headdress. His attention returned to the girl. The lie he told held kernels of truth. Walking away, he approached his collection, trailing a finger along the cranium of the nearest skull. As he awaited her

170

response, a slow, sinister smile crept across his face. Despite her initial fumbling, her words grew surer, stronger with each attempt.

He inhaled, scenting smoke. He looked around and saw the shimmering red lights of the wards etched into the walls, ensuring his protection from her power. Moving slowly, he paced the room, stealing glances at her amber glow. Waves of golden light slithered across her skin. The wards muted it, but the amber of her once dark brown eyes was unmistakable. She was what the rumors spoke of. A child of Huitzilopochtli. A demigod. A bastard. How she came to be and what happened to her mother was unknown. What he did know was that her existence would be brief.

"Again," he said, as he bobbed his head to the cadence of her words. "Again!" he demanded. The flow felt like a prophecy. The girl's ignorance of her abilities was a gift. A hint of divinity braced her words, making them echo.

He made the girl repeat the prophecy thirteen times before he ended their session. He reminded her that he would visit her later to collect the day's offering before sending her away. A reward would be waiting for her once she returned to her chambers—a puppy his guard had collected during their siege. A Xoloitzcuintli. It was a fitting gift for the child. The breed was known to his people as guides of the dead into the afterlife. The puppy was a salve to the wounds he'd left on her spirit. It was a useful tool, ensuring her obedience, which added to his power.

The Toltec watched the girl and her guard until they vanished from sight. Once he was certain they were far enough that he could not be heard, he strode across the room to a large turquoise curtain, which took up an entire wall. He fished around the edges, found the cord, and drew them back, revealing an obsidian mirror. Unlike a normal mirror, it showed no reflection. Framed in tezontle rock, the carvings in it showed hummingbirds, much like the ones he saw in his dream. They were flying into the sun, their feathers untouched by the sun's fire. The Toltec ran his fingers across the scene, marveling at its simpleness. The mirror was one of four he'd acquired through spies and delivered by runners. They varied in size. He also procured a small collection of tomes, all detailing various magics. Magics he would study until he found a spell of transference. Soon. Soon, he would attain his destiny.

Flexing his shoulders, he moved closer to the mirror. Peering into its murky depths, he said, "Eye of the thirteen heavens, grant me a vision of what is to come." The surface rippled. Soft clicks echoed through the barren chamber as it built the image in response to the Toltec's question. A glistening black relief appeared of the Toltec on the summit of the Sun Pyramid, with a blood-red sun shining behind his head like a crown. The mirror's magic was lifelike as bits of color manifested. Blazing orange symbols along his arms and bare chest burned bright in the rising smoke. He rubbed the sleeves of his robe, reveling in the texture of the carefully crafted marks of the stolen spell.

"You possess the white hummingbird. The power of the sun is yours," the mirror said as the image faded. "Take care and heed the words of Huitzilopochtli, or the conqueror will become the servant."

The Toltec frowned. The mirror's message was confusing. It had changed the moment the girl entered the capital. He looked over his shoulder toward the path the girl had taken. Anger rose as he thought of the power the girl possessed. She was an orphan and a female. Females were not meant for such an honor.

He held out his hands. His palms tingled. A priest like himself understood the ways of Huitzilopochtli, his will. He understood the people, knew what they wanted and what they needed. He glanced up at the high window. Deep red, purple, and yellow light filtered through the clouds. The silver men would help him succeed. To ensure his success, he housed the silver men's king in his secret chamber. At the right time, they would rise. The rest of the visitors would arrive on the day of transference. Until then, he would faithfully attend to his priestly duties.

# TWO

*T*he guards shoved Cuicatl into her room and the flap snapped back into place, offering her a semblance of privacy. She didn't know much about the capital except what her uncles Chicahua, Atlocoya, Ilhicamina, Cuallea, Ahautzi, Eztli, and Guatemoc told her. All seven of them said the same thing.

*Never let anyone outside of our family see your mark.*

If only she'd listened, she thought, as her thin fingers sank into the folds of her huipil. Her bare feet tapped against the tepid stone floor and soon after, Cuicatl paced. Warning after ignored warning cycled through her mind with every step.

Her rebellion cost her.

Cost them.

If she had not followed her uncles to the market to meet the Toltec's emissaries, her family would still be together. Misery bubbled up, forming a knot in her chest as the image of her uncle Guatemoc's capture resurrected in her mind's eye. Her uncle Guatemoc was the largest, oldest, and kindest of the seven. An ex-warrior, whose body was a mural of scars. His most prominent scar was a crescent gash that stretched from his left shoulder and ended under his rib cage. It was a day he said the honor of war had left him. Not because he had survived, but because, for a moment, he spoke with their god. Once he had healed, he became a runner for the king. Running freed his mind. After a few years of running, he was granted a release from his duties. He then discovered his true love—tending the floating gardens, chinampas. Raising things. Giving life filled him with a deeper purpose.

Her uncle Guatemoc would say, "If it weren't for the chinampas, we would be childless." He would grin big and bright and gesture toward whichever brother was in the room when he recycled his story. "It was if our god placed you in my arms," he would mimic cradling a baby. "A child with the mark of Huitzilopochtli nestled in feathers amid our crop of amaranth! At the dawning of the Tonalpohualli, no less. A Sacred Year, indeed."

For three years, Cuicatl enjoyed a peaceful life with her uncles. Like any parent, her uncles had rules. All of them depended upon her staying hidden.

"Little bird," her uncle Guatemoc would say before pressing his finger to her birthmark. "When others see this, they will either worship you or hurt you." His eyes would water before he planted a kiss on her forehead. He worried over her like a father. Now he was gone. Her heart stuttered in her grief.

Her carelessness delivered her to the Toltec.

A guard outside her room coughed, startling her into motion. She scurried across the room and settled into the corner next to her sleeping pad. A pile of clothes littered the floor. She sat huddled next to the pile with her back toward the door, extending her legs slightly before she released her bounty. A piece of obsidian fell from the folds of her dress. It was one of the many mirrors the Toltec kept with him. The small ones he carried in a pouch around the capital. In the few days she'd been in captivity, the Toltec kept her close, always covering her from head to toe in a shroud. He offered up explanations for her presence, using the mantle of ritual. His response always appeased the curious. They walked away, leaving him to do what he did. Evil. She'd seen him slip away a few times, always under the cover of shadow, where he talked to it.

She stared at it. It didn't look like much. Her hands flexed along the tezontle frame, and she took a deep breath before she touched it.

Trembling fingers connected with the mirror's surface. It was smooth. It felt normal, so why did the Toltec inquire of it?

Cuicatl ran her fingers along its face. The obsidian was warm. She lay her palm flat against the obsidian surface, instantly snatching it away at a familiar throbbing. Beneath the black surface, something beat like a heart. Everything in her wanted to throw it away and run, but she couldn't.

The Toltec had said, *"They're alive."*

Which of the seven had survived? She stared at the mirror resting against her upper thighs. Could it tell her the fate of her family? Her fingers curled into fists, which she pressed against her pelvis.

Warm breath on her neck startled her. The mirror slipped from her legs, but she managed to catch it before it crashed to the ground.

"Nawal," she hissed under her breath.

A black hairless pup trotted into sight. Its large ears perked up, twisting toward her as if asking her to say his name again. His tail wagged as he leaned his head toward the mirror in her lap and sniffed.

"No Nawal," Cuicatl told her pup. "Please be good."

Nawal yipped, then lay down, resting his head on his forepaws. His tail stilled as he watched her.

She leaned in, narrowing her eyes as she stared at the obsidian mirror. What did the Toltec say when he looked at his reflection?

Cuicatl searched her memory for the right words. There were so many the Toltec forced her to remember. The ones she needed were the ones he used when he thought he was alone.

She tilted her head, hoping the words would find her ears and make themselves known.

"Mirror." His leathery voice would sing the word. Cuicatl did the same. Her voice soft and careful, she said, "Eye into the thirteen heavens, grant me a vision of what is to come."

The Toltec would press his head against the mirror. Cuicatl did the same, surprised at the warmth emanating from it. She did not flinch away from the thumping heartbeat against her forehead, which tingled from the contact.

What could she ask the mirror? She wondered as she dragged her finger along the mirror's frame.

"Eye of the thirteen heavens, are my uncles okay?" Her words poured from her lips. Something wet splashed against her stiff fingers. Cuicatl angled her head, brushing her cheek against the collar of her dress, soaking up the tears gathered there. Now wasn't the time for her to cry. She had to find out what the mirror could do. Maybe it could help her like it helped the Toltec. Maybe if she asked it the right questions, she would find out what happened to her uncles. Her family.

"Please, eye of the thirteen heavens, help me find my family," Cuicatl pleaded.

Nawal whined. He wriggled and stretched toward the obsidian mirror. Nothing happened to it that Cuicatl could see. She adjusted it, propping it so it lay flat on her thighs and the top of it balanced on her knees. She peered into the glossy black surface, hoping it would reveal its secrets, but there was nothing. Why wasn't it working?

Cuicatl was sure she heard a voice answer the Toltec's questions whenever he held it. She tried the words again. "Eye of the thirteen heavens, help me."

Nothing.

She sighed, laying her forehead against the glass. "Help me," she whispered as hope bled from her. No sooner had the words passed her lips, Cuicatl could have sworn she saw a strange silver light. It flared like a star, then vanished.

"Are you there?" Cuicatl whispered, unsure of what she was talking to or if what she saw was real.

A tiny dot of light appeared. It did not fade but grew to the size of a small bead.

Cuicatl's eyes stung as she stared. She was afraid to blink. The light might go away.

Nawal growled.

"Shh," Cuicatl warned. Her hand darted out, wrapping around his muzzle. "Shhh," she urged again. Nawal's ears drooped and the growling ceased. "Please, be good."

She waited a few seconds, needing to be sure that her puppy would not do anything rash. Nawal resumed his resting posture, settling his head on his paws, and watched her.

She returned her attention to the mirror.

"Speak to me," Cuicatl pleaded, tightening her grip on the mirror. "Please, speak to me," she said again. She refused to breathe for fear she might miss the mirror's words.

The little bead of light drew closer. It smoothed out into a disc which grew as large as her face. And like her face, the disc contoured, gaining full lips and finally a pair of eyelids and brows like hers.

Cuicatl did her best to not lose her grip on the mirror as the image settled. The face in it was not her reflection, but something else. It was neither male nor female, but a sexless image bearing the features of her people.

Its eyes were closed, presenting her with smooth silver lids. What frightened Cuicatl was the mystery of what hid beneath them. Her instinct screamed for her to run, but if she ran away, she'd lose her chance at discovering the fate of her family. She inhaled deeply, praying for courage as air filled her lungs, then exhaled.

Soft masculine laughter floated from the mirror, tempting her to drop it.

The mirror opened its eyes, which crinkled at the edges. Brilliant glowing turquoise discs smiled at her.

"Do not be afraid, daughter of the Huitzilopochtli," it said.

Cuicatl stared at the strange face, brows knitted in confusion. There were many rumors about her being the child of a god. She pressed the fingers of her free hand to the mark on her forehead. It was in the shape of a white hummingbird. No one believed it was a birthmark, which it was, until they touched it. The Toltec had heard about it and had his servants wash it. To his displeasure, it didn't wash away no matter how hard they tried. It only made her skin red.

The Toltec did not like her. Her oddness. He treated her hair as if it were a curse. Cuicatl's hair was not the smooth flowing black of her people but a halo of curls the color of sand with a sprinkling of gold mixed in. When she stood in the sun, some said it glowed. But Cuicatl didn't believe it. Hair didn't glow.

"Eye of the thirteen heavens, please help me. My uncles, are they alive?"

The mirror looked sad, choosing to look away from her as it spoke. "They are near, but cannot be with you."

Cuicatl frowned. "You're supposed to help me, like you help the Toltec." She swung her body around, adjusting the mirror as she lay flat on the floor. She propped it against the pile of clothes. "Help me," she said again. "Please."

"Daughter of Huitzilopochtli, do not fret. Things seem hopeless, but not for you. Do as the Toltec says."

Cuicatl pushed up, head tilting in confusion. "But he lies. He made me practice words to tell the people."

The mirror gave her a conciliatory smile. "Obedience serves the purpose of Huitzilopochtli."

"But what he made me practice is wrong." Cuicatl smacked her lips. The prophecy she was to recite to the people didn't taste right. The words were flat. Bitter.

"Huitzilopochtli's will cannot be swayed. Let the Toltec speak through you on the day of the New Fire Ceremony."

Cuicatl wanted to shake the mirror. What kind of spirit or creature would have her lie before their god? The face offered her a wane smile before it faded, leaving her to stare at nothing. She curled her arms around her face and sighed. Something wet and warm slid across her arm. Nawal. She grinned, and he licked her heartily. It was his way of cheering her up. It wasn't long before she giggled, though nothing about her situation was good. She sat up, gathering Nawal in her lap, and hugged him. There had to be a way for her to escape. She lay her chin on Nawal's head, and his big ears framed her face.

Cuicatl adjusted her grip on Nawal and scooted over to her sleeping pad. What could she do? It was up to her to find what remained of her family. There had to be a way to stall. As she began plotting ways to escape, the air in the room soured. She sniffed Nawal, who smelled like the oils she used to protect his skin. She flexed her nose, searching for the source. Rust and spoiled meat.

The sound of pebbles popping spun her around. The Toltec stood in the open doorway. His robes were covered in blood. At his waist was a familiar satchel, which bounced against his boney hips as he took a few steps into her room.

"See," the Toltec gestured toward the mirror. "I have been chosen by the gods." He paused, gesturing toward her. "It's best for you to do as I say," the Toltec said.

Nawal leapt from her arms. He surged forward, snarling and barking, placing himself between Cuicatl and the Toltec. He growled. His little body trembled in his rage.

Cuicatl scooped him up, clutched him to her chest, and backed into the corner, careful of the mirror. Her legs gave out when her back touched the stone wall. She slid down.

Cuicatl felt his gaze on her scalp. She pulled her knees up and held them tight. She winced at the sting from the unhealed cuts on her wrists. Nawal yipped and squirmed from her grasp. Again, he placed himself between her and the Toltec. Cuicatl's heart pulsed like a hummingbird's wings. It wasn't safe for him to challenge the Toltec.

The Toltec moved closer, bringing with him the scent of blood and spoiled meat. His steps were thick and scratchy as he crossed the stone floor. His feet were bare. Blood splatter decorated his face, stained his teeth, and painted his hands.

"It's time for your offering," he said.

Cuicatl pushed herself deeper into her corner, wishing she could pass through the wall to a safer place.

Nawal backed away from the Toltec as well, his rump pressed against her shins as his barking became rabid.

The Toltec stopped just beyond the reach of Nawal's teeth. He crouched, pausing to remove a clay bowl from his pouch. He placed it on the floor, then laid his arms across his knees. His hands hung limp over them. His stench slithered into her corner. Darkness strengthened it, burning her eyes.

"The world starts anew," the Toltec said as he nudged the clay bowl on the floor. "Your offering is pivotal to the New Fire Ceremony." He slid it toward her. "I am now Quetzalcoatl Toltec Tlamacazqui." The Toltec removed a piece of cloth and wrapped it around the blade, then set it on the floor.

"Girl, as you have seen for yourself, I am the voice between our people and the gods." He gestured toward the abandoned mirror. "I only carry out the will of the divine." He chuckled, waving his hands limply at the interior. He gentled his voice, softened his face, and was careful not to smile. "Your offering," he gestured toward the bowl, then at the stained medicinal leaves used as bandages. "Your offering will ensure years of blessings for the people." He paused; his gaze touched the twine composing the necklace from her family, then darted back to her bandaged wrists.

"Hurry child," the Toltec gestured impatiently toward the bowl. "There is much I must attend to before the ceremony." Something flashed across his face. He raised a brow before pinning his attention to Nawal, who let out a low growl.

"Consider your offering payment for allowing you to keep that animal." The Toltec backed away from her.

Cuicatl wrapped an arm around Nawal, using the other hand to clutch her charm—an amber stone with a hummingbird framed by the sun etched in it. Her uncle Guatemoc had carved it for her. Would he take that next?

A guard pulled back the flap to her chamber, interrupting the Toltec's rage. He entered the chamber and bowed his head before he spoke.

"Forgive me, Quetzalcoatl Toltec Tlamacazqui. The priests of Tezcatlipoca have requested your assistance," the guard said.

The Toltec's jaw tightened. Cuicatl could hear his teeth grind as he did a slow pivot to address the guard. "Send a runner with my answer."

The guard waved someone over. A large figure came up behind the guard but did not enter the chamber. There was something familiar about him. He had a crescent scar across his chest. Whoever the runner was, he was tall. So tall that she could only see his chest. His head and shoulders were hidden from her. She wished she could see his face.

"Tell the Toltec Tezcatlipoca that I am honored to join them in preparation for the New Fire Ceremony. After the fasting is done and our fires light Tenochtitlán, I will sit with them and celebrate."

The runner bowed his head, pivoted, and dashed off.

"If that is all," the Toltec said.

The guard cleared his throat, bowed, and released the door flap. Now that there were no more distractions, Cuicatl had to give the Toltec what he wanted, or he would hurt Nawal.

Cuicatl pressed her cheek against Nawal's ear. "Please be good," she whispered and set him down. She crawled forward, stopping before the bowl, and extended the arm with the bandages.

"Good," he said as he took her outstretched arm. The Toltec unwound the leaves, exposing her tender wound to the air. It stung, but the pinch of the blade parting her skin hurt worse. Warm blood flowed. He angled her wrist over the bowl, pulling her arm lower to ensure not a drop missed its mark.

She winced, biting her lip to keep herself from crying out when he twisted her wrist. Her eyes were locked tight against the Toltec bleeding her.

Cuicatl didn't miss his amused laughter. He enjoyed hurting her.

"This is not so bad, child," he said as his grip on her wrist eased. "One more offering," he leaned in and whispered. She flinched away.

He laughed again as he began wiping her cut, then he applied a salve. It stung briefly, but the pain eased.

Cuicatl scurried away from the Toltec as soon as he let go of her. She sat in the corner and watched as he meticulously wiped the blade before wrapping it. He returned it to the pouch, then took up the bowl, his eyes triumphant as he placed it against his lips, turned it up and drank her blood. She shivered as his throat worked when he swallowed. Strange orange light welled up in the marks along his arms.

The Toltec wore his long-sleeved robes, careful to keep his skin covered. He thought no one could see the strange writing, but Cuicatl could. The light shimmering beneath his dark black robes were meant to conceal the marks, but her eyes saw it all. The carvings in the walls, the shelves, and even on the stands that held his ceremonial head-dress. All of them carried an odd smell, too. It wasn't bad, but she sensed it was not a good smell.

The Toltec finished licking the bowl clean and returned it to the pouch. Now that he had gotten what he wanted, he left her without a word as soon as the bowl joined the blade. His dismissal of her was worrisome. Deep inside, part of her knew that once her usefulness ended, any hope of saving what remained of her family was lost.

Misery lay her down, curling her into a ball, and she wept. All she had were the words of a mirror and the promise of a man who had taken nearly everything from her. Nawal came to her and placed his head on her hip. Both the girl and the dog drifted into a deep slumber.

Not long after Cuicatl and Nawal drifted off, a rapid beating of wings joined their soft snores. A glimmer of hummingbirds, five in total, flitted through the high window. They circled each other in a playful dance as they descended. Their dancing ceased as they drifted near the sleeping child. Each bird was unique in its coloring. One purple, another a beautiful blend of green, and another was a delicate shade of pink. The fourth hummingbird was yellow and the fifth was a deep purplish-blue. It landed on the back of Cuicatl's hand. The pink, purple and yellow hummingbirds perched on her head, and the green bird settled next to the girl and the dog. It hopped in a circle until it faced the child. Its little head tilted and turned, examining Cuicatl before it hopped closer. It stopped a few inches shy of making contact. Its wings fluttered. But it did not take flight. Instead, a soft green light surrounded its body, and like a flower, it bloomed. Its incandescent form expanded, stretching until it no longer resembled the tiny bird, and when the light died, a translucent green man sat beside her. He extended a hand, pausing as his fingers brushed against her hair, and shook his head. He could not comfort her. He promised Huitzilopochtli that he would keep his identity a secret until it was time. The remaining four hummingbirds took flight, darting toward the green man. They circled the green man's head, flitting around and through his essence, then back to the child.

The green man kissed the tips of his fingers and pressed them against her tear-stained cheek, then pulled them away. "Be strong, little bird," he said. She would need courage for the days ahead. His fingers twitched. He longed to comfort her, to tell her she was safe and that her family was near, but a promise was a promise. "You are not alone," he whispered as he glanced at the other hummingbirds. He placed his hand over the space where a heart should beat. "We are with you," he said. His form was again washed in a brilliant green light, and when it faded, the green hummingbird hovered in its place. It joined the others, flitting around Cuicatl and Nawal one last time before ascending to the window, where they disappeared into the night.

# THREE

*C*uicatl didn't want to like her dress, but the material was as soft as a flower petal. It glistened in the faintest light, and when she raised her arm, long blue-purple feathers filled in what was normally vacant air. She marveled at the peacock feathers woven into the underside of the sleeves. Her arms resembled outstretched wings all the way to the tips of her fingers, which had been painted the same color as the feathers. Cuicatl didn't know how the women who decorated her body from her skin to the ritual garments concocted the colors and designs, but it felt magical. The women painted her skin from head to toe. The paint held the same sheen as a hummingbird's feathers in the sunlight. Cuicatl also wore a crown of sorts. It was a comb adorned with peacock feathers dyed the same color as the feathers sewed into her sleeves. Around her neck, she wore a pure gold choker, shaped like the sun. A gold loop at the back of her dress had rings clipped to it, each with a long peacock feather attached to it. Amber stones ringed the mark on her forehead, held in place by a honied epoxy. To anyone who glimpsed her small body amidst six priests and a cadre of jaguar warriors, it looked as if they were escorting a divine beast, just as the Toltec planned.

If the occasion for her finery was anything other than carrying out a ritual, she would have twirled around with her arms outstretched, imagining herself a hummingbird. She caught a glimpse of the pyramid at the center of Tenochtitlán, and her childish joy fled.

She swallowed as she considered the journey she was about to embark upon. *I am nothing, but tonight I am the voice of Huitzilopochtli for my family.* Pressing her small hands to the center of her chest, Cuicatl bowed her head.

The drums beat, and the priests surrounding her moved forward. Warriors lined their procession as they crossed the causeway into the streets of Tenochtitlán. It was hard for her to keep pace with them. Their legs were much longer than hers. The ornate sandals she was made to wear were horrible for walking. Every stone and pebble caught in them. Each step she took embedded them into the soles of her feet. She dreaded the pyramid and the steep stairs they would ascend. Her soul celebrated the slab of stone that was pushed aside, revealing a path into the pyramid.

Cuicatl had never been inside a ceremonial pyramid before. She gaped at the narrow stone walls that stretched so high they became shadow. A warrior from behind nudged her, none too gently, urging her to keep moving. After several steps inside, Cuicatl could see two chambers to the left and the right of her. She was led into the one to their left. Once across the threshold, it opened into a waiting chamber with a shelf carved from stone. It was a waiting place for sacrifices. Cuicatl could tell from the fruity scent of her uncle's favorite party drink, pulque. It was strong. Many of her people consumed it at family gatherings, but the priests had a special brew they used for sacrifices. Her nose flexed, catching the subtle but sharp bite of freshly picked chiles. Were they going to kill her? she wondered as her gaze settled on a tray of obsidian blades tucked against the wall on a decorative mat.

What caught her eye and stole her breath was the palanquin. She'd only seen one from a distance when their tlatoani passed through their small village. The palanquin had a painted black throne-shaped chair with brilliant blue and purple peacock feathers along the back. They flared like a peacock preening for attention. The seat looked plush, covered in turquois-dyed cloth. Gold fabric hung in strands along the edges where black tassels dangled. Black sashes piled at the center of the cushioned seat. Cuicatl's gaze followed the sashes to their source. Four sashes, two on each side of the throne. They were tethered to a loop in a solid wood frame which secured the chair. At the bottom of the throne were six large rings, three on each side, which held a large black pole in place. The impatient warrior behind Cuicatl snatched her up and carried her to it. He placed her in the seat and strapped her in. Five warriors joined them, each taking their place alongside her palanquin. They stooped low, took hold of the black poles, and lifted her up as they stood. Her throne jostled briefly as the warriors steadied their grip. Once they secured their hold, her procession continued at a rapid pace up a network of stairs and through a series of passages that Cuicatl was sure no one else knew about. She did her best not to gawk at the paintings and carvings on the walls but failed. They told the story of the priest's work. All of it bloody. All of it at the behest of Huitzilopochtli's blessing.

It didn't take long for her procession to emerge on the pyramid's summit. They passed the king's throne, perched on an elevated plat-form. He liked to watch the sacrifices. A line of warriors stood before the dais used for sacrifices, shielding it from sight. Cuicatl sniffed the air, brows pinched at the absence of blood in the air. Her cadre of warriors pushed forward, hefting the palanquin high for all to see and, as they practiced, Cuicatl raised her arms, feathers unfurled. The light of the moon danced across the stones on her forehead and the people gasped. The warriors before her fell to their knees as her cadre with-drew and set her down. They unstrapped her and the Toltec helped her up. He led her to the steps carved into a short wall. As they ascended them, Cuicatl wondered it if looked like they were floating to the people below. The Toltec squeezed her hand hard, reminding her that she needed to focus. Her promise to him had to be fulfilled. She took her place at his side.

The Toltec stood on the highest step, surveying the crowd. The wall concealing the steps was wide enough for three adults. He took the last step up onto the platform and raised his arms. "The Binding of Years is upon us. We are reborn," the Toltec declared as his arms descended slowly to his sides. "We stand as the first of our god's creations. His chosen people. In the dark, without possessions, naked before the eyes of Huitzilopochtli. We searched." He dropped to his knees, looking earnestly at the sky. The moon was the only light. All the fires throughout Mexica were put out in preparation for the Binding of Years. "Our god, Huitzilopochtli, guided us here with his fire. Led us in battle and gave us countless victories and crowned us with wise kings. Huitzilopochtli has made us a great nation, subservient to none."

The Toltec gestured toward Cuicatl, who stepped forward. As they practiced, she again stretched out her arms, unfurling the winged sleeves, and as the Toltec planned, whispers of supplication were as loud as the roars of charging warriors. It was at that moment the moonlight shifted, setting the well-placed stones in her forehead alight.

The people below, and even the priests sharing the summit with them, lost their voices. Cuicatl took her place in front of the Toltec and prophesied.

"You are the children of the sun," Cuicatl began. She spread her arms out toward the masses below. "Children of the giver of life." She lowered her arms as she raised her head toward the sky. "I have looked upon you. Fed you and have given you kings who have led you to victory." She smiled. It felt genuine as she counted the stars. "Through my priests—" Cuicatl lowered her head regally, waving her feathered arm again at the masses "—you have given me blood to drink." She turned away from the crowd and faced the priests. "I thank you for your devotion," she said before settling her speech on the Toltec.

"You are the most honored among my servants." She said, her stomach churning as the words flowed. "Your voice rings clear and your devotion moves me."

The Toltec bowed in false humility.

"The purity of your purpose pleases me," Cuicatl said as she raised a finger and pointed at the Toltec. "It is my will for you to be the voice of my children." Cuicatl waved her free hand toward the masses below. "I want you to be both priest and king of my people," she declared.

The king rose from his throne and his guard stepped forward, but

Cuicatl motioned for them to stop as she faced the king. "Would you deny me, Huitzilopochtli, my right?"

The king paused and his guards did the same.

"What say you?" The Toltec added, as he rose to stand by Cuicatl's side.

The hum of conversation rose from below as the Toltec moved in front of Cuicatl before the king and his guards and dared them to speak with a look.

"I am the god's chosen," he said as he sauntered around the crest of the summit. The people fell silent as he raised his arms, shaking them toward the heavens. "As the god's offspring declares, I will lead us into the new age." He grinned his ugly grin as he said, "As a sign of Huitzilopochtli's desire—" the Toltec faced Cuicatl."—I am gifted with his divine power." He declared and gave Cuicatl her cue to bow.

She attempted to obey, but her knees refused to bend. Instead of fear and compliance, her teeth gritted and her eyes hardened. She laughed, warmth spread within her chest, as if it were a stock of wood and straw and Huitzilopochtli's words were the fire. Her mouth opened, and the words rolled off her tongue. As she looked across the summit at the priests, dipping to the hidden masses below, and ending with the shocked eyes of the Toltec, Cuicatl spoke.

"Do you believe I would bow to you?" The timbre of Cuicatl's voice deepened, taking on a divine echo as she measured the Toltec with a glance. Her lip curled in distaste as Huitzilopochtli's laughter rumbled in her chest, setting the world beneath her sandaled feet to tremble. "As you make your plans with demons, I, Huitzilopochtli, will let them have you." The last word burned the tip of her tongue. "I will strip my presence from among you." Cuicatl sniffed, squaring her shoulders before spitting at the Toltec. It sizzled inches from the Toltec's bare feet. Her eyes burned amber like her curly crown. The peacock feathers in her crown sparkled like jewels.

"You are not worthy," she said to the Toltec, then looked upon the people. "I am war! I am creation! I am not clay for your hands to mold. In blood, I have made this nation. Through blood, this nation will fall. Your final days will reflect what you have become: arrogant, self-serving, and sick."

Cuicatl stomped her left foot, and the ground from Templo Mayor to the Pyramid of the Sun to the outermost territory shook, and every fire lit. Starting with the great flame that burned on the summit, it spread to the small torches throughout the pyramid and those held below.

"So begins the new age." Cuicatl collapsed, landing on her knees as the light of the Huitzilopochtli left her. Wails, screams and curses rose like ashes into the night. Cuicatl heard none of it as she fell onto all fours. She wanted nothing more than to curl into a ball and slumber, but the Toltec would have none of it.

He shouted from the summit into the sky, fist raised.

"It is as you say, Huitzilopochtli. The age of the people starts now." The Toltec grabbed Cuicatl by the wrist and dragged her to her feet. "Today, I will become the light of Tenochtitlán!" He thrust Cuicatl's hand up with his own. "Your power is my power," he chanted, his tone fractured, creating a multi-tonal echo. The cries from below ceased as he tore his robes away with his free hand, revealing the jagged markings carved into his flesh. They glowed orange like fire.

"Today, I will lead my people into the new age," the Toltec declared.

A quick flick of his wrist and his guards surged forward, executing the king and his guard. They were quick and efficient murderers, liberating the hearts from the newly dead and depositing them at the Toltec's feet. Once the last heart was added to the pile, the Toltec began casting the spell of transference.

The people gasped in unison as the script on the Toltec's body blazed. Starbursts winked, and Cuicatl's body shook violently before it rose. The Toltec's voice rose. Cuicatl's power burst forth in the shape of a spindle of lightning as bright as the noon sun. It coiled around her, climbing slowly toward the Toltec's open palm. The trembling in her limbs intensified as a marriage of sunlight and red flame wrapped around them.

Silence consumed the night as all watched the priest siphon the power of a god.

The Toltec's words gained a steady cadence as what remained of

Cuicatl's power trickled into him. His triumphant smile was as radiant as the light encasing them.

"I am the god of Tenochtitlán," he declared while watching Cuicatl's wide eyes grow slack. He laughed, pleased that his vision had become manifest. His smile waned as Cuicatl's dark brown eyes regained their amber hue.

A predator grinned up at him and Cuicatl's next words stopped his heart.

"Did you think you could outsmart a god?" She said as her power bared its teeth, sinking into his soul. A sliver of lightning pierced the sky, cutting through his body. It was the Toltec's turn to fall. Cuicatl's grip tightened around his wrist and the draw of power intensified. Both their bodies spun in a slow circle as they descended back onto the ritual summit. She stood surrounded by a brilliant light.

The child began reciting the Toltec's stolen spell in reverse, each word perfect. His heart pulsed then stuttered as the power he'd stolen slipped away. Smoke clouded his vision as pain swallowed him whole. He could smell himself burning. Through seams of clarity, he caught sight of the world below. The people. His people were disbanding, running from the horror above.

Grasping the strength that remained, he summoned his guards, who were frozen in terror. His call shook them from their stupor. Instantly, they moved to immobilize the girl. Before a hand could touch her, a ring of fire blazed around the pair, and soon after, the first of the Toltec's guard lost his head.

A battle cry pierced the confused cries as a man, donning the garb of a jaguar warrior, emerged from a chamber to the right of the ritual summit. Nawal, who was no longer a pup but a god's beast, followed him. Nawal was the night in motion, his skin gleamed like starlight where the light touched. Smoke billowed from his open snout as he snarled at the Toltec's guard. He tore into the guards closest to him, pulling their souls from their bodies. Translucent figures littered the summit as Nawal continued his attack. A glimmer of hummingbirds burst from a chamber to the left of the ritual summit. Their little bodies encased in molten light stretched. They grew as the birds arced high above the platform, and upon descent, the light burned away.

Five spectral forms stood dressed in their battle clothes. What remained of the Toltec's guards turned tail and ran. Their terror seemed to incite the five specters, who charged after them.

Cuicatl's grip on the Toltec slipped after the five spectral forms landed. Five colorful starbursts flared, and when they faded, her uncles Atlocoya, Ilhicamina, Cuallea, Ahautzi, and Eztli stood in their war clothes. They were back! In her excitement, Cuicatl let go of the Toltec and began walking toward them. Her gaze darting off in search of her uncle, Chicahua. He had to be nearby. Inside, her chest was warm, and her every step felt as if she were walking on clouds. Her uncles were back! At least most of them. She grinned. Each step became more buoyant as she skipped. A searing pain sliced through the flesh above her right ankle, jolting her to a stop. She fell forward, her knees slamming into the stone. Looking down the length of her body, she screamed again at the thing clinging to her leg.

The Toltec, with his rows of odd teeth and blazing skin, grimaced at her as he sank skeletal fingers deeper into her leg. A grotesque clicking and grunting accompanied his awkward crawl as he attempted to pull her to him. Her ears rung as she recognized the clicks and grunts. They were words. He was reciting the spell.

Nawal howled. He was on the summit, but out of Cuicatl's range of sight. She could feel him as he raced toward her.

What remained of the Toltec's eye gleamed with triumph. The warm floating feeling in Cuicatl's chest morphed into molten fury. How dare he celebrate her pain. Heat radiated like a tiny yellow sun before her eyes, then launched down her body. The little ball thinned and stretched until the end of it formed fingers, taking hold of the Toltec's hand and squeezing. Cuicatl's rage made her numb to the Toltec's stabbing digits. He would pay for what he did to her uncles, to her.

Both the priest and the demigoddess glared at each other as they casted their magic. Cuicatl's fire bit and scratched at the Toltec, loosening his grip on her. She could feel his life force ebb from his body. Flashing her teeth at him, she called to her fire.

"Eat," she commanded her fire, and like an obedient pet, it devoured all of him except his heart.

Nawal skidded to a stop in the pile of ashes that was the Toltec. Swirling ash glittered with bits of blue light. Once they settled, the Toltec's spirit sat in its place. It took a little time for him to understand that he was dead. When he did, he looked up at the rising sun and shrieked. Nawal sat patiently behind him, ears twitching, but Cuicatl couldn't hear a thing.

Something heavy settled on her shoulders and slipped into her skin. The discomfort of her injuries drained from her body, becoming both light and heavy. Her insides again radiated warm and floating heat as she rose to her feet. She limped toward the Toltec's spirit, each step becoming surer. By the time she stood before him, her limp was gone, and when she looked down at him, the Toltec looked upon her with terror-filled eyes.

"Blood is blood," Cuicatl said, her throat scratched at the depths of the voice rolling from her. Huitzilopochtli gave a derisive chuckle at the fallen priest. He reigned in his anger because he did not want to hurt Cuicatl. Huitzilopochtli used her hand to beat against her chest. "Her family is my family," Huitzilopochtli said. "What is mine will not come to ruin."

Cuicatl crouched, feeling the weight of Huitzilopochtli's essence unfurl throughout her body. She studied the Toltec's withered spirit, lip curling at the flicker of rebellion in his gaze. "You wanted a place of glory in the thirteen heavens." Cuicatl grunted. "Enjoy the deepest part of Mictlan," she said.

Nawal grabbed the Toltec's spirit and began descending the pyramid. The darkness below thickened. Wisps of pale gray smoke seeped through a crack forming at its center. Jagged black rock formed the edges as the darkness opened wide like a mouth. Nawal kept going, gaining speed as he neared the abyss. The Toltec's spirit flailed as they descended. Nawal stopped before he reached the mouth of the gaping hole and released the Toltec. His spirit sailed up, arching above the chasm, before plunging into the darkness. Before he slipped from their sight, he locked eyes with Cuicatl.

"I am with you always," the Toltec said, his voice barely a whisper in Cuicatl's ears. The skin above her ankle throbbed in tune with the words. Her five uncles surrounded her, catching her as

Huitzilopochtli left her body. Fresh agony possessed her, making her knees buckle and fail. Gently, her uncles set her down. Huitzilopochtli stepped into her line of sight, kneeling. His bronze skin smoldered as eyes like stars studied her. Cuicatl's gaze traveled along his muscled arms which, like her ruined dress, had feathers along the underside of his arm. Unlike her dress, Huitzilopochtli's feathers were real. His battle armor was gold and glimmered in his perpetual light. Long flowing hair, the color of perfect night, flowed across his shoulders. Huitzilopochtli reached out and touched her face.

"I am sorry for your suffering, my precious one," he said, his voice was like soft thunder. A sad smile dimmed his light. "My blood makes you a treasure for wicked men." He sighed, looking away from her. Cuicatl followed his gaze, a small smile forming as the true beauty of Tenochtitlán expanded under the rising sun.

"My time among men is done."

Cuicatl gasped and reached for him, but he stepped back before she could touch him.

"You are my new fire," he said. "My Alba."

"That's not my name," Cuicatl frowned. She didn't hate the name. It felt more like new clothes. Stiff with little room for movement. "Alba," she whispered, testing it. It sounded nice. Easy on the tongue.

"You are what remains of me," Huitzilopochtli said as he got to his feet. He thrust a fist up toward the sky. A disc of light framed his fist. Tendrils of golden light rippled across his knuckles. "You are my daughter. My Alba."

Cuicatl's lips twisted then parted to protest, but Huitzilopochtli shook his head sharply. "Alba is the only name you will remember." Huitzilopochtli touched his index finger to her birthmark. His touch muddled her thoughts and twisted her insides. She swayed on her feet, but her uncle Guatemoc steadied her.

"A new war rises, and you will be my *macuahuitl*. I send you beyond this time to a new one," Huitzilopochtli said solemnly and opened his fist. A tiny pearl of obsidian formed in his palm. It swelled to the size of a shield and Huitzilopochtli took a knee, holding it forward. The five spectral forms of her uncles flashed, and in their place were the hummingbirds she remembered. They zipped around in front of her, hovering just beyond her grasping fingers. "I'm sending you to a safe place," Huitzilopochtli said, as a familiar face formed in the obsidian mirror. "There will be a guardian, a sorceress of light. She will come for you."

The obsidian mirror grew until it was taller than her uncle Guatemoc.

"How will I know her?" Alba asked.

"Her skin will be the color of stars and her hair will match. You are of my blood, so her magic will be known to you and your magic to her."

"But …" Alba began, but Huitzilopochtli banged the base of the mirror on the stone.

"She will speak to you in our tongue and will teach you hers."

Alba's mouth watered at the questions building inside, but her father growled.

"Do not worry, daughter of Huitzilopochtli. As promised, your family will remain with you for what remains of your journey," the mirror said as her uncle Guatemoc swung her up into his arms. The face of the mirror split. Its pieces fell away. Darkness folded, forming a long spiraling tunnel. The only light Alba could see flowed in from the torches and the moon.

"Be quick," the mirror implored.

Nawal barked. Alba casted a sideways glance at him, her eyes widening as his form became a blob of slick black mud. It quivered and stretched into the shape of a man. When all the quaking finished a familiar form stood beside her. Her uncle Chicahua. He took up her limp hand, gently squeezing it as a humble grin formed.

"I am sorry, little bird," he dipped his head in an apologetic bow. "This is the only way I can remain with you," Chicahua said.

Five colorful hummingbirds hovered around them.

Her uncle swallowed as he looked ahead, squaring his shoulders, and said, "We must become divine to remain with the divine." Chicahua gestured toward the hummingbirds then ran his fingers along Alba's divine mark. "You are both our goddess and our little bird," he said wistfully as his gaze drifted toward the swirling darkness. Light flared under its skin, like lightning threading clouds during a storm.

"It's time," Guatemoc said as he joined them.

Chicahua adjusted his grip on Alba and entered the mirror. His brothers followed.

Obsidian shards boomed as they clicked back in place, sealing them all in. Tiny particles of silver light shimmered around them. When they moved, it felt like they were walking through a cloud filled with crackling lightning. Her skin prickled. Sharp smells made her nose run, and the air stung her eyes.

As they traveled, the sounds outside shifted. Her native tongue faded, replaced by a blend of unfamiliar languages echoing off the walls. Strange noises surrounded them—trumpets, lightning, crashes, explosions—all jostling and rattling her senses.

The strangeness of it all pushed along her temples. As the pressure built, her forehead tingled in the spot Huitzilopochtli touched. The sensation sharpened, spreading around her cranium where it settled in to gnaw at the bone. Her thoughts splintered as the gnawing intensified. She hurt. All of her. From her head, skin, muscles, and bones. How much farther did they have to go until they reached the place her father prepared for her?

Her vision shrank and grew as the amalgamation of pulsing colors dulled. The noises fell away as Alba tumbled into oblivion.

# FOUR

*C*urrent Year
      *Covenant, Illinois*
  *In the alley behind La Comunidad de Corazón*

ALBA KNEW WHAT DEATH SMELLED LIKE, BUT THE PUTRID STENCH pouring into her nostrils was worse. She opened her eyes, which instantly watered. She heaved, coughed, and struggled to breathe. The pounding in her skull added to her agony. Every part of her body felt weighted down with rocks. She groaned, grateful when the coughing had ebbed. It was time for her to get up.

Her fingers twitched. After a few seconds, she flexed her left hand and did the same with the other. She prayed for the strength to sit upright. After a few tries, she rolled onto all fours and vomited. After vomiting, she looked for something solid to lean on. There was a wall behind her. She would use it as an anchor to help the wooziness pass. Closing her eyes seemed to calm the nausea. Using her hands, she felt her way over to the wall then collapsed.

*What was this place?*

It spun in a kaleidoscope of unfamiliar colors. No. It wasn't the world but her head. She clenched her eyes tight, carefully inhaling the air.

*Sorceress of light.*

*Guardian.*

The words pushed to the surface of her mind and hovered like butterflies, refusing to be captured. What did they mean?

*Sorceress of light.*

*Guardian.*

She breathed through her teeth as she grasped for their meaning. Her head ached as she tried to remember why the words seemed so important. Beyond her discomfort, Alba couldn't recall anything but her name.

A rhythmic clank of metal against stone mimicked her heartbeat as she pulled her knees up and rested her forehead against them. Alba's head continued to throb as she paced her breathing. Opening her mouth, she inhaled, ignoring the taste of the air. Her shoulder brushed against a stone slab. Tilting her head slightly, she looked at it. A dark gray stone. She touched it. It was warm, smooth, and not stone. She sniffed, her nose wrinkling.

*What was this odious thing?* She wondered as she carefully scooted away from it.

She counted to seven and began a painful rise. Her discomfort ebbed as she took in her surroundings. It was dark, but the stars were impossibly close to the huts surrounding her. The huts were short and made of vivid white bricks that reminded her of polished bones. Withered balls of white, like dried crumpled leaves, were strewn about. Red cylinders with shapes and pictures rocked under the slightest brush of air. There were clear rocks mixed among the cylinders. Some were jagged while others were flat gleamed under the low hanging stars. The sight was both beautiful and frightening.

*Where was she?*

She scanned the horizon, her brows knitted in wonder at the tall, slender, silver trees that seemed to hold the stars above the vivid white huts. The trees had no leaves, only vines that stretched across the area where she stood. The vines were taut and buzzed like honeybees. Was this the land of floating mountains? Would the colorful beasts with spindly legs and round barrel bodies wander by? Did their feet truly create thunder when they moved? Part of her hoped to see them up close.

Alba moved into the alley. Her limbs trembled with each step. Where should she go? She looked around as she cautiously added distance between herself and the metal structure. There were chambers concealed behind hard flaps on either side of her, all bearing pictures she'd never seen before. Her brows pulled into a V as she struggled to translate the meaning of the pictures. She knew how to read. Her uncles shared that knowledge with her.

What did the pictures mean?

Were they a warning?

An invitation?

Alba's legs carried her to the chamber closest to her. She reached for the flap, wondering if she could push it aside. Before she could touch it, a shrill trilling yanked a scream from her. She retreated, running back toward the odious gray structure. A loud click echoed down the alley's throat, halting her flight. She paused, looking over her shoulder toward the source.

A woman with skin the color of stars stepped from behind one of the rigid flaps. A gust of wind, crisp and strong, flowed through the alley, tossing the woman's luminate-white hair. Alba froze, unsure if the woman was an illusion or if she was real, when the scent of fresh jasmine bloomed.

The woman smiled, took a knee, and stretched out a hand, palm up toward her, and said, "Welcome, daughter of Huitzilopochtli. I have been waiting for you."

Alba wrapped her arms around herself, flexing her toes, but she did not move toward the woman.

"You are the New Fire Huitzilopochtli spoke of." Her words were like music, drawing Alba to her. She stopped just shy of her reach. A soft humming sounded above her head. She looked up to see five colorful hummingbirds darting around just shy of the light. Shimmering feathers gave her confidence, and she took hold of the woman's hand.

"I am Bridgette," the woman said, her cool hands encasing Alba's. Warmth flowed from her hand through her body, pushing away the aches and pains, before it settled in her mind. A soft buzzing rang in her ears. It didn't hurt, but like everything so far, it was strange. The woman was speaking, but it sounded garbled, like she was underwater.

"Daughter of Huitzilopochtli, may I ask your name?"

Alba blinked, unsure of the answer as she stared into Bridgette's silver eyes.

Alba opened her mouth to answer when a second woman burst from a chamber behind Bridgette. The woman was tall, with skin darker than Alba's. Her hair hung in long ropes of black and grey and her clothes were an interesting shade of blue.

The tall woman gasped. Her brows arched over wide eyes the same hue as red clay.

Alba looked down at herself. She looked like a broken bird. Raising her arms, scorched feathers jutted from the underside of her sleeves. Some feathers bent in odd angles. The dress she wore was tattered along the hem. A strange shimmering mark caught Alba's eye. She lifted the hem of her dress and angled her leg so she could get a better look at it.

A narrow black ring coiled around her ankle. Above it, were four small orange circles that reminded her of waning embers. Though tempted to explore the peculiar mark, the sound of a woman's shocked gasp reminded her she was not alone.

"Oh my," Bridgette whispered. Her grip on Alba's hand tightened as she caught sight of the mark before their gazes collided.

"I will do what I can to help you," Bridgette said. Her grip gentled. "But first, I need a name?"

"Alba," she said. The name settled comfortably in her mind. "Alba Huitzilin."

Alba watched as Bridgette looked over her shoulder at the other woman. They spoke in their strange tongue. The other woman left them. Retreating into the chamber behind them.

"Come with me, Alba," Bridgette said as she rose and gathered Alba beside her. "My friend Sister Mary Elizabeth will set up a room for you." She waved her hand at the shapes in brilliant colors along the top of the door. "Here at La Comunidad de Corazón, you are safe," she said and gave Alba's shoulders a reassuring squeeze. Bridgette's magic curled in spindles of shimmering light. "I will protect you, always."

Alba let herself be led into La Comunidad de Corazón.

# ABOUT THE AUTHOR

Meet F. M. Lacey, the caffeinated wordsmith! This coffee aficionado brews fiction with a dash of caffeine, crafting dark urban, dystopian, and speculative tales filled with diverse characters. When not conjuring literary magic, she's busy curating coffee memes, indulging in horror movies, anime, and reading. Spot her at comic cons and nerdy gatherings, bonding with fellow enthusiasts. Originally from Homestead, Florida, she now calls Chicago, Illinois home, where she's tirelessly crafting her next masterpiece. Connect with this imaginative author and dive into her captivating worlds!

Link to series: Biggs & Myer Briefs

KRYSTINA COLES

To preserve her family's rule, a young witch and heir of a noble house enters into an engagement with a charismatic lord burdened with a curse.

Based on the *Bluebeard* fairytale by Charles Perrault. A short story in the *Moonshadow* series.

# ONE

My mother's ladies came in footfalls and whispers—porcelain plates clattering as they collected what remained of our breakfast: scraps of honey bread smeared with butter, nubs of half-eaten strawberries weeping pools of pink juice, teacups drunk to the dregs. A three-tined fork slipped to the floor with a pathetic *clang*.

And I startled, blinking. I'd forgotten myself somewhere between the trails of soft sunlight on the tiles.

The offending girl scrabbled to her knees to retrieve it, widening her eyes when her gaze stumbled into mine. "Forgive me, mi—"

"That's enough, Welyn." A stern voice cut her short.

She pushed to her feet, offered a pitiful dip of a curtsy, and hurried out of the room. And I continued studying the mosaic of light on the floor.

Reality was harsher in the sun.

I wasn't at Renasmere Academy with the other young witches of the winter and water. But neither were the friends I'd made there. Nycta had returned to her home in Tyafae and had scarcely written since. And sweet-natured Cyrie was dead.

"You understand what this means?" My mother's hand touched the curve of my cheek as she continued her lecture, a lithe coil of indigo scales shimmering around her wrist. The little snake lifted its head from inside the silver-embroidered cuff of her sleeve, flicked its tongue to taste the air thick with the perfume of salt and smoke, and retreated to the darkness of her clothes again.

Tamsyn, my mother's familiar. Golden-eyed and venom-tongued, she was as old as the city of Rynmoor itself, passed down through generations of the poisoner women of the formidable House of Torrowin. She'd served my mother well—cut down her enemies in a spectacle of strangled screams and foaming blood. No one ever made the mistake of calling Paia Torrowin subtle.

My mother knelt to stare into my downturned eyes and spoke once more.

"If they can get to you in a school, they can get to you anywhere." She straightened her back and turned to pace the length of the room, the hem of her cobalt dress fluttering behind her like a cloak. And she almost glittered when the thousands of silver moons stitched into the fabric caught the noonday light.

There was never a moment she didn't look beautiful. She bore the traits of the Muyn coven well: hair as dark as ink, framing her narrow chin and tumbling in loose waves past her waist; skin so fair, one could nearly glimpse the indigo of the veins underneath; her lines of her face sharpening into a warrior's nose. She complimented it all in the manner she dressed—in rich browns and gemstone blues fit for a queen.

I wondered what it was like—being so lovely and so feared all at once.

"The headmistress assured me that Renasmere would be the exception." She sighed and picked at the poison-pale blotches in her leather apron as she went on. "And now they have a dead girl on their hands."

My gaze shifted to the window, down to the scarlet bursts of sun-drenched poppies in the garden and the bees that doted over them, and I snatched my quivering lip between my teeth before whispering, "She was my friend."

"She was your shield." My mother looked up sharply, raising her voice as if her words were the only truth worth speaking, and let her hands fall to her sides. "And while—yes—unfortunate, she served her purpose well."

I wrenched my stare from the flowers to look at her, the edges of my vision blurring with tears.

She faltered, collected herself with a long-drawn breath, and softened her tone to a murmur. "We can't risk losing you, Norrie. The people out there—" she glanced over her shoulder, through the glass doors of the balcony and the sun-speckled canals beyond it "—those same families that helped our ancestors build Rynmoor all those years ago, we mean *nothing* to them now." There was a break in her voice. "Not without a Legacy to back our claim to power. And they'll tear this House down on our heads and build another with our bones if we're not careful."

My mouth ran dry.

I could never stomach the talk of Houses and their politics.

I'd heard the story often—how their founders had begun as exiles, wanderers of the eastern wilds. Centuries ago, they'd become the first of the witches. Unpracticed and unrestrained, bringing floods and fires and storms before they'd learned to control their gifts. But the eight kingdoms of the west had no tolerance for the danger of their newfound magic, called it blasphemy, and cast them out. And so they'd fled into the strange east, raised the Free Cities from the dust and the earth, and set the boundaries of their kings aside. Their children, the first twenty-eight born in the new world, bridged both kingdoms and magics. And from them, the Houses came to be. Generations thereafter would inherit their Legacy, a most peculiar gift, the mark of a true heir of those twenty-eight. The House of Notus, the House of Metal and Ice, inflicted their will upon the stars. The House of Thryss, of Wood and the Arcane, the bending of reality itself. But the House of Torrowin, the House of Water and Earth, inherited nothing.

And others had taken notice.

"I understand." I bowed my head, swallowing the ache in my throat. "I suppose...you'll want me to finish school here, then?" Tutors already frequented our gates. They'd come with the doctors seven years prior, stayed long after the physicians' work was done. In the long months after the bombing, my mother kept me from my brother's door. Drew me away with tea parties in the garden, playdates with friends she'd chosen for me. But his teachers were like moths, flittering back and forth from his room in their silver robes, arms heavy with all manner of books and papers, pamphlets and pens. I'd find them lingering in the corners of the house, whispering amongst themselves of the little boy deprived of his leg. Until they saw me, pressed their thin lips into sympathetic smiles, and scattered.

"Well," my mother stifled a noise that almost sounded like a scoff, "you're certainly not going back." She prefaced the rest with a small pause. "But you can't stay."

I sat up in alarm. "You're sending me away?"

"As opposed to what?" She anchored her hands on her hips, her sleeves hanging off her arms like sheets of dark water. "Giving the dissenters another chance at killing you? Or worse, all of us at once? They've already maimed and disfigured your brother."

"Mother." Mysric, who'd been leaning against the dormant fireplace, rubbed his forehead with a sigh and pushed off the mantel, gesturing to his legs. "May I remind you that I'm standing quite ably —and handsomely, I might add—right here?"

She raised her hand to quiet him. "Sit down, darling. You don't have to be brave for us."

He obliged, though a little grudgingly, and massaged his right knee as he sank into one of the twin chaises by the fireplace. The joint buckled on the way down, looking not quite right beneath the woven pant of his navy slacks. And he doubled over to shift it back into place with a bone-chilling *click*.

"I've offered to host the lord of Phaenn at a ball tonight," she said, the words sloughing off her tongue like molasses. "Apparently, he's in search of a wife." She fixed her gaze on me then, and the breath soured in my lungs. "I want that to be you."

She knew full well what that would mean for me. Mysric and I, born minutes apart, had always been told that we would rule together. Me, a Wonder, a wielder of all three magics of our city, and my brother, the brightest scholar I'd ever met. Twin heirs to the seat of Rynmoor. When I was of age and finished with my schooling, I'd take a husband from her choice of respectable men within our coven. But never a lord. Never someone who required, or even wanted, little more than a breeding ground of his wife.

"Mother, y-you can't be serious..." Mysric moved to stand in protest, but his leg, long past its use for the afternoon, wouldn't allow it. And he slumped into the chaise with gritted teeth.

She went on as if he hadn't spoken. "You'll have to charm him first, of course. Girls from the lesser sister cities will be falling at his feet trying to catch his eye. I had a dress delivered to your room this morning. That should be a good start."

"We can't just marry her off to a stranger," my brother pressed further. "What has Father said about this—"

"That's enough from you," Mother turned to snap at him, and he fell silent, the corners of his mouth twisting in a grimace. "You're only here to learn. Do you understand?"

He said nothing else, simply chewed at the dead skin of his lips.

"I sent word to him last night, and we're in agreement." She interlaced her fingers at the sharp taper of her waist. "You'll stay here, Mysric, and continue your instruction as my successor. And Xeanora will secure a strong alliance as the next lady of Phaenn."

Consigned to a life in quiet service, cut at the knees and shackled to a man old enough to be my father.

"I..." My voice began to shake, my hands with it. "I can't."

"Xeanora," Mother said, with an edge of frustration, "the Torrowin claim to Rynmoor has been challenged for the last two hundred years. And that doubt has only grown louder. Mercenaries like the one that killed your friend and much worse will continue to come for us until our position is sure. Until Elynea—wherever she may be—dies, a marriage alliance is our only path forward. If you want this family to survive, I need you to smile and do as you're told. Can you do that?"

I'd believed the rumors they used to tell: that the infant Elynea Torrowin, moon-blessed and first of her House, had been murdered in her crib the night she was born. But I'd seen her—once—when I was little. As a sixteen-year-old specter, a year younger than I was now. Wandering the halls like the ghost of a drowned girl, wet footprints shimmering in the dark. Mother had poisoned her with

Tamsyn's venom, believing her death would rattle her Legacy free and onto our shoulders. But I'd drawn it out of her, saving her life and damning ours, and she'd nearly leveled the house in her escape.

"Yes, Mother." I cast a glance at my brother, but he'd taken up my pastime of staring at the floor, his hands folded in contrition.

"Good. We just need an heir or two." She drew a satisfied breath, unfastened her apron, and draped it over her arm before sweeping out of the room. "Then you and I can poison him when it's over."

# TWO

"*P*resenting Lady Torrowin and her children, Mysric and Xeanora."

I grasped my skirts and the gilded rail, kept my gaze on my heels and the crushed velvet steps. It was a steep descent, a hundred steps at least, from the landing to the ballroom floor.

And every eye was trained on me.

They'd been watching since we'd arrived, whispering their gossip of the Viper of Rynmoor and her brood. They'd say whatever they liked, spin the same stale stories of the happenings behind our doors: how Paia Torrowin had fangs of her own and drank the blood of her servants while they slept, how my brother and I had been born covered in golden scales.

Or the latest: that I'd been the one to murder that poor girl at Renasmere, and that she hadn't been the first.

I excused myself and wandered farther into the room. Mother had chosen the Dome for the occasion: a bubble of wrought iron and frosted glass. Faceted like an expertly cut jewel, its stone floor veined with the clear waters of the River Tel. I crossed one of its many bridges, stared up at the ceiling in wonder.

I'd never seen it like this. Curtains of cream-colored roses draped the walls. Lush and full, filling the room with the sweet, heady perfume of a long-gone spring. Petals peppered the floor and floated in the rivulets, fluttered through the air, and gathered on my shoulders like snow. Blue willows glimmering with lights set every inch of it aglow. Tiered fountains dripped in white wisterias.

A woodland paradise.

I searched the room for a familiar face.

The ladies of the River Court, ambassadors from the other witch cities of the Muyn coven. The thin-nosed Lady Ferafona of Gellion. Young Lady Tenwar of Laethys and her Lord Consort.

I spied a head of platinum blonde hair among the frills and finery. And her dress, like a peacock in a room of bluebirds.

"Nycta?"

The white-haired girl stood at a long table of sweets situated on the outskirts of the ballroom, nursing a piece of fruit glistening in a shell of hard sugar. She'd exchanged her leather gloves for ivory silk. Her academy uniform for a gown as light as breath, in the emerald of the Taenmi witches.

"Nycta?" I repeated.

She looked up, widened her light eyes, and set the confection aside. "Norrie?" Before I could answer, she was in my arms, a constellation of her tears glimmering on my shoulder.

"What are you doing here?" I asked when she let go, my back cool from her touch.

Her gloves did little to disguise it. The chill of Death in her fingers.

"I wanted to see if you were all right." She took a small frosted cake from a glass tower of desserts and handed it to me. "Are you?"

"Lorris and Moranthe Estyr and their daughter, Tannyth."

My skin prickled as I turned.

The Estyr family. They'd come in their mourning clothes, draped in night. Lorris had been more subtle, but Moranthe—she wore a veil that tumbled to the ground and trailed several feet behind her, like a bride at her beloved's grave. Tannyth had dressed in lace, her skirts billowing like clouds of ink in water, the neckline sinking below the hollows of her alabaster collarbones.

The gall alone was enough to make me retch. "Not anymore."

"Gods." Nycta hooked her arm in mine. "They're walking this way."

Lorris had stopped to trade pleasantries with a few lords and their families, some in olive and the rest in cornflower blue. But his wife and daughter had moved on, carving a path straight for us. Nycta quickly turned her back, pretending she'd never seen them, and pushed an overstuffed pastry puff through her teeth, honey dribbling from the corner of her mouth and down her chin. But they were upon us like ravens picking at carrion.

"Lady Ouest." Moranthe was the first to speak. "What a privilege it is to meet the heir of Sylphira the Grim." The lines of her pale face seemed more severe than I remembered, as if she'd pinned her dark hair back too tight underneath that monstrous veil.

Nycta, to their abject horror, whirled to greet them with a mouth full of food. "Madame Moramfee," she managed, spitting crumbs so far, the two retreated a step backwards. "Tannyf. Chommed. What an unusual choif of color."

"When I heard about the gathering—" Moranthe grimaced, fished a handkerchief from the folds of her gown, and brushed a cluster of pastry bits from her shoulder "—I assumed it was a funeral. Miss Xeanora," she said, nodding in my direction, "pleased to see you're well." And then she paused, her next words barbed and drenched in venom. "How are your friends at the academy?"

My neck ran hot. How bold she was, to confess what she'd done to my face.

"A little bored." Nycta reached for a flute of moonflower wine from the table, and the glass frosted over as she raised it to her lips. "But I suppose that's just the company."

Tannyth contorted her pixie-like face in disgust.

But Moranthe was a statue in comparison. "Come, darling. Our time is better wasted with the guest of honor." She let the cut of her gaze linger on me a moment longer, and they both slithered away, their black skirts sweeping after their feet.

I snorted when they were safely out of earshot. "You're absolutely diabolical."

"What do you expect from 'the heir of Sylphira the Grim'?" She brought her voice down to a low rasp. "Why are they here? They tried to have us killed. They *did* kill Cyrie."

A twinge of grief lanced through my chest, and I tried to swallow it away. "Same reason I am, I suppose." I drew in a breath. "The lord of Phaenn is looking for a wife."

Her gray eyes seemed to double in disbelief. "She's marrying you off?"

"Not if I can help it." I closed my mouth around the little cake, the taste of lemon and elderflower seeping on to my tongue. I'd avoid him all night if that's what it took. Or better yet, take after Nycta and send him fleeing in the other direction. I returned to the table to reach for another dessert and pulled my hand back when I grasped someone else's fingers instead. "Oh! Gods…I almost ate you."

"I can assure you, I would've tasted terrible."

My cheeks warmed when I lifted my eyes to his face. He was young, no older than I was, if I could guess. And he favored the Taenmi. Eyes shaped like willow leaves and the color of wildflower honey, bronze skin, and short waves of raven hair—telltale signs of the witches of the woods. But he was clad in cobalt.

*One of the Tenwars' underlings, most likely.*

"Um…hi." It was all I could muster.

His sharp features softened, and he disarmed me with a smile. "Hello."

Nycta buried her elbow in my ribs. And I looked at her, wincing. She tilted her head at two figures in the near distance.

My mother, the Viper, in her silver scales. And another, a broad-shouldered man clothed in autumn brown. He was laughing with her as she led the way, blood-red wine sloshing over the rim of his goblet and splattering on the floor.

I grasped the stranger's fingers again. "Dance with me."

"What?"

"Unless you'd like to see me eaten alive, I'd suggest you hurry."

"Um…" He fumbled around the table. "A-All right."

I pulled him through the willows and into the fray of twirling, gilded bodies. And they blurred around us, sparkling and spinning, all languid limbs and wistful reaching.

"I'm Aeren," he started, and my breath caught in the cage of my ribs when his hand fit into the crease of my back. "By the way." His touch made me shiver, sapped the strength from my knees, and as he pressed closer, his nose a breath away from mine, I wasn't sure how I was standing at all.

"Xeanora." I draped one hand on his shoulder, and we entered into the soft push-pull, rise and fall of a waltz. He seemed tender footed, unsure—perplexed, even—as he navigated the style of the River Court, missing steps and stumbling in the wrong direction. Tannyth, who'd been dancing with a handsome, moon-eyed boy nearby, drifted into our path and choked back a snicker before floating away.

"One of the cannibals, I presume?" He'd barely glimpsed her, and still somehow gauged her perfectly.

I sighed a little. "The worst kind."

"I saw the others, too," he said softly. He'd all but abandoned the waltz, leading me in a different dance altogether. "The ones you're running from."

"My mother." I whispered and chanced a glance at where I'd seen them. They'd cornered Nycta, but she was handling them well, drawing their attention each time their eyes skimmed the rotation of dancers. "And the man she wants me to marry."

His brow furrowed in earnest. "She wouldn't let you choose?"

*What a novel thought.* I shook my head, my voice croaking in my throat. "She *never* lets me choose." We slowed to a halt as the song faded into its final measures, strings quieting, the River Court falling still around us. But I'd hardly noticed them. My heart was beating too fast, too loudly to hear anything else. And he didn't seem eager to let me go.

"I hope, one day, you will," he said, his fingertips brushing down my spine. "Choose for yourself, that is."

My vision swam. "Thank you...for letting me use you."

"Anytime." He murmured as the tips of our noses aligned. An inch closer and—

The chime of silverware on glass.

I averted my gaze and retreated from the lure of his kiss. Mother stood at the edge of the willows with a half-empty flute and sugar spoon in hand, the glassy-eyed lord of Phaenn beside her.

She held the drink aloft to the rousing cry of her fellow nobles. "To

Lord Aflytaer and his health. May this signal the beginning of a long friendship between covens, courts," she paused, her stare settling on my face, "and Houses."

My chest tightened. "Thank you again." I squeezed Aeren's hand and fled before he could respond. To find Nycta and disappear into a corner far from my mother's sight. But the guests pressed in, closed off every route of escape, as they gathered to listen.

"Please," the lord insisted, "my friends in the Rose Court call me Haenor. Paia—" he touched the small of Mother's back, a little too familiar for my taste "—if I may?"

I was shocked she didn't separate him from his hand right then.

But she merely bristled and smiled again. "Of course."

Haenor swept the glass from her fingers, earning a hiss from Tamsyn, and stepped forward. "There's been much talk of an announcement to be made tonight, and I would be remiss if I allowed this moment to pass without doing so." He spoke with the self-importance of a king. His voice alone made my insides squirm. "*The* Lord Aflytaer," he gestured to someone in the crowd.

And I followed the arrow of his hand—to Aeren. I held my breath too long, and the back of my throat burned with the bitter tang of bile.

I was a fool.

"My son," he continued, his voice softened with pride and strong drink, "is in need of a wife. And I am confident that she is in this room." The ballroom stirred with whispers. Girls pining, mothers gasping in delight. "But we won't leave it to chance. Tinnabir, the Perennial Rose, one of the western kingdoms from which our two cities were born, yields to the power of fate. In the assignment of familiars—and those its people are destined to love. The old magic runs deep. Their curse is ours as well. But what of the blessing?" He let the silence linger for effect and motioned to a servant flanking a table nearby. Whatever sat upon it had been covered in a blue veil. The fabric betrayed it, cascaded into its curves. But the domed shape only added to the mystery. "This is our answer."

At Haenor's cue, the servant pulled the veil away, and it slipped slowly from the table and onto the floor.

A bulb of moon-white petals pushed up from the soil of a wide-rimmed vase, a day shy from blooming, encased in the clearest glass. No one spoke, or even deigned to breathe.

"A flower from our ancestral lands." Haenor gripped the crystal knob and freed the blossom of its dome. "It blooms only in the presence of two entangled souls—lives meant to intertwine. And if it opens tonight, there will be a new Lady of Phaenn." This drew a small chorus of impassioned whispers.

And a look of dismay Paia Torrowin could no longer suppress.

"A bride test?" Nycta's voice spat the words behind me. "Is he serious?"

But Haenor never faltered.

Mother cut in to protest. "Lord Haenor, I hardly—"

He didn't let her finish. "Would the eligible young ladies of the court come forward?"

Tannyth was quick to volunteer, pulling free of her escort's arm and rushing to the front of the line by the table. And gripping handfuls of her skirts, she curtsied so low and so long, Aeren's face flushed.

"Tannyth Estyr of Rynmoor, my lord."

"What a fine rose you are. Please, come." Haenor reached into his coat pocket and produced a small, double-edged dagger with a golden hilt. "Blood serves as the key."

"Oh, what fun," Nycta quipped with mock interest. "Maybe he'll stab her and solve all of our problems."

He pressed the tip into the valley of her palm, a small crimson bead bubbling up from her broken skin. I watched, in half-fascination and half-terror as he carved deeper still, until the creases in her hand ran red with blood. But Tannyth remained stoic, even smiled, as she held the younger lord's gaze. She kept it as she tilted her hand over the flower and shed a few scarlet drops over the petals, and the crowd that had gathered round the scene waited in silence. But nothing happened. She turned her head sharply to cast a cutting look at the girls who'd begun to giggle, the blood boiling in her cheeks, and revisited the flower. Squeezed another stream into the soil. Again, nothing.

"Ah. Well..." Haenor stepped in, placed his hand on her shoulders, and ushered her away. "Shall we move on?"

"Lady Ouest of Tyafae." Nycta left my side to break away from the crowd, drawing stares as she offered the perfect curtsy and slipped a satin glove from one of her hands. Haenor primed the blade and reached for her wrist, but she pulled it away. "It's..." She let her voice trail and gestured for the knife. "Best if you don't." He paused, studied her fingers, and pinched the blade, turning the hilt in her direction. And Nycta sliced her hand herself. The blood stiffened in her palm at once, crystalline and frozen. She flexed her hand to crack it into shards of crimson ice and sprinkled it over the unopened bloom.

I held my breath when the flower appeared to shudder, but it remained closed.

Nycta curtsied again, with a comically unbothered grin, and reclaimed her place beside me.

Scores of more girls approached and presented themselves with the same result—cutting and disappointment—until the flower, once white as milk, was drenched in blood, its light perfume now choked with the coppery scent of decay.

Haenor sheathed the dagger in a folded handkerchief and wiped it clean. "Is there no one else?"

I saw my mother's eyes search the room, and I edged backward, farther from the breach in the crowd. If she never found me, I wouldn't have to be tested. Gawked at by the lords and ladies of the River Court while I was appraised like cattle. I worked my way through, weaving past Tannyth and her wounded pride, Lady Tenwar and her husband and their small affections shared in secret, and headed for the nearest bridge.

"I believe," Mother's voice cut the silence, a tinge of annoyance beneath her cool veneer, "you haven't had the pleasure of meeting my daughter. Xeanora?"

I stopped mid stride, steeling myself as I bit my tongue, and whirled to face her.

"Would you come, dear?" She beckoned for me, fixing her lips in a curated grin.

A nide of whispers swarmed at my back when I obliged. But this time, the throng cleared a path for me. Tannyth pushed through and stumbled to the fringe of the crowd to watch with swollen eyes, while the rest looked on in rapt captivation. I tried not to meet their gazes, stared straight on and at the little basin of blood-soaked mulch. It would hurt, I knew. But what gripped me was the terror of what came afterwards. If the flower opened, I'd belong to someone else. And if it didn't...something told me my mother had other, less savory schemes in mind. Nycta waited at the end, unclasping her hands to leave a reassuring touch on my arm. It was cold, almost numbing, but I took comfort in it.

I stopped short of Haenor and his flower, my vision skimming over Aeren's face to his left, and I anchored my hand on my chest and bowed my head. "Lady Torrowin of Rynmoor."

"Milady." The elder lord was in the midst of returning the gesture when I raised my eyes again. "You're as comely as your mother said."

My cheeks seemed to warm with offense, as if he'd meant it as an insult. A clever remark sat poised like a serpent in the pit of my stomach. But I held it back.

"You're too generous, my lord." I feigned a smile in reply.

"If you would," he brandished his golden dagger, "grace me with your hand?"

There was a tension between us I couldn't place, a quiet animosity that traced a chill down my spine. He was daring me—to do what, I wasn't sure. But I wouldn't give him the satisfaction.

"Of course," I said, my tone unchanging, and surrendered my palm.

He took it gingerly, held it with such care, I questioned the immediate disdain I'd felt before. Until his fingers migrated to my wrist and seized it tight as he slit my hand open. I clenched my teeth to the sharp, and then throbbing, pain as it spread like wildfire under my skin, the bite of the air seeping into the seething wound. Haenor wrenched me forward, and I staggered a step closer, the edges of my sight blurring with gathering tears. He guided my hand, dressed in ribbons of my own blood, over the flower. I sucked in a breath, a tear slipping down my cheek, as I listened to the *drip...drip...drip* of my blood falling on the petals. The flower had gorged on all the girls' blood now, its soil swollen and sodden with their offerings. There was no white of its petals, no green of its stem. Only red. Crusting darkly and flaking off in thick, crumbling scales. Haenor slackened his grip on me and stared in anticipation, and I cradled my palm to my chest, my head still swimming from the pain.

But I forgot it, and everything that preceded it, when the flower struggled open.

Once bloody, now clean and aglow, the heart of it limned in the softest, most entrancing light.

My stomach threatened to empty itself when the court erupted in a fit of applause, hurling praises of a betrothal and a wedding and a bride-to-be. I didn't realize my legs had grown numb until Aeren caught me by the wrists and held me upright. He whispered something, so low beneath the cries of celebration, I couldn't hear him. And he repeated himself before I lurched from his grasp and into Nycta's trembling arms.

"If it matters—if it counts—I'm glad it was you."

# THREE

The carriage shuddered each time a new wind crested over the countryside. I braced a hand against the cushioned wall, the plush green velvet squishing through my fingers. It listed in the strength of another gale—leaning so far I was sure it would careen off the path and into the muck and mire by the wayside. The wheels reared up and slammed down onto the unpaved road with a *crack*.

We'd be dashed to pieces if we continued on like this. Rising and falling with such violence, barreling through the maw of a murderous storm.

"We'll be there soon." Aeren reached for my fingers on my lap from the opposite seat, the spark in his honey eyes dimming when I withdrew from his touch and tucked my hands beneath my cloak. He sat quietly for a long while after, kept to himself through the carriage's long struggle through the torrential rain. I peered out the window, at the blurred edges of the mountains in the distance and the trees that bowed in the screaming wind. Veins of white fire cut through the sky in branches, and in the moments before they died, I saw the steep face of an anvil creeping over the ridge. On either side of us, a murky expanse of wind-tossed wheat stretched on to no end. And ahead, the shoulders of two great, black horses as they led the way into the stirring darkness of the night, rain sloughing down their backs and whipping silver streaks across the windowpane.

The plains gave way to a smattering of cabins and farmhouses, and then the shingled roofs and chimneys of a village. Along the road, a procession of swinging amber lights wrestled against the wind. And I drew back, startled, when I realized they were laborers. Woodsmen wrapped head to toe in leather slogged through the storm like specters, thick, slimy mud sucking at the soles of their boots. They were near-faceless, eyes squinting through thin slits in their masks.

I leaned close to watch. "What are they doing?"

Aeren's eyes brightened again, his mouth curving into a lopsided grin as he spoke. "Preparing for the Burning. You came just in time."

"The Burning?" I repeated, turning the words over on my tongue.

"Our tradition," he explained, his voice electric, "to mark the winter season. A hunt at first light and a bonfire at the day's end."

The carriage rolled on, trundling down a solitary road carved into the slope of a hillside. And a great shape rose in the haze of the moors. Grayer than the fog, more foreboding than the storm. The Aflytaer estate. One of the grandest houses west of the mountains.

Its silhouette was sharp and unforgiving. Four stories of oak and river stone, cobbled terraces and jutting decks and balconies. I'd never seen something so palatial—and so intimidating. Lightning cracked the sky wide open, cast the house and hills and garden in searing white. And the sight of the immutable House of Earth and Wood drew a shiver down my spine.

It'd been half-devoured by thorns.

Briars choked the walls like a sickness. A pox of ravenous vines and barbs strangled the eastern half of the garden, swallowed the nearby balconies in ivy and stinging nettles. Tendrils of black spines left strange traceries on the windows.

As if in warning—as if Nature herself had deemed it unworthy of standing.

We ground to a halt, the carriage trembling at the clamor of a horse's bray, and before I could catch my breath, the gilded door swung open.

"Welcome to Phaenn, milady." The footman at the door offered his hand.

I grasped it, his glove slick with raindrops, and raised the hood of my cloak over my head as I stepped down into the sludge of foreign earth. It felt different beneath my feet. My magic seeped into the ground and searched for the familiar, but I found the stranglehold of roots instead.

"Xeanora?"

I looked up.

Aeren. He stood waiting, a hedge of sapphire roses at his back. "Are you ready?"

I let the threads of my magic fade and joined him without a word.

The second of the footmen, a thin-faced youth dwarfed by his leather coat and wide-brimmed hat, unhooked a lantern from the carriage sconces and held it aloft.

It'd been difficult to measure in the darkness, but in the fire's glow, the whole of the garden revealed itself. Walls of vines and branches, seven feet high at least, snaked around the house in winding pathways and dead ends. They appeared to have been sheared cleanly at the top, but the thorns had infested them too, left barbs cutting at the air like razors.

But stranger still, I noticed, there was no opening, no door, no passage to walk through. I looked to Aeren, questioning him with my eyes.

And he smirked, approached the garden wall, and laid his hand among the flowers.

The hedge gashed apart like an open wound, thousands of tiny brambles and thorns scurrying sideways and longways. I almost shuddered when, in the thick of night, I realized they reminded me of spider's legs. Slithering and stacking upon each other, until they settled in an endless arbor of vines and a path cut through, straight and narrow, toward the towering doors.

Aeren hesitated on the threshold, snapped the stem of a rose, and offered me its rain-kissed head. "My garden is yours."

Our fingers brushed as I took it, my breath catching at the accidental touch.

"Oh!" I lifted my hand to my face and examined where the thorn had torn the skin. Two white, ragged edges in the mound of my palm leached with blood.

"Gods…" He hastily produced a handkerchief from his cloak and closed the space between us. "May I?" But he didn't wait for me to speak, staunching the cut and mopping up the blood that had streamed in pink, diluted lines down my wrist. "You're not a true witch of Phaenn until you've hurt yourself in the fields at least once," he quipped and tied the handkerchief over the wound. "Shall we?" He slipped into the arbored path, and I trailed after him, stealing a glance over my shoulder when the footmen and horses disappeared with a lash of the reins. My heart skipped as the hedge stitched itself closed behind me.

My fate was sealed.

"This way." Aeren's whisper carried far in the silence. We'd been cut off from the storm, from the cold and the shriek of the wind. Even the rain was nothing more than a mist in the maze.

I pushed my hood back from my hair and followed.

The twin doors had been carved into the shape of a maiden crowned in laurel and daisies. She looked serene, her closed lips curled in a welcoming smile. Aeren fit the teeth of a brass key into the lock at her waist and turned it. And her breast opened up as if she'd been sliced from head to navel, a sliver of the glimpse inside splitting her smiling face in two.

He held half of her for me, and I stumbled into the shadows ahead of him. I blinked my eyes to the blackness and breathed in a mouthful of dust motes and chilly air. The room was filled with silhouettes, soft-edged and distant. They might have been ghosts, and for a moment, I'd convinced myself that they were, quiet and still as they watched me from the darkest corners.

I jumped with the groaning slam of the heavy door.

"Welcome to Leafaire." Aeren's voice tangled itself in the rafters and hung in the air long afterward. "Do you like it?"

My vision came into focus.

Windows as high as the ceiling, curtains drawn to shut the moonlight away. The reddish-brown panels of a wooden floor. Furnishings that appeared untouched, unused for some time. The dark devoured it all, save the small flame from a lone candle by the door.

It was almost...sepulchral.

And in a hue I hadn't expected. "It's all..."

"Blue." Aeren shed his cloak in the antechamber and stepped into the foyer ahead of me, swiping the candlestick from its table and brandishing its wavering light above his head. "It's the roses—we grow so many. No one knew what to do with them for ages. Now, we use the dye in the petals for everything."

*The ball.* Amidst the chaos that followed, I'd forgotten. He'd been wearing blue that night.

He skimmed his fingertips along the curve of the banister when he'd reached the stairs. "It looks sorry now, but I promise, it's nicer in the day. I'll give you a tour when the light can do it justice. But you're welcome to explore until then." He lit the way up the staircase, threading a lambent path through a series of winding corridors decked in shadow. We climbed another, and another, passed runs of carved wooden doors that flowered by some untold magic, until he slowed to a stop at the relief of a woman adorned in delicate clouds of baby's breath. There was something familiar to her, as if I'd seen fragments of her face on someone else.

"Is that..." I started, my voice trailing.

"My mother," he whispered in answer, soft candlelight flickering in her sculpted features. "These were her chambers."

"What happened to her?"

"She died when I was seven—in her birthing bed, along with my sister."

Every muscle in my body tensed.

He glanced down at me, his freckled cheeks flaring. "N-Not here. Sorry, I didn't mean to frighten you. Different room, different floor entirely." He waved his hand over the door, warding off the specters that had edged into my imagination. "If it comforts you at all, I've never seen a ghost in my eighteen years." He turned to admire her likeness again. "Just traces of her: the notes she left behind, dogears in books she never finished. Leafaire was hers. Our ancestor, Olyphae the Kind—she determined it'd be passed through the matriline. And it had been—for two hundred years. I'm the first lord of this House." He pressed his palm to the door and gave it a gentle push. "I think it's been without a lady long enough."

A great white sheet, as light and sheer as gossamer, hung still over the bed. Thin and silvery in Aeren's candlelight, it wavered slightly, like a cobweb shuddering against the faintest breath. He set the light on the nightstand, gripped fistfuls of the fine material, and tugged hard. And it slid away from the bedframe in cascades, filling like a sail before it pooled at his feet. The wood was dark and seamless, with four slender posts coiling into spires and the image of a wild-eyed woman carved into the headboard. From where I stood, it appeared to be a single piece, bereft of the usual pocks of nails or studs, and I wondered what kind of giant they'd slaughtered to make it. I stepped forward, ran my fingers along the weaves and whorls of golden thread in the sheets.

"My father sent most of the servants home before we left for Rynmoor. They'll return come sunrise." Aeren spun the shroud around his arms and discarded it on the chair at the vanity by the opposite wall. Then he took the candle and seeded the cold wood of the hearth with half a dozen tiny flames. "But I'll bring something up to you once you've settled in. The lord's chambers are in the garden wing, but the thorns are…a bit more of an issue there. I've been staying in the adjoining room, so if you need anything—if you're upset or frightened—I'm a word away." He poked at the kindling with an iron rod until it hissed and spat embers. "This should keep you warm until morning. Did you bring any sleeping gowns?"

I shook my head, silent, and gripped the silver handle of my small satin case. Mother had been eager to send me off, given me a bag with a spare dress and a brief goodbye. My things would follow me here in the days to come, but for now, I'd have to wait.

"Take a look through the chest. There may be a nightdress or two." He stood, turning his back to the fire as he wiped his hands clean. "My mother's parties were…notorious. Goose chases in the garden, archery in the parlor. One night, she filled the ballroom with water, and they raced each other in very large wheels of cheese," he said, striding for the door, so nonchalant, I couldn't determine if he was joking. "Poor drunks never could find their way home, so she'd let them stay until morning. Probably for the best, honestly."

"Why's that?" I asked, unable to hide the amusement in my voice.

His eyes glinted something roguish as he caught his hand on the doorframe, his lips curling into a crooked smile. "They kept getting lost in the maze."

HE RETURNED WITHIN THE HOUR, OUT OF BREATH, BEARING A PLATE laden with all manner of brightly colored sweets. His linen shirt had slipped to one side and exposed the skin of his shoulder, the laces in his collar dangling loose over his chest. "Here you are. Madame Dey made them for the Burning, but I don't think she'll notice if a few disappear."

Something told me she would.

He'd piled on more than I could ever dream of eating: spiced biscuits and hand pies sprinkled with coarse sugar, tiny cakes adorned with bristle berries and dollops of cream.

"Thank you," I said and pushed to my feet from my seat on the edge of the bed, grasping a handful of my nightgown when it slid down too low.

He set the plate on the nightstand. "There's a clasp or two hidden in there…Would you like my help?"

I nodded, holding my arms and turning my back to him, and I shivered when I felt his breath on my skin.

His fingertips danced over the opening, pinched at the fastenings until he'd connected them all. "There…" he said, but his warm hands lingered, the pad of his thumb skimming the nape of my neck.

I glanced up at him from over my shoulder. He was even more beautiful in the dark—bronze in the firelight, hair tumbling past his chin, shadows cutting against the angles in his face. We were so close. Everything inside me ached to lean into his lips.

He leaned in. I retreated, averting my gaze.

"Forgive me." He cleared his throat, his face flushing as he rounded the bed in his flight to the door. "I-I overstepped. I'll see you… tomorrow then?"

"Aeren," I called after him, "wait."

He stopped, his willow eyes wide. "Yes?"

I parted my lips to speak, to pour out every feeling he'd left in his wake and rid myself of the weight. But I thought better of it. "Good night."

He closed his mouth in a half-smile. "Good night, milady." And then he was gone.

IT RAINED WELL INTO THE NIGHT, THE BONES OF THE HOUSE OF EARTH and Wood trembling with the primordial call of the thunder. It came in deafening waves, split the drumming of the rain.

And kept me lying awake.

I wrinkled my nose and sat up, the sheets sinking from my shoulders and pooling in my lap, and I swung my legs over the side of the bed and slid to my toes. The floor was warm underfoot. Flames still lashed at the walls of the hearth across the room. I walked to the chest at the foot of the bed, took a satin robe, and slipped my arms through the sleeves. And I lit a candle and crept silently into the hall.

Leafaire was a labyrinth of intertwining corridors and sweeping landings, winding staircases and burnished redwood floors. Raised from the earth in turrets and gables by at least a hundred hired hands and adorned in tapestries of umber and emerald thread, the manor gave the daunting air of a castle and not the House it'd been so fondly called. Everything I wandered past seemed to dwarf me: the rose-bled drapes staked into the paneled walls and pooling in bruise-blue ripples at my feet, the floor to ceiling windows those same veils darkened.

I ran my hand along a muraled wall, let my fingertips skim the frightened face of a buck immortalized on the wood. Its demise dressed in sapphire, red-capped men with lustful eyes, hacked at its throat while hunting dogs gnawed on its thrashing legs. It was part of a greater scene, lurid in its many strokes and colors. There was the woman carved into Leafaire's doors—whom I'd later recognized as Olyphae the Kind—and the founding of Phaenn. Demonstrations of her Legacy over nature, the book of magic tethered to her soul. The paint seemed to crack and dull the farther down I strayed, give way to the cruel hunger of the vines. They strangled the doors, sealed some of them shut. Save for one, where the corridor came to an end. I fit my hand around the knob, pushed the door open a little … and immediately shut it.

There was a group of women—I'd counted six—standing together in a corner of the room. I pressed against the wood to listen for their voices.

Silence.

I turned the knob again. Cold air leached from inside, seizing my arm with shivers. It rushed over me when I let the door swing wide, and I gave myself to the chill as I crossed the threshold. There, on the far wall, was my face in shards—a thousand times and a thousand more, staring back at me from rows of looking glasses overgrown with thorns. Some were cracked, silver frames so old and tarnished, they hardly shone in the moonlight. I shook my head free of the eerie sight and settled my gaze on the six silhouettes.

The figures convening in the darkness—they were dresses. All abandoned in varying stages of completion. Unfinished hems and basted seams. Propped on half-mannequins fashioned from wood and wire.

I drew closer to study them. They'd been made with the silk of the wood witches, dyed in the colors of Phaenn and its neighboring sister cities: Nymofren, Tyafae, Renarch, Noxos, and Laethys. And embroidered, like my mother's clothes, with hundreds of little crests. They would have been beautiful. I wondered who they'd belonged to—why their creation had never been seen through to the end.

"Satisfying your curiosity?"

My heart stopped at the sound, and I spun, gasping in a breath. "Lord Haenor—" My voice lilted with a nervous laugh. "You scared me. I thought everyone was asleep."

He was leaning in the doorway, wearing the shadows like a cloak over his shoulders. "Apart from you, I see."

"I don't sleep much."

Cyrie's face flashed into my memory, and I saw her hair fanning into her gaping mouth, frost crusting in a handprint around her neck.

I hadn't slept peacefully in a while. "I thought I'd explore a little. Learn my way around the house."

He peered down his nose at me and the gowns at my back. "And you settled in this room?"

"Is that a problem?" I stiffened, steeling myself against his narrowing eyes.

"Not every door is meant to be opened," he said. There it was again, the challenge in his stare.

"Aeren said I could go anywhere I wanted," I replied, unwavering.

"I'm certain *Lord Aflytaer* would feel more comfortable if you spent the evening in your bed." He beckoned me forward, snaking his arm around my shoulders when I obliged. "Come, milady. It's not safe in the dark."

# FOUR

*T*he winter sun filtered in through the curtains, covering my face in a lacework of dappled light. The room had turned gray with the morning, the air crisp and still. It chilled my lungs when I breathed it in, leaving the warmth of my bed to look through the glass doors and past the balcony overlooking the storm-swept hills. A thick pall of fog hung low over the moors, grasping at the hills like the hand of an ancient god. I rubbed my eyes and squinted at the blurred shapes peeking through the haze. And my heart quickened in my chest when I could have sworn I saw a malevolence of ghosts in the mists.

I turned away from the balcony and reached for the cerulean robe draped over the bed. "Aeren?" I threaded my arms through the sleeves and tied the sash at my waist, stepping up to the connecting door. "Are you awake?" I called through it.

Nothing.

I knitted my brows together and raised my hand to knock. "Aer—" The door yielded, creaking open at my touch. I pushed into the silence and slipped inside.

The room was empty.

They gave him away—the unmade bed underneath a canopy of

polished branches, the desk covered in scraps of scribbled parchment in the corner. They were puzzle pieces, hints of the parts of him I'd yet to meet. I drew forward and let the air warm me from the inside. It smelled like him—cinnamon and autumn leaves and fresh embers from a tended flame. I stepped along the sapphire walls, past the fireplace where fragments of wood and ash still smoldered, and wondered.

*Had the hunt begun so early?*

I stopped.

There, in the farthest corner of the room, stood a large mahogany tub—raised several inches from the indigo floor and stained a rich maroon. Even from a distance, I could see the runes in the wood.

Rolisen magic.

My father, a Rolisen by blood, had taught me a few when I was little—one for protection. The other, healing. But stepping closer, I didn't recognize any of these. One, in particular, a crude muddle of slashes and arcs, repeated too often to be ignored. And the longer I stared, the more they looked like antlers. I looked down at the sudden clink of glass against glass and pulled my foot away from a row of bottles on the ground, kneeling to steady one of them when it bobbled on its base. There were five, sealed tight and dyed a different shade of blue.

I lifted the last from its place and turned it over in my hands. Letters, not runes, had been etched into its face, and as I traced the grooves and whorls with my fingers, I read the word aloud. "Pelwyn."

"Excuse me, milady."

Someone cleared their throat behind me, and I shot up, leaving the bottle on the floor.

A boy, no older than fourteen or fifteen, stood in the doorway. He looked as if he'd stepped out of the mural leading to the mirrored room—buttoned in a black hunting coat, a crimson cap fit snugly over his head.

"Please," I interlaced my fingers. "Xeanora."

"Gaereth..." There was a long, uncomfortable pause. Then he dipped in a bow. "Milady."

My tongue teased the inside of my cheek, but I let the annoyance pass. "It's a pleasure to meet you, Gaereth. Would you happen to know where Aeren—Lord Aflytaer might be?"

"He took to the woods early this morning." He started for Aeren's desk, seizing the wooden hilt of a knife lying among the scatter of papers, and returned to his defensive stance in the door. "But his lordship forgot his hunting blade. He sent me back to retrieve it."

"I can bring it to him." The corners of my mouth drew up in a smile.

But he shook his head, pressing his lips together in a tight line. "It's best for a woman to stay here … To spare your sensitivities."

I blinked, my face suddenly warm. "My *sensitivities* and I insist."

A young woman in brown stumbled into the doorway, gasping in mouthfuls of air. "There you are, Lady Torrowin. Maery, at your service." She breathed and curtsied low, the auburn hair left out of the plaits around her head tumbling over her shoulders. With cheeks like lilies and willowy limbs, she looked more like a lady of Phaenn than I did. She carried a bundle of fabric in her arms, layers and layers of spun silk and embroidery. She swayed on her feet under the weight, caught herself leaning, and straightened herself out again. She averted her fox-like eyes from the bottles when I noticed her staring and raised her burden with a smile. "I'm meant to dress you for the day."

"Thank you, Maery. Gaereth." I sharpened my tongue as he turned to flee. "You can leave that with me."

The boy hesitated—something my mother, the Viper, would have never allowed—and surrendered the hilt into my open hand. "Yes, milady."


"WE RECEIVED THE FIRST OF YOUR THINGS EARLY THIS MORNING," Maery said, taking the last of my hair and weaving it into a net of gilded braids. It was warm with her leaning close and working so intently. The last hour had seen us sitting at the vanity—her fingers winding and plaiting, adding color to my lips and the corners of my eyes. I studied myself in the mirror when she left her chair to retrieve a parcel of folded satin from the wardrobe. My nightgown lay discarded on the bed, exchanged for the layers of an earth witch. The first was barely visible, sheer and gold with gathered sleeves. The second, a loose viridian shift tied at the waist. And the last—I suspected newly made—a long, open tunic of midnight blue, embroidered with vines and branches of golden roses.

"I thought you'd like to wear a piece of home today." She smiled upon returning, and as she let the fabric fall away, green and silver glinted in my eyes.

An heirloom comb. A work of glimmering vines and gemstone blossoms set with tiny sapphires and emeralds.

Maery sighed when the sun found it and cast pinpricks of iridescent light all over her hands as she placed it just above my ear. "It's beautiful. I hear all the girls in Rynmoor look like princesses."

"That's...not mine."

Her eyes went wide. And before I could blink, she'd untangled it from my hair and stuffed it in the folds of her dress. "Forgive me." She bowed her head, her jaw quavering into her chest. "My mistake."

"It's all right." I reached for her wrist from over my shoulder. "Maery, you'd tell me if there was anything wrong, wouldn't you?"

"Of course, milady." She pulled free and carried on, gathering hairpins and tins of powder and setting them in their rightful place, but never meeting my eyes.

"Is there?"

She paused. "Pardon?"

I turned to face her this time, steeling my voice as I asked again. "Is there something wrong?"

Her smile faltered. "The hour is quite late, milady. Lord Aflytaer will be needing his knife."


MAERY LED ME AS FAR AS THE LABYRINTH'S END AND NOT A STEP MORE, promising to linger until I returned, and watched me cross the meadow to the swathe of trees in the distance. I gathered my skirts to one side as I trampled a path through the high grasses, barbs sticking and pulling threads in the hems. Most of it was dead. The ground was just as choked with bristles as the House, slithering into the forest in a trail of ruin. I followed it to the edge of the wood, drew in a breath, and entered.

Pale sunlight dappled the sylvan floor, shifting with the caress of the wind in the branches overhead. The forest ran thick. There was no break in the trees in any direction. Roots exhumed themselves from the loam and mud. I meandered deeper, opted for leaping from one root to the other rather than being sucked down into the earth with each weighted step. Until I found a small footpath worn into the ground and clung to it, taking care not to stray and lose myself in the wilds. The woods were eerily still. I didn't realize until now that I hadn't heard a sound. No creatures chittered their morning greetings, no birds hung their song on the air.

I halted when I felt it.

A predator. Silent and close. Stalking me in the trees.

I raised Aeren's dagger and whispered into the ground with my magic, reaching deep and sure, and closed my grip around the earth beneath the killer's feet.

"Xeanora..."

I whirled in surprise, my call to the earth retreating into my fingertips so quickly I lost my footing and staggered backward.

"You shouldn't be here." Aeren. He straddled the path in his hunting clothes, his face severe, a longbow strapped across his back.

I wrinkled my forehead. "What do you mea—"

Something lashed at my ankle and seized it tight, and I managed a small cry before I was wrenched to the ground with a *slam*. Whatever breath I had was knocked clear of my lungs, and I clawed at the mud for purchase, straining to scream, as I was dragged several feet backward.

"Xeanora!" Aeren shouted and bounded after me, fumbling for the dirk at his thigh.

"Aeren!" I sputtered a mouthful of dirt and blood as bristles sliced at my cheeks. Brown leaves fluttered around me, scattering in the air like moths and breaking apart in my hair. I twisted onto my back and kicked at the vine coiled around my leg, my skirts hiking up above my stinging knees. "Let go!" I screeched and hacked at it with Aeren's dagger, but it only pulled me faster, through the muck and the moss, past faerie rings and roots, and down onto the cool bank of a pond dark with grime and silt. Aeren dashed out of the trees and to the edge of the water, throwing himself into the mud to lunge for my hand. But he grasped nothing but the air between us, and before I could hold my breath, I was in the water. It shocked my senses as it filled my nose and mouth and left me writhing in the darkness. I fought against the pull, sinking deeper and deeper still, farther from the light of the surface and the garbled echoes of Aeren's screams. The pond's face broke over and over, rippling around him as he leaped in after me, lost his breath, and dove again.

Something roiled in the pit of my stomach, white hot and raging as I flailed my limbs and shrieked. A storm of bubbles swirled from my lips. And the water changed, rushing and tearing the cold stillness with a torrent of waves that seethed around me. I kicked my legs again, spending the last of my strength, and this time, a current gripped my body and raised me out of the darkness of the deep, spitting me above the surface and into Aeren's arms. I dry retched into his chest, gasping as I clung to him, and he held me there for a moment, fitting his chin over my head.

"Are you all right?" he asked when we separated, palming my arms, my shoulders, my neck, and pushed my grimy hair back from my forehead streaked with pond scum. "Are you harmed?" His fingers settled on the hollows of my cheeks.

"I'm fine." I exhaled, gathering myself, and cupped my hands over his. "I'm fine."

His mouth crushed into mine, recklessly—and so quickly, I almost thought it'd been an accident, or some waterlogged dream. But when he withdrew, his cheeks flushed, his ragged breath warm over my parted lips, I knew that he'd meant it. I pressed into him, stole a kiss of my own. He leaned backward in surprise, the wan light of the morning sparkling in the amber rings of his widening eyes. And he took my face in his hands, streams of water leaking through his fingers as he pulled me into another. I could've anchored myself to his lips—forgotten my short-lived terror, the bone-deep chill of pond water cutting at my waist, the trill of morning birds overhead.

His back suddenly went rigid, his fingers stilling on my cheeks. And he raised his mouth to my ear to whisper, "Don't move."

"What?" I flinched and flexed the hand that had held his hunting blade. But the weapon was gone, lost to the water.

"Your magic," he said, near breathless, through swollen lips. "Reach into the earth. Can you feel it?"

I closed my eyes, my chest still rising and falling in erratic gasps, and let my power branch into the mud squelching underfoot. It warmed my fingertips, electrifying every inch of my skin. And I saw the entire forest floor in flashes. Mice in their burrows, birds pecking at a scatter of fallen seeds.

There, where the thick of the woods gave way to the bank. Four hooves.

Aeren slowly nocked an arrow, water lapping quietly at his thighs, as he stepped to the left, inhaled, and released.

A wail in the distance. And the *thud* of something heavy collapsing in the dirt.

"The Deathwood—it's dangerous." He lowered his bow, solemn, and slung it over his shoulder. "I should've told you sooner."

"The Deathwood," I repeated, keeping close to his side as we sloshed out of the pond and onto the muddy shore. My dress, in all of its layers, clung to my legs like wet parchment. "That's what you call it?"

"It's what we *all* call it." Aeren trudged on, just as heavy-sodden as I was. "There's...a lot you should know." His voice trailed as the sound of guttural bleating grew louder. And suddenly, we came upon it.

A stag, writhing on its side, the fletching of an arrow jutting from its neck. It was heaving, its large ribcage filling and emptying again in quick succession. It blinked its dark eyes as we approached and wheezed out another blood-curdling moan.

"Easy..." Aeren softened and knelt beside it, placing his hand on the creature's muzzle, and removed the small knife from its sheath on his thigh. "Thank you for your sacrifice."

I shuddered when he dragged the blade across the animal's throat, the edge catching flesh and sinking deep. Bright red rivulets leaked down his fingers as the beast slumped over and keened its last. An ugly, garbled cry. The noise was awful—the vilest sound I'd ever heard, and it haunted me long after the thrashing had stopped.

"It's all right," Aeren whispered as he looked up, the breath rattling in his chest, and he offered me an outstretched hand. His palm was slick with blood. "It's over now."

If it had burned any brighter, I would have sworn it was the sun. It blazed in a tower of fire, its flames like golden strokes, painting the night in amber. I closed my eyes to the scattering embers and leaned into the rippling air, the wind thick with apple-scented smoke. I'd never felt so warm, so free. All of Phaenn had come. The woodsmen had traded their axes for flutes and strings. Their wives laughed and ate and drank with each other on woven mats and pillows. And children crowned in braided cornhusks and dried branches danced and leaped in rings around the fire. Hundreds of silhouettes, spinning and stumbling and singing.

I watched the skinned corpse of an animal turn on a roasting spit nearby, its flame-shriveled eyes peering back at me through the smoke. "I was taught the stag was sacred to the Taenmi."

"It is." Aeren sat beside me, a blanket draped over his shoulders. He raised the edges, leaning in to envelop me with it.

I huddled close. "Then why kill it?" I knew no other coven as well as mine, but it seemed strange, nonetheless. Like slitting the throat of a patron god.

"It's our source of strength. We hunt it once a year—at the turn of winter," he explained, his honey eyes lingering on the crease of my mouth. "And when the killing's done, we take its flesh and eat it. The power lives on inside us—keeps us strong until it's time to hunt again."

Haenor staked the point of his knife through a shred of roasted meat and fit the morsel between his lips, a trail of grease leaching down his chin and glistening in the firelight. "It's how we survive."

There was something disconcerting in his smile, as if he planned to carve pieces of me to eat as well.

"Welcome home, my lord." A silver-haired woman tucked a wicker basket brimming with oversized produce under her arm and bent to offer Aeren her hand, the lines in her rounded face deepening with her smile.

He squeezed her fingers with a grin of his own. "Thank you."

"You've picked such a beautiful bride." Her eyes, brown irises edged with the gray of old age, lit up at the sight of me. "You'd best start sewing soon. She deserves something just as lovely as that face." She palmed a swollen fruit from her basket, placed it in his hand, and disappeared into the amber-limned crowd before he could respond.

"Madame Dey." Aeren murmured, watching her leave. "She's wonderful, isn't she?"

But I'd stopped listening. "What did she say?"

"An old custom—from Saian, the kingdom in the trees," he stuttered and shifted his legs, his face beginning to flush. "The groom makes the wedding gown for his bride."

I stared at the cinders fluttering to their tiny deaths in the dirt, and my thoughts turned like a watermill in my head. A chill whispered down my spine in spite of the fire. "Oh."

"Have you tried anything?" He changed the subject, puncturing the rind of the fruit with his nail and tearing the peel away.

"I…"

"Here." He pulled a section off and held it to my lips. "You must be hungry."

I closed my mouth over it, my tongue darting over the tip of his thumb, and tart, crimson juice ran down his hand. The piece burst between my teeth, fragrant and sour and cloyingly sweet.

I clung to the taste, sucking at the inside of my cheeks.

He licked his fingers clean with a chuckle. "It's good, right? Some of us were given an unusual gift. It lets us work in any of the United Cities. Whatever's asked of us, we can do. And we bring back what we learned when we come home. We learned *this* from the botanists in Laethys."

I swallowed the last of its ruby-colored flesh. "Do you have it?"

"Would you like to see?" Aeren wrapped his wedge of the fruit in a handkerchief and set it in his lap. "It might be better if…" He raised his hand to my face and hesitated, his voice catching in his throat. "May I…touch you?"

I nodded without a word. He pressed forward, and my breath hitched when the pad of his thumb brushed my lower lip before settling on my cheek. My head swam at his touch, cast my vision in shadows. And when the ground trembled, I half-believed I'd imagined it.

But it was Aeren, reaching into me—and using my power as his own. I let out a small gasp when he retracted his fingers.

"I should confess something," he started, then stopped, as if he was searching for the right words. "The test at the ball—it wasn't what my father said it was."

I wrinkled my brow. "Then what was it?" It'd convinced me and everyone that night that we were destined. It was all the confirmation my mother needed to send me away.

"A measure of your magic. The house—" he raised his stare toward the silhouettes twirling among the embers "—this city. They're cursed. They have been for a year now. I wanted to make sure my wife-to-be would be strong enough to survive it—survive *her*."

"The Bone Woman." Haenor answered before I had the chance to ask.

"All of the United Cities have their own stories," Aeren rushed to explain. "You've heard of the Fog Catcher—in Thieri?"

I nodded. Every coven knew of him, shared their whispered warnings—the bogeyman in the mist, stealing children away in the night.

"This is ours." The apple in Aeren's throat trembled as he swallowed. "She still comes for us, sometimes, after all these years."

"As she did for Lyali." Haenor added. "His *first* betrothed."

My heart quickened in my chest.

Aeren took my hands in his, tightening his hold as if I might slip away if he let go. "That's why you can't go into the Deathwood."

He told me then of the plague of thorns she'd laid on the House. How she'd taken the first of her victims.

Of a boy bewitched by a beautiful girl. How he labored for a year to satisfy her vanity, bringing flowers to her doorstep each morning. And how, in the dead of winter, she promised her hand to him—if only he'd bring her one more flower. One twice as lovely as the others, just as she had thought herself to be. The boy pledged to do just that, wandering through the ice-stricken land until he came upon the wood and ventured into its shadows. He found a clearing there, and the most peculiar flowers in bloom. And he plucked one and planned to return home victorious. But a girl lived among those flowers—a girl far more enchanting than his beloved. And she convinced him to stay the night in her cottage in the woods, only to eat him up come sunrise and leave his bones to be found by woodsmen in the spring. His skeleton lodged beneath the bark of a tree, his jaw ossified in a scream.

THAT NIGHT, I VISITED THE MIRRORED ROOM AGAIN. TIPTOED THROUGH the darkness and past the mural slithering with vines. But when I opened the door, there was nothing. No dresses. No mannequins. Only the shattered looking glasses and the thorns that strangled them on the wall. I pushed back one of the curtains from the run of lancet windows and gazed out into the moors.

There was more to Phaenn and the House of Earth and Wood than I could've ever known—more than I was *allowed* to know.

A shape emerged from the shadows of the Deathwood. Half-alive —swaying and stumbling. I watched as it dragged its feet through the clearing, towards the groves of moon-drunk roses. I drew back, my blood running cold when the figure lifted its face to stare at the window.

Aeren.

I sprinted from the glass with my candlestick in hand, out of the room and down the thorn-bitten hall to the stairs. And grabbing a fistful of my nightgown, I tore through the dark, past the silver-limned furniture that lurked like phantoms in the night. I threw open the garden door and a winter wind swept over me, whipping at my face and cutting against my shivering legs.

"Aeren?" I called to him from the doorway, holding the flame to the darkness.

He staggered around a corner in the maze of hedges, lurching a few steps and smiling weakly as his legs buckled beneath him.

"Aeren!" I set the lamp on the pavement and broke into a run, catching him before he could crumple to the ground. His body grew slack and heavy in my arms, and he sank to his knees, pulling me down with him. My fingers met something warm and slick on his back, and my heart dropped into my stomach when I brought my hand to my eyes.

Scarlet.

His head lolled against my chest.

I kept it steady, smearing bloody fingerprints on his cheeks. "Aeren, you have to stay awake for me." I tore my gaze from his pallid face to scream over my shoulder. "Somebody!"

"What is it? What's happened?" Haenor dashed into the garden like a wild-eyed man, waving a lantern in his nightclothes, a handful of servants trailing behind him. He lowered the light and made the sign of the gods when his stare skimmed over the horror on my face...and something else.

I followed his line of sight to the shadows of the labyrinth.

A clew of brambles barreled down the garden path. Black as bile, hissing through the brittle grass, they snapped at Aeren's ankles, drawing blood, and snaked around his waist to tug him from my arms. I fought them, even as tendrils seized at my wrists and slit crimson stripes down my fingers.

"No!" I pulled free and shrieked as they swallowed him, dragging his body into the hedge. I drew the moisture from the air and folded it into itself a thousand times until the layers formed the razor's edge of a blade. And I lashed it forward into the thorns, slicing through the vines like a knife through an artery. They splintered, withering and sloughing off of him like shriveled limbs.

"Son!" Haenor scrambled to the heap of crumbling vines and bleeding flesh and tore at the bristles, and he held Aeren's limp shape to his chest when he wrenched the young lord free.

I fell to my hands and knees, gasping.

The curse of the forest. It'd come to us.

I struggled to my feet and strained a step. But before I could take another, I was face-down in the mud, my legs locked in a vise. I shredded my throat with a scream as a horde of vines ripped me through the hedges and the yellowed grass of the meadow.

And into the heart of the Deathwood.

# FIVE

y eyes fluttered open to the golden glow of lantern flame, and I winced, sitting up slowly, and grasped at the ground for purchase—only to crush handfuls of rose-colored petals instead. They littered the sylvan floor beneath me, made every step feel like floating. The surrounding trees were heavy with intact blooms, the air thick with their fragrance...and the scent of fresh bread. I blinked, gathering my senses.

And I remembered.

Aeren in the garden. The thorns at his throat. The vines tearing me from my feet and dragging me into the Deathwood.

*I was in the woods.* My blood chilled, grew colder still when I turned and found myself standing at a cabin door. It'd been left slightly ajar, as if someone had been waiting for company.

*Waiting for me.* I dared a step forward.

And a voice, soft and sweet, called from the shadows within. "Is there a viper at my door?"

I drew back at the sound.

But it merely laughed and spoke again. "Do come in, my dear. I'm not the one who bites."

I steeled myself, pushed the door further open, and crossed the threshold. Candles wept in every corner—in the rafters dripping with herbs, on the table laden with copper cauldrons, fit into the empty spaces of the shelves teeming with jars of clouded glass. They burned low, throwing the room into darkness each time their little flames wavered. A figure worked in the lambent light, filling the silence with the din of silver and copperware at the stove. I saw nothing but her back—long, raven hair piled in curls atop her head, a threadbare shawl cascading over her shoulders and skimming the cold dirt of the floor.

But I knew who she was. "You're the Bone Woman."

"I've never liked that name. It somehow makes me sound...old. Does it not?" She tilted her chin in my direction.

And I caught a glimpse of her smile. Full lips and a mouth of flawless teeth—not at all the pointed edges I'd expected.

"Call me Faedraigh," she said. "I like it much more."

I sidestepped around the table, the warmth of my magic gathering at my fingertips. "Why did you bring me here?"

"Did I?" She turned then, gave her face to the flickering light. It stunned me—how beautiful she was. Eyes like hazel and mahogany skin. A hundred years my senior, but frozen in her youth. It was no wonder men followed her to their deaths. "I don't believe I did."

"Then who..." I started, my voice trailing. No one unfortunate enough to meet the Bone Woman ever left the Deathwood alive. She had no reason to lie to me now.

"Tea?" She lifted a kettle from the stove and poured me a cup when I didn't answer, cutting the stillness with a giggle at my hesitance to take it. "Not to worry," she whispered, as if sharing a secret. "I'm not the poisoning kind."

"If you didn't bring me here—" I stared into its amber surface, searched the ripples for an answer "—then who did?" Her hand glinted silver in the corner of my vision, and I raised my eyes and startled at the dagger grasped in her slender fingers.

But she turned it over in her hands and offered me the hilt. "I know every poor soul—remember every face I've given to my trees. All but one. I wonder why that is."

And I recognized the markings etched into the wood.

Antlers.

# SIX

*I* saw the Deathwood's edge just as a light rain began to thrum on my temples, the cool beginnings of a winter storm trickling down the nape of my neck. The ground softened beneath my bloodied feet, and blades of wet grass tore and clung to my ankles. The sky growled low and deep, something sinister stirring in the thick of the clouds overhead. I braced myself against a vicious lash of freezing wind. I held my arms as another gale sliced at my cheek, whipping my hair into a violent frenzy about my face. I shivered and stumbled into the dark maw of the garden labyrinth, threading my way to the House and wandering into its night-kissed halls. The plague of thorns had eaten nearly everything—slit the curtains open, blacked out the windows like hordes of flies on a corpse. I saw no face as I climbed the stairs. Heard no voices. The air was still and sweet with decay.

No longer a House, but a mausoleum.

Aeren's door yawned wide at my touch, and I stepped inside, tracking grimy footprints across the hardwood floor as I approached the scarlet basin in the center of the room. I turned each of the bottles over, straining to read the names in the darkness.

Vaera. Kaeti. Chalcedony. Jo-zen. Pelwyn.

And I uncorked the fifth and tipped it slowly over the bath.

A stream of red.

It slipped through my trembling fingers and shattered at the bottom of the tub in a mess of sapphire glass and crimson foam.

"Xeanora?" Aeren. His weak voice rasped from the corridor. "Is that you? We've been looking for you in the woods all—"

I whirled at his silence.

There, in the dark of his doorway, he stood, his flaking lips knitted together in a frown. "Night." He barely looked like himself. His face glistened with burgundy cuts, already stiff in their healing. His clothes hung off his bleeding limbs in scraps.

"What did you do?" I took another bottle from the floor and raised it by its neck.

He faltered and ran his hand against the doorframe, trailing blood with his fingertips. "I...borrowed their magic to...to stave off the curse. But they weren't strong like you." He flashed a fleeting smile, crimson seeping through his teeth, before frowning again. "They all... died. Burned up from the inside out. Their blood...still works. But I have you now." He stumbled into me and seized my shoulders, fouling my mouth with the taste of iron when he crushed my lips in a kiss. "We can fight it off together."

"And Lyali?"

He pulled away, strings of pink spittle clinging to his chin. "What?"

I didn't blink. "I spoke to the Bone Woman. She never took her."

"That *bitch?*" he uttered with something resembling a garbled chuckle. "You believe her over me?" A shaft of lightning set a nearby window alight in an instant of searing cyan fire.

I ground my jaw. "I do."

His arms fell to his sides in defeat, his willow eyes colored with mourning as he whispered, as meek as a little boy, "I thought you were different."

"Son, I—" Haenor darted into the doorway, and the lines in his face hardened at the sight of me—and the bottle clutched in my fingers. "You stupid girl."

I was ready when he lunged for me, dashing around the tub and through the connecting door into my bedroom. I fled down the stairs and into the freezing night, into the thick of the vines and twisted

246

branches of the labyrinth. The rain came down harder, slicking my hair to the nape of my neck. I slipped and fell in the loam, and as I scrabbled to my hands and knees, I grasped something stiff and cold in the soil. An alabaster arm. Severed at the joint, fingertips black and frozen.

All the girls who'd come before me. He'd used them up and cast them aside, gorged his roses on the husks of their bodies.

I fumbled to my feet and sprinted under the garden arbor, through the high grasses thrashing in the wind, past the tree line and into the darkness of the Deathwood again. I yelped when two hands gripped my hair at the root and jerked me backwards.

Haenor.

I dug my nails into his fingers, scratching hard, and he cursed as my hair slipped through his fists. I'd only stumbled forward a few steps before a shadow came down on my head. Then I was on the ground again, doubled over in the muck. He wrenched me onto my knees, and I saw my face in the curved blade of a farmer's scythe.

"My son," Haenor grunted as he pulled my head back, stretching my neck as far as it would go, "was fond of you." He brought the edge to my throat, tearing skin, and my eyes watered as it stung. Blood ran in rivulets down my collarbone, bejeweling the front of my night-gown with crimson blooms. "You could've lived if you'd just shut up and done as you're told."

My hand brushed Haenor's thigh, a surge of magic bleeding through my fingertips.

There was a soft gurgling at first, barely heard over my heart's frantic beating and the pounding rain, and then, the rush of falling water. I turned when Haenor's grip on me fell away, crawling back-wards as he crumpled to his knees, his head tilted back too far, as dark water gushed from his mouth. His burbling screams quieted, his dimming eyes still wide with terror, and he keeled onto his side and never moved again.

I was my mother's daughter now.

I turned and ran deeper into the forest, as far from the Aflytaer estate as I could flee. Until my legs couldn't hold me any longer, and I collapsed against the gnarls of a tree, gasping with burning lungs. The ground stirred underneath my feet, and I stepped back as the tree yawned open, splintering like a cage of broken ribs. Hunks of moss dropped from the bark like discarded flesh and gathered at my feet. And with a long, chilling groan, its dark womb spat a heap of bony limbs and rags into my arms.

Blood red sap had sealed its eyes shut and fouled its clothes. Long, black hair lay matted down its back and face. For a moment, I thought it was dead. Until the creature cleaved the night in two with a scream, clawing blindly at my shoulders. The ragged nails cut deep—left scarlet crescents in the sleeves of my shift as I held it.

"Lyali!" I called her name over the howling wind. But she fought me still, shrieking and writhing in my hands. "Lyali!" I gripped her hard, her arms slick with sap, and shook her. And a final cry died in her throat. "Let me—" I sucked in a breath. "Let me help you." Her eyelids peeled apart, and I stared into her pale green eyes. They'd lost their shine, dulled over time in the darkness. Wide and wild. And full of terror. I knew that look too well. "This is what he did to you?" She collapsed into my chest with an earsplitting wail, her withering body trembling in the cold.

"Xeanora..."

I looked up at the sound of wet leaves squelching underfoot and ushered Lyali toward the shadows. "Go. Hide."

Aeren stumbled into view, looking more and more like a madman as he approached. "There you are. Come home with me. We can talk." He frowned when I didn't respond. "Please don't say you're afraid of me." He followed my eyes to the axe in his hand and gave a hollow laugh, tossing it into the mud. "For gods' sakes. Stop being irrational. Come home. Please?"

Lyali edged into the path between us, her hair streaking down her face.

"Lyali." Aeren seemed to sober, his shoulders tensing, as he spoke her name. "You should be dead."

She said nothing—only stared.

"The curse—it didn't start until..." he murmured, mulling it over, and looked up when he realized. "It was all you, wasn't it? Thought you'd punish me for what I did?"

Silence still.

"It was your fault. Tell her," he spat, but the tremor in his voice betrayed him. "You never listened to me." He turned to me, feral with desperation. "She never listened. But the people loved her anyway. More than they loved me. But she wasn't the lord of Phaenn. It was me. Me! I had to make her go away..." Aeren breathed, his eyes dark, and reached for the axe's handle. "And I'd do it again."

But before he could raise the blade to her, a horde of brambles shot up from the ground at his feet and impaled his body, black tendrils curling at the crimson blotches that flowered in his clothes. I looked away when he sputtered blood and went rigid in the moonlight, and only listened as he sank and disappeared, lifeless, into the rain-pitted earth.

Dawn gilded the sky by the time Lyali and I found our way out of the Deathwood, shades of rose and gold streaking over the gables of the House of Earth and Wood. The vines on its façade had gone. Shriveled up in the darkness with Aeren's and his father's sins, disappeared by morning light. All that remained were the scars—sickly, sallow imprints on the walls.

And hedges of swollen, sapphire roses.

# ABOUT THE AUTHOR

Krystina Coles is a young adult author with an affinity for dark fantasy, world mythology, and gothic horror. She discovered her passion of writing between the pages of Greek myths and Nancy Drew novels—which influence her stories to this day. She currently lives in her hometown of San Diego, California, where she bakes, sews, and haunts her neighborhood at night.

Check out the Moonshadow Series.

R. L. MEDINA

Trapped in a dark fae court, where shadows come alive and danger hides behind illusion, a teen struggles to recover her stolen identity.

Can she remember who she was before it's too late?

Or will the memories lead her to a truth much darker than her prison?

# ONE

*here am I?*

Everything is quiet. A blinding light surrounds me. It's so bright, it hurts. I clench my eyes shut, then slowly open them again.

The room comes into focus. There's a large bed with a sky-blue comforter against the white wall. Sunlight streams in from the window to my left. To my right, a little desk sits in the corner with stacked books and papers spread everywhere. Above the desk there are photos of smiling strangers.

If I turn, I know I'll see a closet cluttered with clothes and a long mirror hanging on one side of the door.

I know this place. I've been here so many times, and I know what comes next.

As if on cue, footsteps echo behind me. I don't move. They never see me. Sometimes it's the man. Sometimes the woman. Today it's the boy and the little girl.

They're sad—they're always sad. The girl starts crying and the boy, who looks barely older than her, hugs her. He says something to her that I can't hear. I move closer and reach for them, but I know they can't see or hear me. I'm a ghost in their world. I can only watch.

Watching them makes something crack inside me. A lump lodges in my throat. I blink.

*It's just a dream. This isn't real. Wake up.*

"Rosie, wake up!" a little voice echoes in my thoughts.

The room disappears, along with the strangers. I wake with a gasp, sitting up too fast it makes my head spin.

Black, ink-drop eyes stare into mine. "Were you dreaming again?"

I'm shaking, still recovering from what I've seen. Meriwether hovers above me, her dark blue fairy wings making a humming noise as they flutter in the air.

"Come on! Come see what the imps have done," she says, waving for me to follow.

Her long, white hair glows in the dim light as she floats in the doorway. My door is open. My breath catches in my throat.

*Why?*

I push the heavy blanket off and swing my legs over the bed to stand up.

"Meriwether, did you open my door?" I ask, knowing full well that's impossible.

It can only be opened from the inside.

She frowns at me. "Of course not. It was open when I got here."

Ice fills my veins. Anything could have gotten in while I slept. A dwarf, an imp, or a gargoyle. Even the pixies and other fairies are dangerous.

Meriwether gives me a cautious look. "Princess Maloret wouldn't let any of her court harm you, Rosie. Not... horribly, anyway. She has rules, you know."

Her words are not comforting. I know very well the 'rules' the fairy princess has in her court. There are places in her castle where she can't *or won't* guarantee my safety. That's why I mostly stick to the rooms I know.

"Come on! I want to show you," Meriwether says, waving at me impatiently.

Her gossamer dress clings to her small dark frame, the hem hanging low past her bare feet. Rubbing the chill from my arms, I follow her, throwing one last look back at my room.

Shadows splay across the stone wall behind my giant bed. One waves at me with its claw-like hand. My stomach clenches with dread.

Princess Maloret is back.

Suddenly, following Meriwether through the dark castle sounds like a really, really bad idea. I could run back to my room and shut the door, but that wouldn't stop the fairy princess from finding me. There's nothing she likes better than games, and hide and seek is her favorite.

I can't escape her.

So, I keep moving, one hand on the stone at all times. The wall is ice cold, but I don't dare let go. I don't want to lose my way.

"Meri, slow down!" my voice hisses and echoes through the pitch-black hallway.

I hear the steady fluttering of her wings and watch as her shining silhouette grows closer. She pauses right above me and gives me a sympathetic look. "Sorry. I forgot how slow humans are."

Flames from the wall torches light all once. Fire flickers against stone, highlighting Meriwether's glowing dark skin. She turns and leads the way, slowing her pace for me.

I follow, one careful step at a time. Soon, the ground slopes, and we make it to the stairs. The smell of smoke and sugary treats fills my lungs. My stomach rolls at the scent. When was the last time I ate? I can't remember.

Unlike the other creatures, I need food, but the food in Princess Maloret's court is dangerous. There's always a ninety-nine percent chance it's poisoned or cursed. I honestly don't know how I've survived this long, but then again, I don't know how long I've been trapped in her castle. There's no way to know.

Without Meriwether's help finding food and avoiding the others, I don't think I'd still be alive. But even she can't protect me from the princess.

We make it to the next floor and the air grows slightly warmer. Still, the chill and dampness around us make me shiver. My thin nightgown does little to keep out the cold, and coats and blankets are scarce in the Court of Shadows.

"Look!" Meriwether's voice startles me.

Her voice echoes around us, fading as it travels farther away. We're standing just outside one of the princess's lounges. The smell of candle wax and wood polish hangs in the air.

Carefully, I lower my head under the arched doorway and follow Meriwether into the room.

At first, I think it's empty, but then I spot something in the corner. Broken shards of wood gleam in the candlelight. The imps have destroyed another spinning wheel. I don't know whether to be upset or relieved. Spinning is one of the tasks the princess gave me to keep me 'busy.' As much as I hate the tedious work, sometimes I'm rewarded with edible food, but the biggest benefit, if the princess approves of my work, is going outside. It's my only chance to escape the gloom of the castle.

Meriwether glides to my side and shakes her head at the mess. "Stupid imps."

She turns to me, black eyes staring into mine. "Do you think we can fix it?"

Her hopeful tone makes me smile. Before I can say no, a loud cackle comes from the hall. More laughter follows, along with heavy footsteps and the unmistakable sound of claws scraping against stone.

"Hide!" Meriwether instructs me before she races to the doorway.

I look around at the empty room. There's nowhere to hide. My heart pounds wildly as the footsteps grow closer. I can't let them find me.

# TWO

*I* crouch in the corner of the room, back pressed against the cold stone wall. My teeth chatter together. I hope they can't hear it.

Meriwether's voice comes from the hall. She's speaking their language, so I don't know what she's saying, but I know she'll do her best to keep them from finding me.

*Go. Just go.* I wish them away.

My breath comes out quick and shallow, the sound so loud in the quiet. I clench my eyes shut and wait.

It's not until the footsteps and scratching fade away that I open them again. A loud sigh escapes me.

*Safe. For now.*

Something moves underneath the broken wood in front of me. I reel, nearly hitting my head against the wall. I watch as shadows burst out of the pile. They're long, thin, and smoke-like as they writhe and grow before me.

I sink further to the ground and cover my face with my hands.

"Rosie!" Meriwether's voice catches my ear.

I turn to see her flying toward me just as the last shadow creature emerges from the broken spinning wheel. Pieces of wood fly around the room. I barely have time to protect my eyes before they hit me.

Then, a sharp laugh comes. My stomach rolls with dread. I know that laugh.

*Princess Maloret.*

She emerges from the shadows, making the dark creatures disperse. They fill the room with their eerie presence. Meriwether is at my side now, her little hand on top of my head.

"Stand up, Rosie," she hisses urgently.

I don't want to. I want to go back to my room. Back to sleep. Back to my dream.

"Oh, dear. What's wrong with her?" Princess Maloret asks, giving me a mock-pitying look.

Her bright purple hair is loose around her, moving slightly as her thin shoulders shake with laughter. She's dressed in a sparkly purple tube top with tight black pants and giant silver boots.

"I was at a funeral," she says, noticing my stare.

I try to stop myself from looking up, but can't. My eyes meet hers. Like Meriwether, the princess has solid black, pupilless eyes. There's a coldness in their inky depth that sends a shiver up my spine.

Her skin is ghostly pale, and though she's much bigger than the fairies, she's barely my height. She looks like she's my age—sixteen. Or at least that's the age I remember.

Apart from her creepy eyes, the princess almost looks human, like me, but then she smiles.

Her lips spread and stretch unnaturally across her face, revealing her tiny, pointed teeth. "What's the matter, Rosie? Bad dream?"

I can't answer her. Though I've seen her countless times, I can't stop the terror seizing me. I'm a mouse caught in her trap. My survival instincts scream at me to run. Hide. Cower.

All of that is useless.

This is her court, and I'm just her plaything.

Shadows of all shapes and sizes spread out around her, making the room grow even colder. One edges close to me, dark claw opening and closing. I steel myself for its icy grip.

Before it can touch me, Princess Maloret waves it away. All the others disappear with it.

She sighs loudly and crosses her arms over her flat chest. "Isn't there something you want to ask me?"

I glance at Meriwether. Her blue lips are pressed together in a thin line. She doesn't look at me. Instead, she's watching Princess Maloret. Fear shines in her eyes.

"Well?" Princess Maloret's voice grows harder.

I turn my attention back to her. There's only one question in my mind.

"I ... My door was open," I finally get out. My voice is hoarse and barely audible.

Have I always sounded like this? I can't remember.

The princess arches a delicate brow at me. "Is there a question in there, Rosie?"

Heat spreads through me at her taunting tone. I hate the way she toys with me. My fingers curl against the stone floor I'm still sitting on.

Amusement flashes on her face, and I have to force myself not to lunge for her and wrap my hands around her throat. It would do me no good. First off, it would be incredibly stupid. Second, she would probably enjoy it.

Meriwether flits closer, the bottom of a velvety wing touching my exposed shoulder. It's her way of comforting me.

Princess Maloret watches us with a smirk. Everything is a joke to her. I've never seen her truly upset before, nor do I want to. She's dangerous when she's in a good mood.

Emboldened by Meriwether's touch, I push myself off the ground and stand to meet the princess's stare.

"Why was my door open?" I manage to ask, my voice stronger.

She nods in approval and flicks her wrist, casting more shadow beasts. They leap from the ground and move in a frenzy around the room.

"Come," Princess Maloret commands.

At first, I think she's talking to the shadows, but then her dark eyes turn to me. My stomach lurches. I glance at Meriwether, who hovers by my side, a worried look on her face.

"Let's talk somewhere ... more comfortable," Princess Maloret adds, nose scrunching as she takes in the room.

Her eyes dart to the spinning wheel pieces scattered all over the floor. She gives me an amused look. "Was that me, or was it broken before I got here? Didn't like your spinning task, huh?"

"I didn't do that," I reply quickly, hoping she believes me.

A wicked grin spreads across her face. "Now, now, Rosie. You don't have to lie to me."

Meriwether flies closer to her. "It's true, Princess. It was the imps. I saw them."

My shoulders loosen in relief. Thankfully, my fairy friend can vouch for me. Unlike humans, fairies can't lie. Or so I'm told.

The princess frowns at Meriwether's words, then shrugs her thin shoulders. "I'll just have to bring another one."

Without waiting for a response, she turns and sweeps out of the room. The shadow creatures follow close behind her. Flames flicker against the stone walls as if warning me. My eyes meet Meriwether's.

She waves me forward with a grim look. Though she doesn't speak her fear out loud, I know what she's thinking, because I'm thinking the same thing.

What does the Shadow Court princess want with me?

# THREE

 $\mathcal{M}$ eriwether and I follow close behind the princess, careful not to bump into the shadow beasts that surround us. I don't know if they're there to ward off the other creatures or to make sure I obey the princess's command. Their presence gives me goosebumps.

My stomach is in knots, hunger and dread swirling together. Coldness sinks into my skin. I desperately want to go back to my bed and bury myself under the blanket, but a tiny part of me is also curious.

Princess Maloret was gone for a long time. Maybe she brought food back this time. My stomach rumbles at the thought, loud in the silence.

The princess pauses and turns back to look at me. "Humans are so needy. So fragile," she says with an amused laugh.

It's something I don't need to be reminded of. *My mortality.* Every day in her court is a lesson in survival, and I can't remember a life before.

Did I have one?

My mind goes back to the dream. There has to be a reason I dream of that room and those people, but the harder I try to remember the scene, the more it fades away. Was the room blue or white? The images are blurry in my head now.

One thing I do know is that I'm cursed.

"Did you have a nice trip, Princess?" Meriwether's melodic voice interrupts my thoughts.

Princess Maloret snorts loudly. "I was at a funeral."

Meriwether flinches at her tone. "Oh, right. I'm sorry for your loss. Was it someone very dear to you?"

The princess laughs, a sharp, biting sound that bounces around the dark hallway and rings in my ears. The shadow creatures shake and jerk, eerie mouths open in silent laughter.

I glare at the back of Princess Maloret's head. Someone is dead and she's cackling like it's the funniest thing in the world.

*Crazy bi—*

She turns to me, smiling as if she can hear my thoughts. I share a glance with Meriwether. The last time Princess Maloret came, she ordered me to spin yarn while she told me about her misdeeds.

*Stealing. Lying. Tricking. Killing.*

She's only part fairy and not bound to honesty like the others. What the other half of her is, I don't know. Demon, maybe?

And it isn't just my life she toys with. She has a long rap sheet spanning years and years. I don't know how she gets away with it. Worse, I don't know how I will ever be rid of her.

"Here we are," the princess announces, abruptly cutting off my thoughts.

We're standing in front of a room I don't recognize. A dining room. My eyes snap to Meriwether. Is it a trick? Or are we really eating?

The long, ornate table fills most of the room. Above, a giant chandelier glows, bathing everything in a bright yellow. Dark wood chairs surround the table, monstrous faces carved into them.

"Please, find a seat. You too, fairy," Princess Maloret says with a smile.

She motions us forward, and the shadow beings spread out, blocking the doorway. My steps feel wooden as I head for a chair. My heart races.

I don't remember if we've done this before—eaten together? Is that what we're doing? I'm so hungry, but I'm also on guard.

I know better than to eat her food.

Meriwether flies to the seat beside me, a worried look on her face. Does she think it's a trick, too? I want to ask her, but there's no way to do that with the princess watching.

I feel her eyes on my back and her presence makes me shudder. The shadow creatures disappear with a soft hiss, the sound filling the silence.

Princess Maloret strides over to the table, boots slapping loudly on the stone floor. She ignores my questioning look and takes the seat directly across from me. Folding her hands together on top of the wooden table, she watches me.

"It was me that opened your door, Rosie. I'm sure you already know that," she begins, turning and snapping her fingers into the air.

A fairy flies into the room and bows in mid-air. "Yes, Princess?"

"Bring us something to eat and drink," the princess replies, eyes still on me.

The fairy spouts something off in their language, eyes flitting to me and Meriwether. I watch for Meriwether's reaction. Her face is blank during the exchange.

Princess Maloret claps her hand, the sound loud. The fairy leaves in a hurry, wings humming as she goes. Meriwether wrings her hands together atop the table and doesn't meet my gaze.

What is going on?

"Sooo, Rosie," the princess catches my attention. "Don't you want to know why I opened your door?" she continues, lips quirking into a smile.

Of course, I do. She knows that, but I don't want to give her the satisfaction of seeing me squirm. Forcing my face into a blank stare, I shrug.

Amusement flashes across her features. "I think it's time for you to join the others."

Meriwether gasps beside me.

*Others?* Her words strike an icy fear through me.

"Princess Maloret, surely you don't mean ... the rest of the court?" Meriwether asks in a shaky voice.

The fairy princess glances at her. "I wasn't talking to you. Keep your blubbering to yourself or leave us right now."

Meriwether stiffens at the warning in her tone. My fingers curl against the table. The wood is cold to the touch and solid, reminding me that this is real. All of this is real.

"The others? Why? Why now?" I ask, hoping to take the attention off my fairy friend.

Princess Maloret meets my gaze. "You'll see. I've given you more than enough time to get acclimated to my court. It's time for you to become more familiar with ... everything. Seeing as you'll be here on a permanent basis."

My throat goes dry. *Permanent.*

She grins. "Don't look at me like that, Rosie. This is what you chose, after all. Isn't it?"

*Is it?* I can't remember.

# FOUR

*P*rincess Maloret's words still ring in my ears as the fairy servant returns with several others. Between them, they carry a tray holding a tall, lopsided cake. Pink frosting drips from the top, splashing on the stone floor.

"Cake? Well, aren't you lucky, Rosie," the princess says, waving the fairies forward.

They set it on the table in front of me. A strong scent of bubble gum comes from the spongy-looking cake. The smell is so sweet and so strong it makes me nearly gag.

I meet the princess's stare over the cake. Her wide grin makes me nervous. She isn't going to force me to eat it, is she?

Her smile fades. "Eat it. I know you're hungry."

There's an edge in her voice I haven't heard before. I glance at Meriwether, my chest tightening. Her face is grim. It could be poisoned, or it could be harmless. There's no way to know without taking a bite. Which I won't.

Princess Maloret shoots to her feet, her chair scraping against the stone. "Not so hungry then."

She turns to the fairies still hovering in the air. "Take it away."

They rush forward to obey her. My stomach rolls with dread as I watch them struggle to lift the tray back up and carry it out of the dining room.

Did I make a mistake? Have I offended the princess? My throat turns dry. Will I be punished?

Her face is a blank mask and her black, pupilless eyes stare back at me. Meriwether shudders in her chair, her wing brushing against my bare arm, tickling me.

"Oh, Rosie. Rosie. Rosie. What am I going to do with you?" Princess Maloret asks, leaning over the table toward me.

I flinch.

She smiles and drags her finger through the pink frosting that spilled on the table.

Sucking the pink substance from her finger, she shakes her head at me. "You're very difficult, you know. I should rid myself of you, but I just don't have the heart."

Her grin widens, sharp little teeth gleaming under the chandelier light. A tremor runs through me. I glance at Meriwether, but she's watching the princess with a fierce look on her face. She wants to protect me. She would do anything to help me, but she'd be powerless to stop the shadow princess. I wouldn't risk her life, anyway.

"You're lucky I'm so kind," the princess continues, still smirking.

I don't respond. What am I supposed to say to that? Kind is the last word I'd use to describe her.

*Cunning. Dangerous. Cruel.*

She sits back in her chair and sighs heavily. "This is exactly why I opened your door. If you're going to stay in my court, you need to start making yourself more at home."

"What if I don't want to stay in your court?" The question escapes me before I can think better of it.

Meriwether sucks in a sharp breath.

Princess Maloret cocks her head at me, studying me as if I'm the strange one. I'm struck by her otherworldliness just as she's struck by my humanity. Her dark inky eyes bore into me, and it's all I can do not to shrink under her gaze.

She waves her hand in the air, conjuring smoke-like shadows around her. They shake the chandelier with their wispy claws and dance against the stone walls. Their bodies stretch and transform into giant, grinning faces.

"You can't leave my court. That was the deal, Rosie. Don't you remember?" Princess Maloret taunts, snapping my attention back to her.

Heat spreads across my skin. Of course, I don't remember. She took my memories. I only have her word, her claims that I chose this. That being a 'guest' in her court is what I wanted.

I can't imagine why. Was my previous life so terrible that I gave it up for … this?

"There is always another way out of our deal, but I'm not sure you're ready for that," she says in singsong.

She wants me to ask her what it is. I won't. I already have a good guess at what she's talking about.

The only way out of this 'deal' is death.

Smiling, she shrugs her shoulder. "I've been more than patient with you. Things are going to be different from now on. No more hiding away and brooding about. You're going to be a part of my court. An *important* part."

Not waiting for my response, she rises to her feet and waves her hand at the shadow creatures. They stand at attention by her side, towering over her.

"Since you don't want to eat, we'll move on to the next thing. But first, you need to change."

She makes a face at my nightgown as if it's the ugliest thing she's seen. "Come on."

I don't listen.

Meriwether flutters beside me, close enough for her velvety wings to touch me. She's trying to help me, but I can't make my body move.

The princess's words worry me. What is she going to do to me? Is she still upset at my refusal to eat the cake?

She grunts. "See what I mean. Difficult. Get up now or I'll help you." Her words are sugary, but there's a tightness around her eyes. Her sharp little teeth are bared.

I glance at the shadow beasts closing in. The room grows ice cold.

Before their claws can reach me, I stand. My heart pounds wildly, the sound filling my ears. I don't know what game the princess is playing now, but I refuse to let her see my fear.

"You have to remember, Rosie. I'm not the bad guy here," Princess Maloret says, staring hard at me.

A scoff escapes me. She's stolen me away from my previous life, stolen my memories, and keeps me captive in her castle. If that's not classic villain MO, then I don't know what is.

She smirks. "Believe it or not, I'm trying to save you."

I don't believe her.

The smile she gives me is predatory. She's the cat and I'm the mouse. I don't trust her, and though every warning bell in my head is ringing, I follow her as she leads me to the doorway. The shadows dance around us in an excited frenzy.

Whatever she has planned next, I'll survive it. I've been lucky so far.

# FIVE

*I*'m standing in a room full of mirrors. It's a room I've tried to avoid at all costs, but today, I have no choice but to follow Princess Maloret inside. Meriwether hovers above me, her reflection fractured by a crack in the corner of the mirror we're looking into. It makes her look faceless.

I turn my attention back to my own reflection. The baby-pink dress I'm wearing makes me crinkle my nose. It's lacey on top with a puffy bottom. It doesn't feel like me. Then again, I don't really remember who I am. Did I wear stuff like this in my previous life?

My doppelgänger stares back at me from all the mirrors. Though, instead of showing the same image, I see different versions of myself. In one, my black hair has turned to silver and my brown skin is wrinkled, but my eyes remain the same.

*Big. Brown. Sad.* I can't remember why I'm sad.

In another mirror, I'm crumpled on the floor, my eyes wide open in death. My mouth is slightly parted.

I tear my gaze away from that reflection and suppress a shudder. There's a reason I avoid this room of horrors.

"Much better," Princess Maloret says, meeting my eyes in the mirror.

She nods in approval and waits for me to speak. I want to ask her what's going on, but my throat is dry, and the words are stuck.

In all my time here, I can't recall ever dressing up for her like this. Meriwether nods along, her pretty blue wings fluttering and filling the silence.

The princess folds her arms across her chest and clears her throat. "Now, before we rush off, let me ask you this. Would you rather have the gift of good thoughts or beauty?"

I frown. "What?"

Her thin lips quirk into a smile. "I can make you the best singer or the best dancer. Or make you popular? Rich? What do you desire most?"

This question leaves me stunned. I don't trust anything she offers me, yet a part of me wonders if she really has the power to grant me these things. Or this could be another trick. Another game. The princess loves her games.

She snorts and shrugs her shoulder. "Think about it then. You don't have to answer right away."

Turning to look at her own reflection in the mirror, she leans closer and purses her lips. "I can't show up to the party like this. I'm going to change. Meet me in the ballroom."

Her eyes flit to Meriwether and then back to me. "She knows where it is."

Meriwether nods her agreement as the princess sweeps out of the door. I stand in front of the mirrors and take a deep breath. My head feels dizzy, and my stomach aches with hunger.

*A party.* A party usually means food, but in this case, I'm not so sure that's a good thing. The image of the cake flashes before me.

"This is very strange," Meriwether says, breaking the silence.

I turn to face her as she glides beside me.

"Do you know what she's up to?" I ask.

My question echoes back, sounding loud and hollow.

Meriwether shakes her head. "No, but I'll be there the whole time. I won't leave your side. I promise, Rosie."

I smile. "Thank you."

Sighing, I draw my shoulders back and motion for the fairy to lead the way. "We should go. I don't want to upset her."

My friend nods, dipping lower as she flies to the doorway. I follow. The puffy train of my dress scrapes against the stone floor.

Meriwether guides me through the twisting halls and sloping stairs. Coldness presses in around us as we make our way through the dimly lit castle.

I try to remember if I've seen the ballroom before, but keep drawing a blank. In a castle this size, she could have more than one ballroom. Voices drift from up ahead, their guttural and melodic sounds clashing together.

A party means I'll have to mingle with the others. The dwarves, imps, fairies, and pixies will all be there, I'm sure. Will the gargoyles join in as well? With Princess Maloret in attendance, I know to expect the shadow creatures. She rarely goes anywhere without them.

Meriwether told me the princess's power is shadow magic. What that means, I'm not exactly sure, but I know it means she can conjure horrible things out of thin air. The shadow beasts that look like black smoke but aren't. They're solid sometimes, and their touch is always icy. A kind of cold that cuts right through to your bone.

The voices grow louder as we approach. I glance back at the hall we've come from. The candles have gone out, leaving nothing but darkness behind us. In front of us, the flames flicker against the gray stone.

My dress scrapes along the ground like claws against stone. The eerie sound echoes around us and makes me cringe.


FINALLY, WE MAKE IT TO THE BALLROOM AND A LOUD GASP ESCAPES ME. It's unlike any other part of the castle I've seen. The floor is a shiny, sparkling gold and the ceiling is impossibly high, sunlight streaming in from the glass roof.

Instead of the princess's usual bones and gloomy décor, everything is bathed in sunshine and gold. Gold statues of long-limbed elves and their smaller fairy counterparts line the room.

At our arrival, everyone turns. I freeze, cowering next to Meriwether as all eyes land on me. The creatures that loom before us don't belong in this sunny room. Giant, oily-black gargoyles hover in the air along with the fairies and pixies. Dwarves and imps crowd the floor. All but the naked gargoyles are dressed in tattered suits and moth-bitten dresses much too large for them. Most of the court is missing limbs and covered in scars and scratches. Their voices blend together, sharp and guttural.

They are creatures of nightmare, and the hostile looks they give me make me shudder. How does the princess expect me to fit in among them?

Meriwether flies in front of me, her presence a lifeline I cling to. Unlike the other fairies, I know I can trust her.

She holds out her hand as if to ward them off, but they laugh. A harsh, inhuman laugh that chills me to the bone. All at once, they swarm toward me.

# SIX

$\mathcal{I}$ can't move. I'm frozen to the spot, and my eyes clench shut, my heart in my throat. There's no escaping the horde of creatures barreling toward me.

"Get back," a steely voice cuts through their snarls and squeals.

As one, they obey, heads bowing and bodies lowering.

I'm trembling. I feel like I'm suffocating. The dress is constricting, making it hard for me to breathe.

Princess Maloret strides in and pauses to glance at me. I don't know what to make of her serious look. She's never serious. This scares me even more than the room filled with her monsters.

"Come along, Rosie," she orders, sweeping through the room in her extravagant black gown.

Meriwether flutters above me as we follow the princess. Walking between them, I feel safe. As safe as I can possibly feel in the Shadow Court.

The room is crowded with creatures, and the clashing scents of rot and sugar are so strong I can barely breathe. Eyes follow us as we make our way through the giant ballroom. For a minute, the grotesque faces that surround us blur and flicker.

*You don't belong here.* The words come to my mind, surprising me.

The face of the little girl from my dream flashes in my mind. Who is she?

Who am I?

I try to remember, but the harder I try to focus on her, the more she slips away. She's just a dream. This castle—these creatures—they're real.

We're at the giant throne now, and Princess Maloret orders a fairy to bring in a chair for me. Meriwether will have to stand or hover in the air. I try to catch her attention, but her eyes are glued to the princess, a worried look on her face.

My stomach rolls. If she's concerned, it's for a reason. The princess's words from before echo in my ears.

*Things are going to be different from now on ... You're going to be a part of my court. An important part.*

The fairies return with my chair. Its legs are tall, making me tower above the princess. I climb into it and sit, feeling ridiculous in my puffy skirt.

"Bring her something she can eat before she passes out." Princess Maloret sends the fairies out again.

The thought of food makes me nearly weep with relief. How long has it been? I open my mouth to thank her, but stop myself.

Heat spreads up my neck. It's not right. I don't remember my previous life, but I don't think I ever cried at the thought of being able to eat.

I've grown so dependent on Princess Maloret that I've become grateful to her for basic needs.

*Things are going to be different from now on.* Her words ring in my mind.

*Yes. They are.*

I don't know how, but I refuse to let her rule over me. To toy with me. I must have had a life before, and it had to be better than this. I'll do whatever it takes to remember. To free myself from this curse.

The food returns, and I glance at Meriwether. She gives me a subtle nod.

*Not poisoned.*

It's all I can do to not tear into the delicious smelling meat and potatoes. I don't care where it came from or how it was made. I probably don't want to know. I use the fork and knife I'm given and eat from my lap, slowly, trying to savor each bite.

All my focus is on my plate. I tune out the noise and sights around me. Thankfully, the princess lets me eat in peace. Once my belly is full, I'll be ready to hear what she has to say.

Too soon, I'm finished, and though I want more, I don't dare ask. It could come spoiled or poisoned.

Time seems to drag on as I sit beside the silent princess. Meriwether continues to hover next to me, and I give her a sympathetic smile. Her wings must be tired by now.

A sigh escapes me.

I don't like parties. At least not this kind of party. Music blares from invisible speakers, the notes sounding flat and off. It strikes my every nerve and makes me grit my teeth. The creatures are dancing together, their movements jerky and forced. Princess Maloret's shadow beasts join them.

How long do I have to be here? I glance at the princess as she lounges on her throne.

Her black eyes meet mine. A knowing smile is pasted on her face. Anger rolls through me, making my fists clench.

Surely, there's a reason she has me dressed up and sat here on display. But she isn't forcing me to dance or eat from the dazzling buffet set out for the others. The food is glamoured, I'm sure. What looks like a feast fit for royalty is probably rotten and putrid. Poisoned.

The sun is still shining through the glass roof, but my body tells me it's long past daytime. There are no clocks in the Shadow Court. Time here seems irrelevant. Though, right now, it feels as if I've spent the whole day sitting in the ballroom.

Finally, after what feels like a lifetime, the princess stands, and the music ends. Everyone stops dancing and turns to her, waiting.

She gestures to me with her hand and addresses her court. I listen with growing dread as she launches into a speech that I can't understand. Beside me, Meriwether's face has grown pale.

The creatures hiss and whisper together all at once. Their reaction scares me. What is she telling them?

My stomach churns, the food from earlier feeling heavy now. It's all I can do to hold it in and not hurl over the side of my tall chair.

Princess Maloret glances at me, smiling as she finishes her announcement. The ballroom erupts in a mixture of roars and squeals. My ears ring.

"What did you tell them?" I ask, my voice hoarse.

Her eyes bore into mine. "I told them to welcome their new honorary princess. Smile. I've made you a permanent member of my court."

*Princess. Permanent.*

The words echo in my mind. I turn, hang my head over the side of my chair, and empty my stomach.

# SEVEN

My stomach is still queasy and my body is weak. Princess Maloret's announcement rings in my ears as the music restarts and everyone celebrates. She made me an honorary princess of her court. I don't know what that means, but I know I don't want it.

I want to go home. But where is home? Does it still exist? Did it ever?

Questions race in my mind. Meriwether hovers beside me, saying something, but I can't hear her over the noise of the crowd.

I struggle to climb down from my chair, desperate to leave. Return to my room and my bed. I don't want to be here anymore.

I can't be here.

Just as my feet land on the floor, Princess Maloret grabs me by the wrist, her grip like steel.

"Not so fast, *Princess*," she hisses out the word, a cruel smile on her face. "Tell me what you desire most in the world, and I'll grant it."

"What I want most is to go home!" I blurt out, trying to pull my hand out of her grasp.

She laughs, and all around us, the creatures echo her with their strange sounds. Meriwether flits above us, wringing her hands nervously.

Princess Maloret clucks her tongue at me. "This is your home, Rosie."

"It's not! It can't be," my voice wobbles, making me sound pathetic.

She grins. "There's only one way to break your curse, dear girl. But to do that, you'll have to slay your biggest dragon, and I don't think you're ready for that."

Her words make me frown. *My biggest dragon?*

I don't even know what to make of that. Before I can question her further, she releases me and saunters away. Her shadow creatures follow her, slicing and snarling their way through the crowd. Pained cries and fearful shouts rise above the music.

I rub my wrist from where she grabbed me, nausea rolling through me. Her words replay in my mind.

*Tell me what you desire most in the world, and I'll grant it.*

Was it a trick? Another game?

A deep sigh escapes me. I'm tired—so tired—of the princess and her tricks. My eyelids grow heavy and I'm vaguely aware of Meriwether motioning for me to follow her. My legs are shaky with exhaustion as I move toward the fairy.

The sound of the others and the music fades as I make it to the hall. I blink slowly and wait for my eyes to adjust to the darkness. Meriwether's velvety wing brushes my shoulder, making me jump.

"Come on, Rosie. I'll get you to your room." Her words sound muffled. Far away.

The thought of my bed urges me forward. My dress scrapes along the castle floor, filling the silence. All I want to do is throw myself down on the mattress and hide under the blankets. The events of the day have left me unraveled. Scared.

*An honorary princess.* What does it all mean? What will happen now?

I push away the questions and suck in a lungful of cold air. I don't know how I'll break free of this curse, but I know I'm the only who can. No one is coming to save me. Meriwether, as much as she would like to help me, can only tell me so much. To get the answers I need, I'll have to leave my room. Explore more of the castle, which I've been too scared to do. I need to go where I haven't gone before.

A thought strikes me. Why not go now? It's the perfect time while everyone is busy in the ballroom.

"Rosie?" Meriwether calls me, noticing my pause.

I look up at her. "I'm not going back to the room yet."

Her head cocks at me, her lips pursing in confusion.

"Meri, does the princess keep any kind of … I don't know … record of her curses? Anything you think would help me break mine?"

Meriwether doesn't answer. She gives me a solemn look, her eyes drilling into mine. "You want to break your curse? That's risky, Rosie. Too risky." She shakes her head and wrings her hands together.

My heart sinks. If my only friend won't help me, I don't know what I'll do.

"Come with me. I think I know something that might help you," Meriwether says, turning in the other direction.

I pick up my gown and hurry to keep up with her. My heart hammers in my ears. We'll have to be quick about it because there's no telling how long the party will last. What if we run into other creatures lurking in the castle? The ones not invited to the ball?

A shudder runs down my spine. I don't think I want to see the monsters that even the princess avoids.

We race down the dimly lit hallways. Snarls and moans echo from somewhere in the castle, making the hairs on the back of my neck bristle. Meriwether sets a pace I can barely keep up with, but the thought of the princess finding me pushes me forward.

All too abruptly, the fairy stops, and I smack into her. My face collides with her velvety wings.

A tremor runs through her.

"Meri?" I whisper in the dark.

She doesn't answer. Something wet falls on my bare shoulder, making me yelp. I blink against the dark. "Meri?"

A rushing sound fills my ears, and more water pelts me. Rain, I realize.

I gasp. "Are we outside? How did we—"

Meriwether's icy hand covers my mouth. "Shh."

The urgency in her tone kills my excitement. The few times I've been allowed outside the castle, there was still daylight. I've never been outside at night.

Though the air is much warmer now, a chill fills me.

"I'm sorry, Rosie. I shouldn't have brought you here." Meriwether's words are laced with fear.

"What do you mean? Why? Where are we?" My questions are carried by a huge gust of wind.

My gown is soaked, weighing me down.

Meriwether glides closer to me, her body trembling. "I'm—"

An ear-splitting shriek cuts her off. My heart drops to my stomach.

We're not alone.

# EIGHT

*T*he smell of rot makes me gag. It's so powerful it makes my nose and throat burn and my eyes water. Rain roars all around us, a heavy curtain that would be impossible to see through even if it wasn't pitch black already. I'm soaked through, and the weight of my gown holds me in place.

I can't move.

"Hurry! You have to find your name, Rosie. I'll hold off the guardian for as long as I can," Meriwether's voice whispers in my ear, low and urgent.

"What?"

"I'm sorry. I should have told you sooner, but I was too scared. And now ... oh, there's no time now! The roses. They hold the names and identities she's stolen. Find yours!"

Before I can ask her more questions, Meriwether is gone. Gone to face whatever monster is lurking in the darkness. Fear ripples through me. She'll be torn to pieces.

"Meri!" I call out.

She doesn't answer. All I can hear is the rain now. Did the creature leave? Did it take Meri with it? Should I go after her?

My friend's words replay in my mind. *The roses. They hold the names and identities she's stolen. Find yours.*

How am I supposed to find anything in the darkness? A shiver runs through me. Everything feels hopeless. But I can't just stand here and do nothing.

There's no one coming to help me. No rescue. I'm on my own, and if I want to break this curse, I need to move. Now.

I will myself forward, dragging my heavy dress with me. I strain against the weight. In the darkness, it's impossible to see where I'm going, and though I try to picture the layout, I can't tell where I am.

*Roses.* Where were the roses? I can't remember ever seeing them when I was outside. A shaky breath escapes me, getting lost in the heavy rain.

At least it's not freezing like it is in the castle. Is the party still going on? Has the princess noticed me and Meriwether gone yet?

*Meri.* My throat turns dry. I hope she's okay. I don't want to imagine the alternative.

Pushing away the dark thoughts, I press on.

It feels as if a lifetime has passed and still I've found nothing. There's nothing but darkness and rain. Why haven't I run across anything yet? Should I turn around and try the other way now? How far have I gone?

Rain continues to pour and weigh me down, as if it's actively trying to keep me from my goal. In this strange place, it very well could be alive and working against me. The rushing sound of it fills my ears.

Struggling, I move forward. Even if I wanted to go back, I wouldn't know how. All that exists in this moment is the darkness and rain. Both feel like enemies I have no hope of overcoming.

My mind drifts back to my dream. Pieces of it start to form together, but before I can remember much, they shatter once more and fade away.

What if that is my past? What if that is reality, and this castle, the princess, is the nightmare?

*What do you desire most?* The princess's words ring in my head.

A sob breaks free. What do I want?

Wind blows against me and knocks me to my knees. I sink, dress and all, into the thick mud. I'm shaking now, body exhausted. I can't keep going.

I want to go home. This place can't be where I belong. Why did I ever agree to come here? The image of the little girl and boy flash in my mind. I can't remember who they are, but I know, deep down, they are important, and I am important to them.

They are waiting for me. I just know it. I can't give up.

Will all my strength and a load groan, I struggle back up to my feet and push myself forward. I will not be her honorary princess. There's nothing she could offer to make me stay a moment longer. I have to get free.

I take another small step, my legs nearly collapsing. My hand wavers in front of me, looking for anything to grab on to.

Thorns pierce me. I suck in a sharp breath. The roses!

*Ellie.* The name pops into my mind. Images flash before me. A giant house with a picket fence. A stern-faced woman and a mean-looking girl. None of it seems familiar.

It's not the right rose.

Ignoring the pain shooting up my arm, I keep going. I reach for the tops of the flowers, hoping to avoid any more thorns.

Nothing happens when I touch the petals. Dread unfurls inside me. It only works if I prick my finger.

By the time I'm done, my hands will be a bloody mess.

I find the thorn and tap it slowly. Another name pops into my mind. More images I don't recognize.

Blinking against the darkness, a wave of despair washes over me. How many roses will I have to search through? This is impossible. I'll never find mine in time. Any minute, Princess Maloret will find me, and it will be too late.

And Meriwether … a sob escapes me. Is it already too late for her?

Pushing away the dark thoughts, I move forward, forcing myself to continue. If this is my only chance to break the curse, I have to try. What other choice do I have?

Heat rushes through me. I can't stay here any longer. I refuse to be the princess's plaything any longer. Whatever life I had before, wherever I came from, it had to be better than this miserable place.

Numbness fills my hands, and a thought strikes me. What if the roses are poisonous to the touch? What if all of this is for nothing?

The thought of dying here, in the darkness, with no memory of who I am, makes me shudder. An ache spreads in my chest. I have to keep going.

I touch another, then another. My head is spinning from all the names and memories that are not mine. Nausea rolls through me. How many lives has she stolen? What happened to these people? What will happen to me?

All of a sudden, the rain stops, and I pause. My shallow breaths echo loudly in the silence. I blink, trying desperately to see against the darkness. Nothing.

A sharp laugh cuts through the air. Ice fills my veins. I know that laugh.

Princess Maloret is coming. My time is up.

Quickly, I reach for another rose.

*Please be the right one.*

# NINE

ain flares through me. A wave of shock ripples through me. A name flashes in my mind.

*Aurora.*

The faces from my dream—the boy and the girl—flicker before me. The same room. My room. All at once, I remember everything. My house. My family. My life.

With all the good memories come the bad. The hopelessness. The emptiness. A sadness that I could never shake no matter how hard I tried. The wish to end it. End all the pretending and trying. To finally be done with everything.

Rain drowns out the broken cry on my lips. I remember it all now. I remember why I made the deal with the princess.

"Ah. You found your rose," her voice echoes behind me.

The rain stops suddenly as I turn to look at her. The sky brightens, revealing her silhouette as she walks towards me. She's still dressed in her black gown, her creepy eyes on me.

She smiles. "Do you remember now, Rosie?"

"That's not my name."

Her grin widens. "No, it's not. Aurora. It means dawn, doesn't it? Do you think your parents pictured this when they named you?" She gestures at me with an amused laugh.

"Pictured me here, kidnapped by some crazy fairy? No, I don't think so."

She cocks her head at me. "You came here willingly. Don't you remember? You were a burden to your family. Always bringing everyone down."

I glare at her. "My family loves me."

She arches one eyebrow at me. "Maybe. But can you love yourself?"

Her question rings through my ears. I stare down at the rose in my hand. My fingers are red with blood, and a numbness fills me.

The last thing I remember before coming here was writing a note. A goodbye note, trying to explain to my family why I had to do what I was going to do. A lump grows in my throat. Tears blur my vision.

What did they think of the unfinished letter? My disappearance? Did they think I ran away?

Running wouldn't have saved me. Even coming here to this strange place, I couldn't escape it. There was something broken inside of me that I could never fix. I could never be the smiling sunshine girl they wanted.

"I can take it all away. The memories. You can stay here in my court. Be an honorary princess. We would accept you for who you are. Who you truly are."

Princess Maloret's words interrupt my thoughts. I glance around at the gloomy garden and black castle behind us. Maybe this is where I belong. The Court of Shadows. Maybe I do belong here with all her dark, broken creatures.

"I can even bring your little friend back," the princess continues, her lips spread into a cold smile.

*Meriwether.*

My heart sinks. She sacrificed herself for me. To help me find out the truth and escape this place. How could I ever repay her? Could she really be gone?

"Now that you've had time to think it over, do you have an answer for me?" Princess Maloret asks, black eyes drilling through me.

I stare back at her, fighting the urge to shudder.

"I don't want to be your honorary princess." My voice echoes around us, carried by the wind.

A shiver runs through my still soaked body.

The princess laughs. "That wasn't the question. Let's try this again. What do you desire most in the world, Rosie?"

She throws her hands up and a crackle fills the air. I flinch and close my eyes, waiting for a blow, but nothing happens.

I open my eyes to see a familiar figure hovering between us. My breath catches.

"Meri!" I step toward her.

Something is wrong. Her little body jerks and shakes, her blue lips morphing into a silent scream.

"Stop it! What are you doing to her?" I whip toward Princess Maloret.

"Do you want me to bring her back? Is that what you desire most?" the princess taunts me, eyebrow raised.

I turn to Meriwether again and watch in horror as my friend transforms into one of the grotesque shadow beasts. Its mouth spreads into a cruel smile.

Bile fills my mouth. Meri is gone. I'm certain of it now, and guilt and anger swirl inside me. It's my fault she's gone. Tears blur my vision.

It's too late for me to save her. Even taking what the princess is offering wouldn't truly bring my fairy friend back. It would only be a trick, I'm sure.

Blinking back the tears, my hands clench into fists. "You're a monster."

Princess Maloret laughs. The sound is sharp and shrill, ringing through my ears. Anger rolls inside me. It's all I can do to not lunge for her.

"Maybe, but I can accept myself for who I am. Can you say the same about yourself?" she asks me, her lips still turned up in amusement.

She lets out a loud sigh and motions to the castle behind us. "I'm not the enemy here. I brought you here to save you. What you were about to do, dearie—there's no coming back from. Not even with all the magic in the world."

I don't answer. What she says echoes through me. Maybe in her own twisted way, she really does believe she's the hero in this, but deep down, I know she didn't save me.

"If you go back, you can never return here. And you will be going back to the same life. Facing the same dragon. What will you do when it gets too hard? Because, trust me, it will get hard. Do you really think you have what it takes to survive?"

A lump grows in my throat. I swallow hard, eyes burning hot. "I don't know," I answer honestly.

The same hopelessness fills me. The same darkness. I don't know what my future will hold, but I know I can't stay in her court.

Her hand lashes out. She grabs me by the wrist, her grip icy and steely. Black, pupilless eyes bore into mine. "What do you desire most in the world?"

I don't know what to say. Asking to go home didn't work last time, so how do I get away? Suddenly, realization dawns on me. The dream. This is the dream. Or nightmare, really.

A tear runs down my face. "I want to wake up."

The princess smiles. Then everything turns black. Alarm fills me. Was that it? Was that the right thing?

# TEN

*a* bright light surrounds me. So bright, it's blinding. I blink against it, trying to let my eyes adjust. A groan escapes my lips. I turn my head, pain slicing through me at the movement.

Where am I? What happened?

I'm lying on something large and soft. A bed. My bed. I sit up too quickly, dizziness washing over me.

There is the window from my dream. The desk. The closet. It's all here.

I give a strangled cry. I'm home. How? Pain throbs in my temple as I try to piece back the fading memories.

Princess Maloret. The deal. Her court. Meriwether. The roses.

It all comes back to me, images flooding in and my emotions clashing together. The question the princess asked me echoes in my ears.

*Do you really think you have what it takes to survive?*

I survived her court, and yet, somehow, I think that was easier. I'm back home now, and though I've grown from my experience, I'm still me.

Aurora. More cloud than dawn.

*You will be going back to the same life. Facing the same dragon.* Princess

Maloret's words ring in my mind. For all her tricks and games, I know those words are true.

*You can never return here. What will you do when it gets too hard? Because trust me, it will get hard.*

That I know is true too. I know better than anyone that life is not all sunshine and rainbows, but it's also dark and hard. Sometimes too hard. All the memories from before crowd my mind.

The constant feeling that I'm broken and a disappointment to my family. No matter how hard I try to fit in and pretend I'm happy, there's still a part of me that is stuck in the shadow. While my time in the Princess's court showed me I'm stronger than I thought, I know I'll still have to struggle with my dragon. One day at a time.

I don't know what struggles lie ahead for me, and I don't know the secret to survival, but I do know that I want this life—my life—more than anything. The good and the bad. The sun and the rain.

The sound of footsteps coming toward my room breaks through my thoughts. My heart leaps into my throat, and I jump to my feet as the door opens. A smile breaks on my face. Now I'm awake.

# ABOUT THE AUTHOR

R. L. Medina is a Bolivian American Fantasy author. When she first learned to read at age six, she vowed she would hate it forever. That hate quickly turned to love (or obsession) and by age eight she was filling every notebook she had with her own stories. Now she juggles her time between a busy seven-year-old and all the quirky, diverse characters that demand her attention. When she's not exploring all the Sci-Fi and Fantasy worlds in her head, she enjoys life with her family in the Sunshine State.

**THANK YOU**

Thank you for embarking on this enchanting journey with us! As independent authors, your support means the world to us.

Your reviews, shares, and word-of-mouth recommendations are invaluable to us. They not only help us understand how our stories resonate with you but also assist in spreading the magic to more readers like yourself.

We invite you to stay connected with us online, where we share updates, behind-the-scenes insights, and glimpses into our creative processes. And while you're at it, don't forget to explore our other works.

Sincerely,

K. R. S. McEntire

Montrez

Alicia Ellis

E.M. Lacey

Krystina Coles

R. L. Medina